skin
GAME

skin
GAME

A SIN CITY INVESTIGATION

J.D. ALLEN

MIDNIGHT INK
WOODBURY, MINNESOTA
MIDNIGHT INK

FIRST EDITION
First Printing, 2019

Book design by Bob Gaul
Cover design by Shira Atakpu
Editing by Nicole Nugent

Midnight Ink, an imprint of Llewellyn Worldwide Ltd.

Library of Congress Cataloging-in-Publication Data
Names: Allen, J. D., author.
Title: Skin game : a Sin City investigation / J.D. Allen.
Description: First edition. | Woodbury, Minn. : Midnight Ink, [2019] |
    Series: A Sin City investigation ; #2.
Identifiers: LCCN 2018041423 (print) | LCCN 2018042602 (ebook) | ISBN
    9780738755892 (ebook) | ISBN 9780738754048 (alk. paper)
Subjects: | GSAFD: Mystery fiction.
Classification: LCC PS3601.L4188 (ebook) | LCC PS3601.L4188 S57 2019 (print)
    | DDC 813/.6—dc23
LC record available at https://lccn.loc.gov/2018041423

Midnight Ink
2143 Wooddale Drive
Woodbury, MN 55125-2989
www.midnightinkbooks.com

Printed in the United States of America

To Dad.

I love and miss you every day. Thanks for the love of story and the gift of words and the strength and courage to use both.

DAYS LIKE THIS ONE made being a PI suck. Jim Bean dragged a dirty sleeve across his brow as he bent over and dipped a tattered brush into a paint bucket for the three millionth time. He peered through a jagged hole in the wooden privacy fence surrounding the target's dilapidated house as he straightened. This guy had been a rotten pain in his ass for days. More like a pain in his sore back. He stretched. Vertebrae popped in complaint.

Bribing the body shop owner to let him paint the dumpster had been a stroke of pure genius. What he hadn't thought through was the actual work of painting the stinking thing in the sweltering Vegas heat.

As if it was his goal in life to paint the perfect dumpster, he coated it in navy blue, then forest green, and now it was about to be finished out in a very nice Boy Scout beige.

The ruse had served well as cover but was killing his left wrist and lower back. It was better than the alternative, which had been to hang around this alley sitting on his ass in a car. Too obvious. Besides alerting the target to his presence, the act of spying on someone's back yard in this neighborhood might not have been so good for Jim's long-term health. People got dead around here fairly often. He didn't want to be added to any police statistics this week.

Given that his wrist felt like it had been used to paint the outside of the MGM hotel instead of a six-foot-by-four-foot dumpster, he really hoped that Edmond Carver made a mistake soon. Thus far, Jim had evidence that this outstanding citizen was most certainly dealing drugs, had a taste for ugly prostitutes, and ordered lots of cheap pizza—information Jim might be able to sell to a prosecutor at some point in the span of Edmond's burgeoning criminal career. However, none of that was the evidence Jim was currently being paid to gather. Standing out there sweating was getting old, but it was a job he had to do. He needed to replenish his cash flow.

"It's all about the money," Jim muttered as he slathered on a little more paint. Let the cops take Edmond down for pushing. All he needed was to catch the creep holding something heavy or shooting hoops with one of the other losers on the block—anything that might prove he hadn't slipped a disc tripping behind a blackjack table. Bye-bye workmen's comp claim.

A car pulled past his position and parked not far from the dumpster. Interesting. No need to run through the list of cars he'd mentally cataloged over the last couple of days. No way this screaming-yellow compact was on that list. In this kind of neighborhood, he saw cheap auction rejects or pimped-up land yachts. This brand-new compact did not belong to one of the local residents.

A well-made woman unfolded herself out of the small door, tripping on her heels and grumbling as she did. She was checking a slip of paper as she stretched to retrieve something from the passenger seat. Jim couldn't help noticing the nice curve to her ass, but more interesting was why a chick dressed like she belonged in a fancy office was making her way to the gate of Edmond Carver's house.

He missed getting a good look at her face as she stepped out and turned. Probably shouldn't have been watching her ass so closely. Rookie mistake. Jim Bean was no damn rookie. His intuition twitched, making his stomach tighten.

He checked his back. No one.

Edmond stuck his crooked nose out the door. She managed to talk him out onto the concrete porch. Then, like a mother scolding an unruly child, she kept advancing on him, causing him to back his way along a rusted porch rail. He looked like he was about to run from her. They moved out of the line of sight afforded by the busted fence. If Jim wanted to see more, he'd have to be a little more obvious. Dammit.

Maybe this Edmond character wasn't as dumb as he looked and had hired himself a lawyer. Jim checked his back again, the alley to the east. He was still alone. No one paid attention to a guy in dirty painter's overalls and cap. He stepped over so he could get a glimpse of the pair. He edged closer and pressed his ear to the wood fence. The new position gave him a fresh nose full of stink.

He could only see her back. She was really working it, using her body, inching right up in Edmond's face. The drug dealer kept backing away and shaking his head. His hands were up, showing her his palms. "I ain't done nothing, lady." Jim finally was able to make out Edmond's argument as his back hit the wall at the end of the cracking concrete porch. "You'll have to look somewheres else."

The vocabulary on this one. Jim huffed and tucked his paintbrush into the little bucket he'd been using. There was only so much this guy was going to take from the woman before he pushed back, and that might be Jim's best opportunity to get his money shot. Can't beat up an attorney, or whatever she was, if you have a slipped disc. He turned on the video camera disguised in an empty can of paint sitting on the far corner of the dumpster as she moved in even closer.

She poked his chest. "Where is she?"

"Lady, I can't tell you what I don't know."

"You know. You were the last one to leave her a message at work."

"I don't know what you're talking about." He tried to move around her, but the woman stepped in his path. Jim smiled.

"I have cash." She started rummaging through her bag.

He'd give it to the woman—she was no wuss. He watched her butt move as she talked with her hands.

"You don't get it. I have to keep my mouth shut or else my ass will be missing too."

"So you do know something?"

"No. I don't know shit about shit." This time he did push past her.

She swung him around by grabbing his arm. Jim still couldn't see her face. "I'll go back to the police station. I'll tell them your name and number were on her desk, that you were working on something with her."

"I don't need no trouble with the cops, neither."

"Fifty." She counted out the cash. "Tell me and I go away. What was my sister up to? Where is she now?"

He held up his hands again.

"She's been gone a week. I don't have it on me, but I'll get more cash. A hundred."

Edmond eyed the bills. She was waving cash out in front of a creep. Something like teasing a bull with a red cape in this slum. This chick was gonna get herself rolled. Action!

Jim didn't need to hear any more. She was going to push Edmond over the edge. He grabbed his remote monitor and sank to sit on his heels on the far side of the dumpster, out of sight. Soon he'd be able to get away from the disgusting thing and have a cigar to celebrate a lucrative job with a big bonus. He watched the feed from the camera on the small monitor. For the love of poker, he needed Edmond to do something, anything resembling exertion or exercise.

"Give me the bonus money, baby," he whispered. "Go ahead, asshole, grab one of those metal porch chairs and wield it at the woman like you're on daytime TV. Grab her purse and run." Not that he really wanted her to be hit with it or anything, but whatever happened here was out of his control. Those chairs must weigh thirty pounds each. Edmond waving one around would garner Jim that fat bonus from the casino trying to get out of paying the scum a compensation claim.

Sadly, Edmond did none of that. Instead he silently shook his head and shrugged. His expression was strangely apologetic. The woman let her head fall forward. Her shoulders drooped. It was a touching thing to see her make her final plea. It was like watching a low-budget silent film, maybe even entertaining if it wasn't for the fact he was also watching his payday slip away. Jim could only imagine her tears. He hated crying women. Apparently, Edmond Carver did too. He caved. Told her something. She wrote it down and gave him the cash.

Fuck, he didn't want to put a fourth coat on that dumpster. All he had left was pink paint and he suspected the shop owner would disapprove.

She turned to leave in a flurry of swirling hair. As she stepped off the end of the dilapidated porch, she looked directly into the camera. Shock jolted through Jim Bean, numbing his fingers. The monitor slipped from his grip. She was still on the screen, wide green eyes boring into him from the past as the expensive piece of equipment hit the crumbling pavement, cracking the glass.

Erica fucking Floyd.

FIRST A DRUG DEALER'S house and now the Peppermint Pony? Jim watched Erica enter one of the trashiest strip clubs in town. It had been a feat to gather his wits and his equipment in time to follow her from Edmond's. What was Erica Floyd up to and why was she here looking for her sister? Last he'd heard Erica was working for some investment firm in Boston. And her little sister, Chris, was still in school. Not that he was keeping up with the traitorous bitch. His job was to know things, so he knew things.

She drove in and parked right up front. No way this was a mistake. From the parking lot, it was clear this was a seedy place. The large building sat a few miles from the Strip in an area that may have once been a thriving business park. Now it was run-down and most of the buildings were crumbling ghosts with empty parking lots. Weeds were all that thrived around here these days. Weeds and the Peppermint Pony.

Jim pulled open the blacked-out glass door. She was at the counter and glanced at him as he entered. He was still in the ridiculous painter clothes and he pulled the stained hat down and found something interesting to stare at on the floor so Erica couldn't get a look at his face. Fortunately, the entryway was narrow, musty, and dark.

Glenda was working. She was a wrinkled, craggy old woman whose head was covered by an orange-and-gray camouflage bandana. She sat behind a display counter with cigarettes and T-shirts for sale. Frowning, the woman was leaned back against the wall behind an outdated cash register with her arms crossed. She regarded Erica rather suspiciously.

"I'd like to speak with the manager, please." Erica's voice hadn't changed over the years. Its jazzlike tenor made the hairs on the back of his neck twitch. He scratched at it to stop the urge to grab her and…strangle her.

"The manager, huh?" Glenda looked to her left, into the darkened club. "He'd be back by the Far Bar, most likely."

"Oh." Erica looked very unsure as to what to do next. "Thank you."

"Ten bucks," Glenda barked before Erica could pass her by.

"I'm not here for the, um…entertainment." She stiffened. "I need to ask the manager a few questions."

"You go past me, it's ten bucks." Glenda's overly red lips thinned. "I don't care what you're here for."

Erica stomped past after tossing a bill on the scratched-up counter. Jim removed the hat and gave Glenda a wink and a twenty as he eased into the club. It paid to be nice to people who saw things. Glenda saw a lot of things.

As expected, Banks was lurking right inside in his usual spot, leaning against the half wall separating the hall to the restrooms and the main room. The goon was huge, but he wore his suit and spiked hair like the best of the pit bosses in the big casinos. On the rare occasions he smiled, you could go blind from the glare off the gold.

Erica found her way to the Far Bar. Wasn't hard. A glaring neon sign marked its obvious location. The unimaginative name in blocky text cast a red glow on her hair as she waltzed to the bar.

Before deciding where to land himself, Jim scanned the room. It was midafternoon and slow. Two tables up close to the action by the main floor were occupied. A group of college-age boys were getting lap dances off toward the adjacent wall. Over there, it was dark and a little more private for those on the shy side. Jim would've liked to sit there, cloaked by the dark, but it was too far from Erica.

He moved as close to Erica and the conversation she was having as he could. One of the dance stages came pretty near the Far Bar, where Erica had hesitantly slid onto a bar stool. She sat stiff and spoke to the scruffy bartender. Jim eased into a table not far from the brass pole. Checked his exit routes. Banks seemed the only threat, but Jim counted him as two.

A couple of old guys were shouting over the music, holding a conversation with the stripper as she dangled from the brass. Regulars. The trio should be enough distraction to keep him from being noticed.

Then again, Erica was within seven feet of him in the lobby and she didn't have the slightest clue. No way she even knew he was living in Vegas now. More interesting might be how she'd react if he did walk right up to her. He rubbed his unshaven chin. He was older, grungier, and living a new life as private investigator Jim Bean. Would she recognize the young man she'd known as Korey Anders in his paint-smeared face? His jaw popped as he clenched his teeth tightly at the sound of his given name echoing in his head. Korey was dead to him. Erased. Replaced.

Time had been good to Erica. Her hair was a little shorter, but her athletic build was still evident even through the stuffy business attire. Maybe she carried a few more pounds than she had in college, but who didn't?

He pulled his flask from his boot and took a good long shot of Scotch. Banks frowned at him from the side but didn't make any indication that said he gave a rat's ass about what Bean was up to. Nope. He seemed as intrigued by Erica Floyd's presence in his bar as Jim was. If Erica's sister had been here for some reason ... The hairs on Jim's neck stood up again. Trouble was brewing. Jim suspected Hurricane Erica was about to slam into him in Vegas just as she had done in Columbus eight years ago.

He fought back the consuming anger it had taken him years and court-mandated classes to get past. But memories rolled right at him like a storm. He had no way to stop 'em. All he could do was take cover. He took another shot and tucked the silver flask back into his boot. *That* wouldn't work either. He couldn't drink away the repercussions of that late-August night back in Ohio. But he had tried.

The loud techno music the girls were gyrating to couldn't begin to drown out the memory of the sound of his door being pounded on in the middle of the night.

Jim shook his head. He didn't want to relive it again. But sometimes it happened, replayed over and over, a jukebox with only one song. *Push all the buttons you want, buddy. Patsy Cline and heartbreak is all you get.* Seeing her standing there, arguing with the bartender, brought it *all* back.

He closed his eyes and memories pummeled him. Police pushing past him. Being slammed onto the cold tile floor. Arms being wrenched behind his back, shoulder tendons straining. Guns aimed at his head. Shouting…

He'd been half asleep and in his boxers but not dumb. He relaxed as the police pinned him down on his kitchen floor. So unreal, he could have sworn he'd been watching it happen to someone else. He'd even considered it a prank until he felt the bite of the cuffs and the roughness of the officers yanking on his arms.

Arrested? Him? A criminology master's student. A candidate for the next FBI class. They had the wrong man.

Once the questioning started they would realize it. Right?

But that wasn't how it had played out, was it?

The questioning wasn't the end at all. The nightmare had just begun.

"Bean." He wrenched himself from the images, back to the present and back into the club, as Toyota poked his shoulder. The portly stripper stood in front of him. Her round, overly tanned breasts were positioned right in his face. Jim blinked and wondered at the irony of a girl shaped something like a car actually naming herself after a car. "Where you at, sweetie?"

Nowhere I want to be. "Reliving the end of my youthful innocence."

She tilted her head as if for an instant she considered delving deeper into the subject, but she nodded instead. "Dance?" Evidently his problems were not on her give-a-shit list. He almost chuckled.

He glanced back at the bar. Erica had turned and was looking around the room. He pulled another bill out and tucked it into Toyota's G-string. He could watch Erica from around the girl's generous hips.

He retrieved the flask and took the last draw off it, wishing it held just a little more.

"Banks is gonna kick your ass if he sees you with outside hooch." She turned sideways and did a move designed to show off her flexibility, her hips and shoulders moving in different directions, making her midsection slide close to his chest.

Jim glanced at Banks, who was now frowning at Erica. The big man looked pretty intimidating when he was unhappy. He pulled out his cell and punched at it with a sausage-sized finger. Awkward. Slow. A text.

Jim set the silver container on the table. "Wouldn't want to get your boss man's buzz cut in a twist."

On second thought, maybe he did. With Banks no longer paying attention to Jim and his contraband Scotch, he was busy watching Erica, and Jim was none too happy with that. No one wanted to be scrutinized like that by this guy.

Banks then glanced down. Jim could see the cell phone light up in his paw of a hand. The big man nodded as he looked down at his screen. Jim sucked in a deep breath and turned his attention back to Erica.

Banks pulled away from the wall and trudged toward Erica. Jim closed his eyes. Fought feeling things he'd long ago buried. Jim should hate her. He *did* hate her. She'd played a huge part in destroying his life. He didn't want to be involved with this. He had another job to be doing.

She'd said her sister was missing.

Two jobs, really. What the fuck should he care what Erica or Chris had gotten themselves into? If the trail led from Edmond

Carver to this joint, it was likely Chris had turned junkie and come to Vegas. What did he care?

Banks loomed over Erica's shoulder. She turned and gave him a very businesslike smile. She was in over her head.

Too damn bad...

"You could give a girl a complex, Bean." Toyota thumped his chest with her thick fingers.

He found himself looking at her naked breasts again. He felt no need to apologize. "I paid you. Do I have to watch?"

"I guess not, but—"

"Move." He pushed Toyota out of his line of vision. Erica was no longer at the bar.

"You're an ass."

"I hear that a lot." He stood and twisted to see the entire club. He'd gotten caught up in the past, and the present was getting away from him again. Hadn't done that in a while. The thought made him twitch. Erica and Banks were nowhere to be seen. As a matter of fact, most of the staff had pulled the find-somewhere-else-to-be act.

He should walk right out that front door and let Banks do his worst with the traitorous bitch. That was exactly what a smart man would do. Not his business.

He turned to make his way back to his truck. Getting roughed up by a bouncer might serve her right. She'd abandoned Jim back when he was Korey Anders. She'd broken his heart and his general belief in people. Why should he stick his neck out with Banks—and, more importantly, Banks's boss—for her now?

"Goddammit." He stopped, staring down at the division of the dark club and the light of day. It was a line in the sand waiting to be crossed.

If someone was going to scare the crap out of Erica Floyd, it should be him. *He* deserved that revenge. No counting the times he'd thought about inflicting some kind of revenge on her and Gretchen Bates in the years right after the arrest. He stepped away from the light. He was not about to let Banks take the opportunity from him.

"That hurts." Erica was on her tippy toes as Banks dragged her down the narrow painted cinderblock hallway cluttered with closed black doors. The private rooms for private dances. "I don't suppose you're the manager of this fine establishment, are you?" she squeaked out as he yanked her around a corner.

Jim pulled back before Banks spotted him.

"Do you know Chris Floyd?" he heard her ask Banks.

What kind of mess were the sisters mixed up in that had Banks knocking Erica around? Holy hell, Jim needed to leave. Banks wasn't only a bouncer in this tacky strip club; he also worked for Zant. Casino owner, mobster, racketeer, and all-around bat-shit crazy Andrew Zant. And that meant Banks did all kinds of things. The big boy was like a human utility knife Zant wielded as needed. Like roughing up people who owed Zant, as Jim well knew, since he currently owed the casino owner a huge debt himself. A debt that he'd chipped away at but was almost sure would never be forgiven.

"This is very eighties-movie cliché. You know? Being taken out back by the bouncer." She was nagging at him as he pushed her forward. This time her shoulder hit a stack of boxes. "Hey. Lug Nut. You can't do this!"

Aw. Fuck. Erica was going to destroy his life *again*. Not that this shit of a job and a city was much, but it was his now. He cringed as he heard her squeak and the unmistakable sound of a body hitting the wall.

Jim took a peek around the bend in time to see her kick back at the huge man as hard as she could, jamming her heel down his shin. Banks's grunt of surprise and pain was not accompanied by a loosening of his grip. On the contrary. Next, she flailed her free arm in attempt to scratch and claw any part of him she could reach. Her efforts to break free would be admirable if they weren't so pathetic. As it was, she was just pissing him off.

"Fuck me." Big Banks snatched up her other arm and shook her like a ragdoll. "Hold still, dammit."

Jim saw the moment Erica realized how bad this situation was. Her face paled and her eyes widened with an adrenaline rush of fear. He knew the feeling. Her toes would be tingling with it, her heart racing so that she could hear the pulse of blood in her ears. Though Jim doubted she had the time or inclination to study how her terror was affecting her body functions.

This is the dirty side of Vegas, girl. And you walked right into it. She let out an ear-splitting scream. *That* would be useful in the back of a club pounding techno music turned up to hellish levels on the other side of the cinderblock.

He had no real choice. He may be an ass, but he wasn't leaving Erica to Banks or Zant.

"Fine." Banks's voice was low and even. Jim saw it coming; Erica did not. Banks smacked her face-first into the peeling cinderblock.

Her body gave up, drooped, but Erica managed to reach for and awkwardly snag the frame of the opening to a room with her fingertips as he pulled her deeper into the bowels of the club. Between his grip and her rubbery limbs, she couldn't hold on but she'd managed to slow their progress a little.

"Stop being such a pain." Banks shook her hard. The door slipped from her weak grip. Her head looked like a wooden puppet moving in slow motion as she looked back at Banks's large leathery face.

"Dammit," Jim muttered. He moved swift and silent, glad for the element of surprise. Banks would never expect to be bum-rushed in his own place. Jim took advantage of the big guy having both hands full.

He had to jump to get onto Banks's back. The man must be six-foot-six. Not having a better solution, Jim wrapped his arm around the man's thick neck, cranked it tight with his other hand, and hoped for the best.

Erica fell out of Banks's grasp and against the wall. Good start. Now all Jim had to do was hold on and keep pressure on Banks's larynx until the man's oxygen-deprived brain started to falter along with his strength. With any luck, the oaf would pass right on out and Jim could slip away without having his identity disclosed.

"Korey?"

Jim glanced down at the heap of woman trying to right herself against the wall.

"Shut up," he said to Erica as Banks tried to turn to see him. Jim had him tight. Fighting a monstrous boa constrictor would be easier than bringing Banks down. At least a snake wouldn't hold a grudge or be likely to beat the crap out of Jim later. It was taking all his strength to maintain the correct position to cut off Banks's air and keep his big head facing forward.

"Leave off," was all Banks managed to say before launching himself backward and slamming Jim's already aching back into the cinderblock. Jim almost let his grip lessen with the force of being sand-wiched between a behemoth and the brick, but he held fast.

"Korey Anders. Is that really you?" She was sitting and rubbing her bleeding forehead. Her eyes looked crossed. No wedding ring.

Evidently, Banks was losing his patience. He turned in a circle with Jim still on his back. With a ham-fisted move, Banks tried to fish his revolver out of its holster. Jim grabbed his thumb and twisted with a pressure move. Judo 101. Banks lost his grip on the weapon. Jim took the gun as easily as shaking hands.

And with a good arching swing, he popped poor Banks in the sweet spot. The big man tried to hold his ground. He stumbled a few steps forward before his knees gave and he crumpled into an unconscious pile between Jim's feet.

"Oh, crap. Korey." She looked up from Banks and her mouth fell open. Her eyes were still dilated, but she looked better.

If she called him by his birth name again, he might whack her with the gun butt. Korey Anders had ceased to exist in Columbus eight years ago. He'd worked long and hard to become Jim Elwood Bean and establish his identity, his reputation, and his business. Well, his reputation wasn't stellar, but he got the job done. Lawyers loved him for getting the dirt they wanted for clients. Housewives with cheating husbands loved him.

"Don't call me that again." He grabbed her hand.

3

HE SILENTLY WATCHED ERICA from the hall, still not believing she was in his house. "Nice place," she said to herself as she surveyed the room. He knew what it looked like. A fucking mess. So what? He needed another drink. She was looking over his office. Her fingers trailed the edge of his desk as she scanned the stack of bills and mail. She'd know he'd changed his name and would figure out he was now in the private investigation field. He wasn't hiding shit from her.

Ms. Annie sat eyeing Erica from atop the center of the pile of junk on the desk. All four feet were tucked up neatly under her body and her ears turned on Erica. Her tail flipped back and forth with a snotty snap. Apparently, his cat did not seem particularly happy with Erica's presence either. Maybe the aloof bitch-cat had some sense after all.

"For someone who constantly went behind me and rewashed dishes or refolded my clothes if I left them in the basket too long…"

she mumbled, still unaware of his presence. But that was a different place. A different life. A different man. He was well aware that his office looked like a terrorist bombed a junkyard.

"From the FBI academy to this." She jumped at the sound of his voice. "Two classes away from a criminology master's when…" When Gretchen had shown up at the sorority house with her face bruised, her clothes torn, her bucket full of lies. And Erica believed them all.

Erica spun. Came to him. "Thanks for pulling me out of there." She cupped his cheek. She'd done it a thousand times when they were a couple.

Time and treachery surged up like bile in this throat. He recoiled as if he'd been slapped. He stepped back, physically moving to put his desk and Ms. Annie between the two of them. He tossed her the bag of ice and a towel he'd gotten from the kitchen. The fake leather office chair creaked as his weight filled it.

"Any hallucinations, dizziness?" His voice was tight, professional.

She smiled in spite of the situation. "I see an angry black cat in the middle of a messed-up desk."

"Annie's my security." He looked around the array of paper spread out before them and shrugged.

She hissed from pain when she pressed the ice to her brow. Her eyes were sad. Tired. He didn't care.

"Gretchen fooled us all. It was crazy," she blurted out.

He held his breath. He did not want to have this conversation.

"You don't want excuses?"

He wasn't sure what to say, so he didn't say a word, sat still, not blinking, with his hands on the arms of his office chair. He could see the small lines time and stress had etched on her face. She looked older, a little vulnerable.

"I looked for you." She started on it again. The excuses. "After the charges were dropped. You just disappeared."

He gripped the arms of the chair. She waited for a response. He finally blinked.

"I'm really sorry, Korey. I could blame youth or fear or ..." Jim saw the tears coming. She glanced around the office to avoid his scrutiny. "I know you wanted to be a politician as well as an FBI agent." Meaning this mess was a thousand miles from all his dreams. "I know it's too late. I know your life was changed with the charges and the publicity. I should have acted differently."

Yeah, she should have defended him from the start.

"My name is Jim Bean." He wanted to move. To put a stop to this right now. There was that small part of him that wanted to hear what she had to say. The rest of him quit giving a flying fuck about her years ago.

"Fine. *Jim.* I'm sorry." She put her hand on her chest, over her heart, like she was pledging to the flag. "I loved you. I wanted to believe you. But Gretchen was in the hospital, the police were every-where, the news crews were already crucifying you, insisting there was evidence. DNA evidence." She shifted. Looked at the bag of ice in her hand. "The entire thing was like a tornado. When you called, you didn't deny it. You didn't deny anything."

There it is. So it was *his* fault? Enough. Too long gone to fix. Too much anger to care what she thought, then or now. Water done dried up from under that bridge. "Why are you here, Erica?"

She blinked, her face tightened. She was getting angry, maybe appalled that her apology meant nothing to him. What'd she expect? He simply waited for an answer.

She fidgeted with the towel. Thinking. "You're right. I'm not in Vegas to give you a long-deserved apology. But you know that." Her face paled. She took in a deep breath as if to steady herself for what was coming next. "I'm here about Chris. "

He knew that but wanted to hear what she had to say. "What's Chris doing in Vegas?"

"After you left, she became a social worker. A while back, she decided there were places outside Ohio where people needed more help. Said there were too many families out here without resources, young girls in trouble." She stood and attempted to pace his office. But with the electronics and props lying around, she could only put together a couple of paces. Now that she was talking about Chris, he could see panic in her eyes. "She's been here about a year and a half." She adjusted the ice. Pushing it into her skin.

"And? How does that get *you* knocked around in a strip club?" His body eased slightly as the subject moved away from their past. Missing person, that was his gig.

"Supposedly, she went to work there. That's what the police and some thug said, anyway. I find it nearly impossible to believe."

She'd stopped next to Jim's desk. His gaze traveled up her body as she hesitated. He might hate her, but obviously, he still found her attractive. When his gaze finally found hers, she smiled at him. She saw where his mind had gone. Fuck.

He frowned, shuffled some papers on the desk. "Go to the cops."

She readjusted the ice bag and pulled on her skin a little too hard. Blood trickled down the side of her eye.

"Cops pissed me off." She flopped herself back on the rickety chair in front of his desk so she could exchange the ice bag for the towel. "They are 'no longer pursuing leads.' Not interested." She winced. "Unless you want to help me, I'm out of ideas and she's still missing."

"Help you?" With a grunt, Jim got up and came around to sit on the edge of the desk in front her. "Not likely." He pulled the towel from her and pinched together her split brow. "You should go get this stitched. Unless you want me to do it?"

"You'd love that, wouldn't you? Leave me a nice jagged scar." She yanked the towel from him. "Just give me a Band-Aid."

That worked for him. He got up to retrieve one from his emergency kit. She was gonna be trouble with a giant, throbbing *T*. And she had the nerve to be mad at him. He would stick a Band-Aid on her ass and send her on her merry way. The past and the fact she was mixed up with one of Zant's minions both pointed in one direction: out his back door.

He'd heard enough. Erica Floyd needed to be gone. He tossed her the bandage and nodded to the door. "Call a cab from the diner on the corner."

Her face reddened as she stared up at him. He remembered that look. Knew the instant she was going to blow. "I know you're mad. I understand how you must feel. But I apologized." She stood and propped her hands on her hips. She was inches from his face. He could smell her lingering perfume.

"And that should fix everything?" He couldn't have stopped the chuckle that escaped even if he had wanted to save her feelings. And he did not. "Do you have any idea what I went through in that hot, airless interrogation room that night? When I was alone and staring at a small window on a closed and locked door." He tilted his head. "Do you?"

She shook her head and eased back into her seat.

"I was shocked as hell. Confused. Pulled from my fucking bed in the middle of the night and charged with rape. Not just rape, no. They'd charged me with first-degree kidnapping with a weapon and sexual assault. And who was I supposed to have raped? Gretchen?"

He said it slowly and leaned in over her, not caring if three years of anger-management classes got blown out the window. "Those were serious charges. Charges that carried life sentences. I was scared. All I had at that moment was you and the *misguided* faith that you'd be on my side no matter what. The knowledge that you'd believe in me."

She nodded and mumbled something that sounded like *I know*. As if she could understand.

"You don't get to understand. I remember pulling at the shackles binding my wrists, straining them, making the steel dig into my skin to prevent the overwhelming urge to vomit from fear, from knowing my life was over."

"I get it."

"No. No, you don't!" He'd yelled it. Yelled it at her. He paced away, braced his weight against the file cabinets with his outstretched arms and faced the wall. He didn't want to look at her. He calmed his voice. "When I called you, it didn't matter what I said or didn't say. You were supposed to be there for me." He shook his head. Remembering the deep-down feeling of his balls being yanked up through his stomach when he heard her speak. "You'd already made up your mind. You'd believed her story. I heard it in your voice." The conversation had been short. He'd needed to know Erica was there, would help him through the mess. It had taken about thirty seconds to know where she stood. The world had gone black.

"I'm sorry."

"*Sorry* doesn't cut it, baby." He looked back at her. Tears were streaming down her face. Fucking crying women. He saw a lot of it these days. Clients. Subjects. This conversation would get them nowhere. He knew it. He'd imagined getting to tell her to fuck off for years. Having the opportunity to say it now felt as empty as it had in his daydreams. He cursed himself silently. "You're bleeding again."

She dabbed at it with the towel. Looked at the evidence of the violence she'd been subjected to. "Why do men have to beat on one another to make a point?"

"Banks beats the crap out of people for a living. He makes *other* people's points."

"Whose point do you think he was trying to make?" She looked up at him as she held the towel, her eyes tired and scared. The sooner she was gone, the better. He could have gone an entire lifetime without looking into those green eyes again. Easier to hate the woman from a distance.

"No telling. Could be any number of people. Banks is an equal-opportunity thug." But Andrew Zant was the one who owned the big man. "Go back to the police. File a complaint. After this, they'll help you find Chris." He looked at the hand on the towel. "Hold that firm."

"They quit looking for Chris as soon as they found out she was working at that strip place." She huffed and let the cloth fall and blood trickled from the cut.

Jim reached down and put her hand back. "They'll keep her on a missing persons list, but too many girls disappear after doing tricks and stripping for the police to keep up. Some get dead. Some move on to another city. I know. Hopeful parents hire me all the time. I'll gladly give you the speech I give them as I take their money. It's not meant to be encouraging."

She stood. "I don't want to hear your speech. I want to find my sister." Her hand dropped from her forehead again.

Jim knew very well where this was headed. He didn't want to say no to her, but he would. What if she started crying again? "Go back to the station. You can press charges against Banks and they'll probably re-open her case since you were assaulted." He turned. "I'll get you a cab."

But she caught his arm. "Kore—Jim." The correction was fast but the emotion in her voice was not to be missed.

He stopped and looked down at her hand. There was blood on her knuckle. She pulled him closer, slipping her arms around his waist. She gripped the muscles of his lower back, pulling their bodies together. Close enough to feel her breasts against his chest. His body roared to life as if it remembered hers and cared little for what his head thought of the situation.

The ghost of their broken lives whispered in his ear. He still wanted her. Not since Erica had he managed a relationship deeper than the occasional late-night booty call. He could bury himself in her heat as he had done years ago. He'd *trusted* her.

A trust she'd shattered. He shook his head to clear the lusty haze in his mind. She'd abandoned him. The one person he'd thought would stand by him for the rest of his life. He thought of the ring that had been in his bedside table when he'd been arrested. The ring he'd hocked to help pay lawyer fees. He pulled away from her. "You need to go."

"I *need* your help."

No way. "There are a lot of PIs out there. Check the phone book."

"I can pay. Three times your usual rate. None of the others will do as good a job as you. I know it."

He barked out a laugh. "What makes you think that? I'm a washed-up PI at thirty-five, sweet cheeks. I drink too damned much. I'm an asshole. I don't want to be around *you* and I don't want *your* money. Don't you get it?"

Mad. He needed to stay mad instead of hurt. Maybe that would make her give up and leave. He wanted to be mad anyway. All of a sudden the bottle of Scotch sitting on the filing cabinet looked real good. He poured two fingers into the dirty glass next to it. Then drank half of it.

"You still want me. I can tell."

She was looking at his jeans. Yep. He was hard. Even if she didn't mean that by her words, that's what her eyes said. He laughed. No hiding that.

"I could fuck you, Erica. I could strip you out of that high-dollar suit, lay you out on that desk, and fuck you." Her eyes got bigger. He swallowed down the second half of the glass. "But that doesn't change anything. I *won't* help you."

Not to mention that Zant would probably kill him right off if he tried to investigate. But the Scotch wasn't fast enough to kill the pain, so he dug deeper for the anger.

"I said I'm sorry. Admitted I was wrong. What more do you want me to do?" she appealed, her eyes filling with tears.

Damn her tears. His life lay in ruins. Not hers. No matter that they dropped all charges six weeks later. In any basic criminal search of Korey Anders, it still came up. *Arrested. Seven-hundred-thousand-dollar bail. First-degree sexual assault with a weapon.* To this day he could picture the headlines in the paper. His mug shot plastered under it. Still see his mother's face when she had come to visit him. Even *she* had been unsure based on the lies the news had reported.

But that wasn't what killed Korey Anders that night. He spoke the words he'd waited eight years to say to her: "*You* believed I did it."

"You wouldn't deny it." She sat back in the chair. "I was surrounded by people telling me to believe it."

"Yeah, well. Now, I'm surrounded by people telling me to take other cases." He gestured toward the cat. She blinked beady yellow eyes at Erica from the desk. "Annie says we're booked solid. So sorry."

He grabbed his cell off the desk, thumbed through the contacts, and found the number for one of the cabbies he used when he was in a tight spot. She poured herself a shot and knocked it back with a cough. He didn't look at her as he arranged for Adair to pick her up. From the diner at the end of the block.

"You really are an asshole." She slammed the glass back on the desk.

"That's what they say. But you were the one who believed a drunk sorority girl—who pissed you off more often than not—over the man you supposedly loved. *I* think that makes *you* an asshole." Wow. That really sounded immature and nonsensical. But he meant it. He reclaimed his glass.

"Fine. Hate me. You're right. I get it. I was stupid, misguided, and mistaken." She stepped back into his personal space. He took another drink. "My sister did not come out here to be a prostitute and you very well know it. She was a social worker." Erica poked his shoulder, making some of the Scotch slosh out. Her eyes were piercing his. "Chris has an advanced degree and a trust fund. Why would she take a second job as a stripper?"

27

He knew none of it made sense. Chris was okay. She had always been nice to him. Maybe he could check it out a little and not let Erica know.

No. What was he thinking? He needed to stay out of this shit. Away from her. "The police will figure it out."

Erica stepped closer. Moving away didn't help, since his back hit the file cabinet. Trapped. She slid her hand under his shirttail and up his stomach. He held the bottle in one hand and the glass in the other. It left him unable stop the trail of heat it made over his skin. Or so he justified. He closed his eyes let his head fall back. Let his body experience her touch. She leaned in, her thighs pressed against his.

"You still want me even if you don't like me."

"No, I don't."

"Liar."

Yes. He was. Traitorous arms spread, letting her even closer. She was seducing him. Movement on the desk caught his attention. Annie had sat up. Her tail was curled around her feet. Her yellow eyes were glaring at Jim suspiciously. Condescending.

"I'll tell you what, Jim Bean." Erica whispered it on the edge of his ear, her lips brushing the rim, making his toes tingle. He squeezed the glass in his hand. "You may not like me anymore. That's fine. But you do still want me." She kissed that spot where his neck and his shoulder meet. "Help me find Chris."

4

HE SHOULDN'T RESIST. Why should he? He'd felt used and aban-
doned when she'd betrayed him. Now he would return the favor.
Do a little digging about Chris and then move on. She'd go back to
Boston.

With a large gulp he finished off the last little bit of Scotch. Direct from the bottle. The glass he held was not needed. The room-
temperature liquid burned his throat as he swallowed. Erica's lips
touched that absurdly sensitive spot on his neck again. His body reacted as if not one moment had passed. He channeled his thoughts
in on that so his head played no part in his existence for a moment.
How far would she really go with this?

He opened his eyes and found her watching him, that jewel-
green gaze as piercing as always, her expression questioning. Her
nails barely scraped just under the edge of his waistband. He didn't
have to look down. He could visualize all of it. Her ivory fingers
against his darker skin.

What he wanted was … her. Her to be in Boston where she be-longed. Out of his life.

"Please." She was pressed against him from chest to ankle. The word was a breath on his neck, her body a temptation. Femme fatale.

His body was overusing blood flow at the moment. His brain moved slow. She knew how to take him right to the edge even with only her touch. She always had. But he was an easy read, like a billboard.

"Erica…" He knew it sounded desperate. He dug his back into the cold metal edge of the cabinets to hold himself upright and looked down at her. As much as he deserved a down-and-dirty grudge fuck…

"No deal."

With more of a groan than he intended, he pulled away from her. Took a breath. She fell back into the chair. Her eyes were about to fill with tears again. Maybe he was an ass. But their past… his pain was not fixable with a little tickle and squeeze.

Annie got up, stretched, and resituated on his desk. She was look-ing down her kitty nose at him. Rarely did she approve of his morals. Tonight was no different. He'd left Erica hanging. Served her right.

She'd walked away when he needed her most. Left him to hang. When he pawned the ring he'd bought for her, he'd been glad he'd never proposed. She strung him along for two years.

Her shirt was unbuttoned, her head cut. She looked at the ground. "Let me embarrass myself before stopping that, huh? A little payback? You enjoy it?"

He hadn't really. Hadn't intended it.

She sniffed and wiped her nose on her sleeve. "I don't care. I'll beg. No time for pride. I need you. Chris needs you."

He felt a wave of shame. He *had* momentarily enjoyed her humiliation. In the end, Jim was not *that* guy. "There's a restroom." He tilted his head toward the hall that led to the rest of the townhouse house. "Go clean up."

She nodded, her face still beet red as she put herself together.

But then there was Chris. Could he tolerate Erica for a day or so until he found out why Chris had disappeared? He needed the cash. Bad. He wiped a bead of sweat from his forehead with a napkin from an old Burger King bag. He tossed the whole mess in his trashcan and plopped to his chair. His space. His life. His crappy office.

The office was really a converted one-bay garage attached to a shitty little townhouse in a shitty little neighborhood. It was the unit on the end of a row. The end where the traffic came and went. Not the end by the pool or the playground. He didn't care about the pool or the playground. *He* was usually the traffic, coming and going at odd hours. His was the corner lot. Faced two streets and an alley behind. Room for all four of his cars parked on the road and the bike in the alley behind. No one complained.

The fuzzy black cat was up on the cabinet now, sniffing around his empty Scotch bottle. "I believe you are absolutely correct, Ms. Annie." He opened his top right drawer and pulled out a new bottle. He cracked the seal and poured another half glass. "I'll have another."

Annie tilted her head and one eye closed as she scrutinized him. Her irritated expression gave Jim the impression she disapproved of his sound reasoning. "I can spend a few days giving her hell and then send her packing. We need the money. Don't give me that look. Meow Chow ain't free."

The cat shook her head and turned tail to wander off toward the front of the house. In the same direction Erica had headed. He took a big ol' swallow. Yep. If he kept this all business and made sure she didn't trample his heart again, this might be a profitable few days after all.

5

HIS PHONE CHIRPED. Text message. Jim looked up to see Erica standing in the hall as he fished it out of his pocket. Her clothing restored. Her expression hard to read. He wanted to say something but didn't have a clue as to what. He read the screen. "Cab driver. He's waiting at the coffee shop."

She nodded. Grabbed her bag. "Are you going to help or not?"

He *could* just drive her to the hotel himself, but that would be too personal... considering. Now that she was standing in his space again, he needed her gone. He took another drink. That's what he knew how to do these days. "I'll start in the morning. Where you staying?"

"The Americana."

A Zant hotel. Andrew Zant's office was on the twenty-third floor. He knew that because he'd been there, on that ugly carpet, looking at that hulking snake in its pompous tank with the Asian jungle plants and the rainforest tree. He'd made a different kind of bargain *that* day.

Zant would keep using it. Keep putting the knife to his throat. The thought of yet another banner day made the Scotch turn in his stomach.

"Banks works for the man who owns that hotel."

"So?"

"You may want to consider changing addresses."

"I don't intend to be here long. You should be able to track her fairly easy, right? She wasn't that complicated a girl." Her head was no longer bleeding, but the bruise on her brow was starting to show.

"You'll have a shiner by morning."

"Perfect."

Unfortunately, tracking Chris might very well be easy. The news would most likely be bad. Very bad. He opened the side door and walked out. Turned right and headed for the Coffee Girl.

She followed. He heard her closing the door behind them, the tap-tap of her dress shoes as she rushed. He glanced at her as she caught up. She looked flushed and beautiful. He had the urge to hold her hand. Habit, he told himself. That's all.

"What about my rental car? It's still at the strip club."

"I'll get it. Don't go back there. Ever."

They crossed Alexander Avenue and turned left. The Coffee Girl was on the corner. It used to be a dirty old greasy spoon Jim had loved. But some out-of-work telecom executive moved out here and bought the place last year after the dot-com bust. He'd cleaned up the grease, painted the inside a cheerful yellow, and changed the menu. Now it was *not* Jim's favorite place. But it was close. So he was now a reluctant regular. Did most his business at the back corner table. And the coffee girl who worked mornings was one of the few people he liked. Her face and smart mouth made the bland organic spinach omelets go down better. That and ketchup.

"You need my number," she said. The cab was sitting in the lot, closer to Jim's house than the front door of the diner. Adair knew what was what. He did not seem surprised when Jim opened the door and motioned Erica in.

Jim got a card from his wallet. It was plain white, his name printed in dark block letters in the middle and his cell number printed on the bottom right corner. "Text me when you're up."

She handed him the keys to the rental car, inspected the card. Started to smile but caught herself. "That's all?"

"That's all." He told Adair where to go and glanced back at her. "Okay?"

"Okay."

"Tomorrow, then."

"Tomorrow."

The cab pulled away. He felt a sense of loss. It aggravated him. He was hungry. He considered the Coffee Girl. Nothing but Tofurkey and salads after breakfast. He'd settle for Scotch. Jim Bean headed home.

He needed a shower. Needed food. Needed to get the memory of her breath on his neck out of his head. He entered the house through the same door they'd left so he could retrieve the Scotch. Annie met him and followed him, weaving through his legs as he made his way to the kitchen. She sat next to her bowl and made a public, boisterous complaint about the empty state of it. He opened the pantry and grabbed the bag of cat chow. It had no weight and when he shook it, only crumbs and dust rattled in the bottom.

Annie mewed her impatience. Jim considered that he may have forgotten to feed her before leaving this morning. "Sorry, baby girl."

The cupboard was bare. The pantry contained only a half box of macaroni noodles, a can of black-eyed peas, and an empty tin of coffee. He moved to the fridge. It was equally barren. On the bottom shelf was a pizza box. Three days old. He retrieved it and inspected the contents. Three slices of sausage, hamburger, and onion. Extra cheese.

Annie jumped on the counter to investigate her options. "How's about some hamburger?" He picked off a piece and tossed it to her. "Sausage was pretty spicy."

She tested the meat. Found she approved. He took a drink and pulled a few more pieces off the pie and put them on the counter. Annie happily ate.

He retrieved his phone and popped a piece of sausage in his mouth. Scanned his contacts and hit the call button.

"Broady."

Jim cringed. He half expected no one to answer the detective's line this late. Broady was an ass. Stupid and mean. Bad combination for someone who was supposed to protect and serve.

"Hey. It's Jim Bean. You're working late."

There was a perceivable sigh on the line. "Yeah. I'm busy, Bean."

"I just need a name. Who's working the Floyd case? Chris Floyd. Missing persons." He kept talking, not giving Broady a chance to deny him the information. "Give me the name and I won't come down there and ask you to pull the file personally."

He'd had a couple of run-ins with the Vegas PD. He knew his rights; sometimes they pretended not to. It got ugly a time or two. Either way, Broady would not want Jim down there hassling him at this time of night.

"You won't show on my shift?"

"Nope."

"Hold on."

Jim heard the click, heard the crappy music. It kept playing. And playing. A Beatles remix, he believed. It shouldn't take this long.

The music clicked off. "No one."

"No one's been assigned?"

"Not exactly."

Jim took another swig. "Not in the mood for games." He was about to get mad enough to go back on his word and go down there and get right in Broady's face. "It's closed?"

"Not one open. Don't see any Floyd on anything open at all."

"How about closed?"

Broady sighed. Jim listened as keys clacked on the old fat black keyboards attached by long twisting cords to antiquated computers. "Nothing. Bye, Bean." He hung up.

Jim looked at his phone. He was sure Erica had said the police had at least looked into it. She would have filed a complaint. That would mean a case file had to have been opened. Case files did not disappear. He paced the other end of his small living room, avoiding a pair of shoes and an Amazon box in his path. The new remote microphone he'd ordered was still in it. He slid it under the end table to prevent stepping on it.

No file. Maybe Broady was being a bigger asshole than usual. The couch felt good as he slouched down to operate the remote. A random sports report came on the screen. The volume was too low to follow what the cute sports reporter was saying. Her eyes were a little crossed, but she looked pretty excited by her news.

————

The phone woke him. Not the ring, although it should have. The thing danced on the coffee table as it vibrated with a metallic clang like an old-fashioned clock with the silver double bells on top. Annoying. Painful. He kicked at it but missed. No use. He was awake and the events of the previous day spilled through his thumping head like a dam breaking.

He rubbed his chin. Next to the phone was the half-empty Scotch bottle and a half-eaten slice of pizza. All the meat was missing, including the sausage. Annie had helped herself to breakfast. Mental note: buy cat food.

The screen said he had two messages and a text. The text was brief, from an unrecognized number. UP AND READY.

Two calls from current clients. One of whom would want an update. An update with news. News that would save them money and an upcoming court appearance. He still had nothing on Edmund Carver's workers' comp fraud. The other was less urgent, a new adultery investigation. The mister was loaded and not careful. The missus wanted proof of multiple affairs. She would get it. Just not today.

He navigated to the text and pushed the tab to add a contact. Her number showed with the appropriate blanks to fill in. First. Last. Address. He typed an *E* and hit save. Didn't want her name and number in his contacts. Didn't want to feel that connected. She was desperate. But he had to bow out.

The thought of being around her, having to look into those eyes, was too much. He could be angry and probably make it through the investigation. Angry was easier to deal with than hurt. Hurt made people do stupid things.

Annie jumped onto his lap. She wanted attention. He scratched her head, let his hand run down the length of her back. Her fur was soft, her purr comforting. The phone chirped again, vibrating in his other hand. Not comforting. Nagging. That one indicated a voicemail. He navigated to the message. The casino client. Pushed play.

"Thanks for all your good work, Mr. Bean, but circumstances have changed. We're dropping the case against Mr. Carver. We cut a check this morning for your current billable hours. Let our accounting department know if I've miscalculated. We'll be in touch."

No update needed. No bonus. Damn. He spent four days painting a dumpster and they no longer needed the proof? This day was starting off with a bang. He'd needed that bonus money.

He made it upstairs to the bathroom and started the water running in the shower. He rummaged through three drawers, found a bottle of aspirin, popped four, and stuck his head under the sink faucet for a swallow to wash them down.

Once in the shower he closed his eyes. The hot water was clarifying. Erica had offered three times his normal fees. *That* would solve some issues. Like paying his rent. But, as much as he needed the money, he knew he was going to pass. He'd give Erica the names of two or three other investigators in the area. He needed away from her.

6

JIM SLID INTO THE usual booth at the Coffee Girl. The farthest from the front door, on an interior wall and close to the waitress station and the alley to the kitchen, which led to the back door. Least desirable for most clientele. Most desirable for Jim Bean.

Sandy came directly behind him with the coffee urn. She poured him a large cup with a smile and a simple good morning.

"You sure you don't want that job?" One of his earlier investigations ended up with Sandy being kidnapped and drugged. Dang close to being killed. He didn't really want an employee, but in the heat of the moment when things had gone bad, he'd offered her the position of his assistant. He could really use the help in his one-man venture, but he wasn't so keen on the idea of someone in his business. Or paying too much attention to how he lived his life.

"Let me finish this semester, then we'll talk about it again."

Same answer as she gave him every week. Seems like a semester should have passed by now. He gave her his best pre-coffee smile.

She retreated without taking his order. He got the same thing every morning: organic spinach omelet, hash browns, and some kind of sausage patty made from soybeans. It wasn't horrible. It wasn't good. It was probably the only healthy thing in his life. It was serviceable and he didn't have to change his routine. Routine was generally not a good thing, but he liked waking up and walking to breakfast. It felt normal, comfortable, in a life that offered little of either.

Jim watched a large silver motorcycle roll into the lot. Oscar. See. Routine wasn't healthy. Oscar Olsen knew exactly where to find him. Not that Oscar was a threat. On the contrary. Oscar was one of the only people on earth Jim called friend.

His omelet arrived. But Sandy didn't bring it. Oscar relieved her of that duty as he strode past. He leaned in, gave her a wink, pecked her on the check, and took Jim's plate.

Double O, as most called him, slid into the vinyl seat across from Jim and plopped the plate down. "Will there be anything else?" He grinned. For a man whose life had taken a far worse turn than even Jim's, he sure smiled a lot. It was annoying.

"A little less cheerful breakfast companion."

"Bad night?"

He thought of Erica, the anger, her so close to him. "Something like that."

Sandy brought his new companion a cup of coffee. He smiled up at her. "I'll have the pancakes and bacon." Which meant some kind of sweet potato shingle that would be the consistency of cardboard and some fake tofu strip, and O knew it. To Jim he said, "You should really go elsewhere for breakfast."

"And give up all this?"

Oscar quit smiling. "I know I've asked you before, but do you want to help out with a couple of my cases? I'm slammed. Can't keep up. Seems half the idiots due on trial last month skipped." He made a face as he took a sip from his cup. "Oh. Yum."

He was right. The coffee was as bad as the food. Maybe it *was* time for a change. And maybe he should pick up a case or two from O. He needed the cash. Owed Oscar some cash, in fact. Maybe he could work it off. "Sure. I need to look into one thing for a current case. Should wrap it up later today."

Double O's face changed. Hardened. He was going for serious, but it looked like he had gas to Jim. "I need you to carry that piece if you're going after skips. They got more to lose than some guy cheating on his wife."

"That depends on the wife, now, doesn't it?"

"Serious, Bean."

The Glock. Still in the box, still on the floor in his office. A gift from Double O. Not gonna happen. Jim shook his head. "Don't need one."

"Tell me that after your ass gets shot at."

"I've managed to take care of things for years without one. If it's my time—"

"Stupid. Your time to go might just be rescheduled for an earlier date if you don't start carrying. If that one's too big, I got a snubby you can have."

"It's not that. Just not my thing." They'd had this discussion before. Jim felt like guns just made it easy to kill a man. If you had to kill, use your hands. Then you'd have time to think about it, to *know* he needed killing. Plus, Jim couldn't hit the broad side of a barn with a shotgun. Oscar had given him some lessons, but his aim was still for shit.

Anyway. He had other things on his mind. "Let me ask you something—you ever heard of a case file going missing from the police database?" He took another large bite despite the fact his morning-after stomach was protesting the dry eggs. He added ketchup. Food was great for a hangover. A greasy real sausage biscuit would be better, but...

"No. Case is opened, it's in the computer. Stays there."

"That's what I thought." Why would Broady tell him differently? It didn't matter. He was going to be off the case. Erica would be using someone else. After he delivered her car and got her out of Zant's hotel. Speaking of ... He texted Adair for a ride to the Peppermint Pony. He'd drive her car over to the Strip, tell her he needed to help out O, and be done with the whole mess in an hour. Grab some cat food and go home.

They sat in quiet as they ate. A little bounty hunter work would be good for him. Maybe a bail jumper might put up a good fight. Give him a reason to break the rules of his anger-management class. He sighed. *Maybe* it was time to leave Las Vegas. Maybe an entire new identity was waiting for him just around the corner. Not just a change of name like he did here. Nope, the real deal. New social security number and everything. But that took time and money to set up. Double O was offering him a way to make that money.

Erica would have to manage this shit on her own.

7

JIM HESITATED AT THE ELEVATOR as a very lean man encased in a shiny dark gray suit stood outside Erica's room with a clipboard. The effect of the suit, slim cut and skinny legs, along with a big face, made him look cartoonish, like the Pink Panther character clad in high-end fabric. Dark gray for the suit, lighter gray crisp shirt. A narrow avocado tie was the only break in the color palette. Vegas.

He bowed his head and checked off something on his paper. "I apologize for any inconvenience. "

Jim knelt down to tie his shoe as the man slinked around the corner toward the elevators on the back side of the hotel. He waited a moment before going to her door to make sure the thin man wasn't going to double back. Not paranoid, just careful.

He knocked only once.

She pulled the door open quickly, surely expecting the thin man again.

"Who was that?" Jim stood there. Her eyes were a little blood-shot, she was wrapped in a towel.

"We have a lot to do today." She looked him over with a disapproving frown before she turned to her suitcase and fished out a pair of slacks and a button-up top.

He did glance down at his attire but offered no comment. "The guy at the door. What did he want?"

She turned back with a snap. Not happy. "Laundry service is behind today. Clean towels aren't coming for a while."

"Bullshit."

"I've been waiting all morning with no word from you. That would get people fired in the banking world. I texted you three hours ago."

"And you said you were ready." He tried to keep from leering at her towel-clad body.

"I *was* ready. I got bored waiting. Then anxious. So I went to the gym." His guess was she'd gotten worried he wasn't coming, angry he hadn't replied to her message, and then scared that she was on her own again in trying to find Chris.

"Where do we start?" she asked briskly.

"From where I was standing I couldn't get a good look at his face. He didn't stop at the next room. Or the one after that. He went straight for the elevator."

"Really? I guess I'm the only one short on towels." She stepped closer to him. He backed away. He wished he hadn't taken her to his house the night before. He wished she was dressed now.

"Have you started?" She came even closer.

"How likely is that?"

"How likely is what?"

"That you're the only one on the floor without towels."

She huffed, backed off a little. "What? I don't care about towels. We need to start looking for Chris. Did you start this morning or not? Since you didn't reply, I was hoping you were already looking for her."

He looked at his feet. "I need to talk to you about this."

"This conversation is going in too many different directions. About the man in the hall, Chris, or last night?"

"Chris"—his brows drew together—"and last night. And that guy being here is a little concerning."

"I'll start with the easy one. The guy is a hotel guy. Doing his job. Next."

His gaze moved away from the top of the towel, where her breasts were pushed up due to the fact that she'd just crossed her arms. "I think you should hire someone else to help with Chris."

"Oh. No, you don't. You cannot back out. Not now. No."

He crossed his arms and changed his weight from one leg to the other. "I have other clients, you know. I can't just drop everything. There are several PIs around here."

She stammered, seeming to lose her confidence. "I ... I knew that trying to seduce you wasn't going to work. That had been a long shot and I panicked. The whole idea was borne more in desperation and desire than a real belief that you would barter for your services with me. I'm sorry."

She paced to the window with a sigh and looked out over the tourist milling about the Strip in daylight hours. "You may be jaded, angry, unhappy, and a jerk, but inside you have always been a good man. Things like that don't change. Character doesn't change."

He wanted to say something about a time she must have felt differently, but she kept on. "This is my sister. She's missing. You've been

46

drunk with her. Hung out at the lake with her. And now you're giving me a bunch of crap about other clients?"

He shook his head. "I told you last night. I didn't want to be around you. I can't be around you." He slid a couple of business cards onto a nearby table. The air in the room was getting hot. "These men are just as capable. Probably more so. They won't start out with all this baggage. It's better for the investigation."

"I can come up with a laundry list of why this would be good. No one will care about us like you do."

He was heading toward the door. His hand made it to the handle. "What makes you think I care, Erica?"

"Ouch. Well. Maybe not for me. I know I fucked up, but she defended you. Chris came to Mom and to me and tried to convince us that you had to have been framed. That the DNA reports were speculation. No one in town would have thought the press would just make up things based on shaky facts and add them to the reports. She was so upset."

"Sexual manipulation last night, guilt trip today?" His voice was hard. Defensive. He didn't move but couldn't look back at her. "You have changed, girl."

"That may have been a bold move last night. I give you that. I *thought* you wanted me as much as I wanted you." She took in a deep breath as if to calm her own anger. "I was trying to get you to let go of your anger and see things for what they are today."

It was all true. And it was nothing he wanted to deal with. He pulled the metal door open and stepped out of her life. It slammed with an echo.

"I was trying to save my sister!"

Jim wished all his feelings were still based in anger. Her last statement echoed loudly down the corridor. Saving Chris. He closed his eyes as he waited on the elevator. The thing chimed brightly with each floor it passed. He balled his fists. Chris. To think that little Chris had defended him to her family. It wasn't so hard to picture once he thought about it. She was a couple of years younger and a slightly smaller carbon copy of Erica. He was sure the girl had always harbored a crush for him. But he didn't want to think on any of that. Wasn't sure he believed the story. Wasn't sure he believed Erica.

He made it out to the casino floor. The clanging of the slots, the tacky carpet, and the weird unnatural lighting always made him uneasy. Walking away was the right thing to do. Being around Erica made him want things. Things long dead.

He passed rows of machines and gaming tables but stopped before a bank of particularly vulgar slots arranged in an oval. Their lights were blinking, flashy and tasteless. On a platform just above eye level sat a fancy sports car. A whole car was displayed, as if someone could win it with a dollar. He didn't care what the make was. It was something he'd never own in his line of business. Stood out too much. Jim liked to blend in.

He dug in his pocket and found his change from breakfast. He didn't care for the slots. Things he couldn't control rarely fell in his favor.

He inserted a single bill. *Sullivan's Fortune* it said across the top of the machine.

He pushed the blinking yellow button.

The missing case file, though. It made no sense.

Two limes and a golden oval.

Loser.

Put in another bill. Zant had to be involved. That meant if Zant caught him poking his nose into things, there would be far-reaching complications. Other lives involved. His deal with Zant was done, favor rendered. Zant was not particularly fond of people going back on him. People died for less. That would be a big gamble. He pushed the button again.

A purple ape. A lime. A double red heart.

Loser.

His last bill. And what was that thin man doing checking out her room? Towels? Bullshit. Erica was in big danger. Chris was probably already dead. These boys didn't play for fun. Jim had to walk away. This time he used the old-fashioned pull bar. Found he enjoyed the feel of it in his hand. Real. Better than a dingy, worn-out button. Felt like he had more control. A trick of the mind. With a good yank, he set the barrels spinning. Of course they were all digital, but they still looked like barrels.

Double heart. Double heart. Double heart.

Fuck. Winner.

With an exasperated sigh he listened to the music the modern casino played out like an anthem. The sound of hundreds of coins falling into the steel bin below the machine. The clanking was accompanied by bells and whistles announcing a winner. This slot had a flashing blue beacon that spun like a searchlight through the fake lighting of the cavernous room. Several people stopped pushing their own buttons, risking losing their own mojo, to inspect his winnings.

When the hoopla finished, he was able to generate a ticket to cash in for winnings. Six hundred and thirty-seven dollars and twenty-two cents. What kind of new math figured that, he didn't know. Didn't really care.

8

HE'D CASHED HIS TICKET and eased into a stool near the end of a remote bar. He could see most of the room. More slots here, built right in the bar top, flashing at him from under the flat soda he'd ordered. You could lose money even in this out-of-the-way corner of the casino. A couple sat at the other end. They looked like they'd been up all night and were still going strong. Dressed up, drinking, and draped over each other. Lovers. Maybe newlyweds.

Jim pulled out his phone and called Noah Miller.

"What do you want?" The answer came quick. The detective's temperament the same as usual—impatient and annoyed.

"Missing case file." Jim answered. "Wondering if that's a common thing in your system." He knew it was not.

Erica slid up next to him, running her hand over his shoulder as she took the seat on the far side of him. He wasn't exactly hiding, but he'd picked a far location, off the normal throughways of the casino. She'd managed to figure out where he was. Her hair was still damp. Her clothing businesslike.

"Not so much." Miller was somewhere loud, construction noise in the background, maybe a front loader. "In the middle of a crime scene, Bean. Is it urgent?"

Miller was a good egg. Big, fit, smart, everything a cop should be. He didn't care much for Jim's methods. "Floyd. Christina Floyd. Missing person. Regular channels say no file." He looked at Erica. She understood his comment to Miller. "I have a good informant who says there was."

"Chris Floyd. The social worker over at Protective Services?"

"Yeah. You know her?"

"We work with that department on occasion. Abandoned kids. Juvies." Someone yelled for Miller over the sound of a diesel engine. He didn't respond for a moment. "I'll check. Call you when I can."

"Thanks." The line was already dead.

Erica was sitting quietly, worry creased in her eyes, nibbling on her thumb. "Thank you."

"Don't get too excited. I'll look into a few things. Make a few calls. There are some very unsavory characters involved in this little drama. I have to tell you, I'm not optimistic, Erica." He tried to make it soft. But how you do that?

"You think she's dead?"

He tried to meet her gaze but failed. "I'm afraid after a week missing and the places she'd frequented, it's hard to imagine a scenario that ends differently."

Her body stiffened, but she didn't cry. She didn't try to refute his account. "Where do we start?"

"What do you know?" He did look up at her. "Everything. Even if you think it's insignificant. Start with how you found out she was gone."

"I got a call from her roommate. She's in L.A. on business. Has been for three weeks. Said she'd been trying to get Chris on her cell for days. No answer. No returned calls. She called Chris's office. No answer there. She got a hold of someone else there who said Chris hadn't been to work in four days. The girl in the office told Chris's roommate that there were three messages on her desk. One was from Edmond Carver. He didn't have a case file with the office, so she figured it was personal and gave me the number."

"So you flew here and tracked him down." He was impressed. And Carver had to be the one guy Jim was tailing at the moment. What were the odds?

She took a sip from his glass. Old habit. He guessed she didn't even think about it. "I did. First thing."

"And he sent you to the Peppermint Pony?"

Her eyebrow sported a nasty bruise, but the little cut had closed and was covered with a small bandage. Now she looked upset. It was a serious situation. Maybe she was considering what he'd said, that Chris was probably dead. "He said he thought she was working there, nights and weekends, that she'd contacted *him* to get the job a month or so ago."

She looks so vulnerable. Jim shook the thought away. "How did she know Carver? Did you ask?"

Erica nodded. "Chris helped him once. He didn't elaborate. I presumed it was with a child custody or something. That's the kind of work she does. Child welfare, family stuff, lost girls."

She meant like runaways, but the implication that *Chris* was now a lost girl hung in the air like the smell of burned popcorn. "Did Carver say anything else?"

"Like?"

"I don't know. Best to ask. Anything."

"He just apologized for not knowing any more. Said he liked her." She looked down.

"Sounds like he knew her fairly well."

"You know how she was. Never met a stranger. Always helping everyone. Loved the underdog."

"Even me."

———

They sat in silence as he drove Erica's screaming-yellow rental car back to Shalamar Avenue. He passed his townhouse and two other streets and parked by dumpsters tucked behind a brick wall. From the main road of his neighborhood, you couldn't see it. He handed her the keys. "Did you see the drugstore we just passed?" She nodded. "Good. Program Adair's number into your phone. If things get dicey, if you get separated from me and I don't answer a text, if I die, whatever the first sign of a problem is, call him. Have him drop you behind that drugstore. Come through the fence here." He pointed to a small opening. "Then you go straight to the airport."

She shivered. "How'd you know he gave me his card?"

"He's a businessman. I plopped you in his cab. You're in a hotel. Chances are you'd need his services again. Chances are he's right."

He walked away. She followed.

He hesitated next to a little sedan parked on the side road of his townhouse. The thing was beige, had no pin striping, only light window tint, and its wheels were dull. There was nothing about the car that would stand out, not one sticker or identifying mark. Perfect for surveillance. "You need anything before we go?"

"Just the bathroom."

Shit. "Oh. Follow me." He continued on and unlocked the door with a remote key that looked just like a car fob.

"I don't remember that from last night. I don't remember much after that Banks character busted my head until..." A flush of pink covered her face and a wave of guilt hit Jim.

"About last night," she said as she followed him into the open door.

They were crowded close in the hall that led from his office to the main part of the townhouse. "Forget about that. We got carried away. I was drinking, you were stressed. It won't happen again."

She laughed, but he saw the hurt. "Sure. Stress." She nodded. He could see she was trying to stay strong under the circumstances. Still no tears. It was a good start. "I need you to help with Chris. If that means I have to swallow some hurt feelings, so be it."

Jim didn't want to even talk about *not* talking about feelings, hurt or otherwise. He gave her a curt nod and headed to his equipment room. "Leaving in three minutes."

9

JIM KEPT HIS EYES on the road as they made their way to the nicer part of town. The part where rows of four- and five-bedroom houses with well-groomed rock garden yards lined up like dominos. Close together and mostly looking as if the developer lost imagination after designing a couple of them. Chris lived in a tidy little apartment complex at the back of the development.

Three separate buildings with two stories each made a U shape around a sparkling pool with a landscaped waterfall. The rear of the complex was closed in by a high stucco wall with large metal pieces of Mexican-American artwork properly spaced out between sections. Large palms and colorful flowers were dripping from pots around the pool. Fairly safe setup for occupants. Any intruder would have to come through the open area by the pool.

They made their way to the address Erica had in her phone. Apartment 232. Right-hand side of the pool. Top floor. End unit.

"You wouldn't happen to have the key?" he asked as he knelt and fumbled for his pick set. This one would be hard. It was broad daylight too. Neighbors didn't like seeing people picking locks.

"I don't, but shouldn't we ask the property manager?"

"Managers like to say no. Especially when you want to get into their residents' property uninvited. Bad for business," Jim said, not bothering to turn around as he strode to Chris's apartment door.

"I'm her sister."

"How would he know if she liked you or not? You could be estranged. Maybe the roommate—you have her number? See if they hid a key."

She tried the knob. It opened. Erica looked as surprised as he was to find it unlocked. She shrugged and opened the door.

The main room was tossed. Not much had been left unscathed. "Wait here. Don't touch anything." He stepped in, taking care not to make any unnecessary noise. This was a pro job. No one would still be lingering, but he poked his head into all six rooms just in case. Only one of the two bedrooms was turned. The kitchen and bathroom had all the drawers and cabinets emptied.

Erica came up behind him. He felt her as she neared. "Still think she turned to a life of prostitution and stripping?"

No. From the looks of things it may have been better for her health if she had. "When you talked to the cops, what did they say?"

"They had opened a case. Checked her work and her apartment and nothing seemed out of the ordinary."

He looked around the ransacked apartment. That was definitely out of the ordinary. Guess it happened after the police checked in on Chris. "When was that?"

"Roommate said she reported it Saturday. I called them Tuesday afternoon, right after I talked with the roommate." She was making her way into Chris's room. His phone rang. The number was blocked. He hit the answer button but didn't speak.

"Bean?"

"You called me."

"Miller." Calling from a different phone. One that wasn't owned by LVMPD. Interesting. "New situation. We're at Chris's apartment. It's been turned. Professionally."

"You would know." True. More than once, Jim had looked for things in a very quick-and-dirty manner.

"And the case file?" Jim passed Erica as she looked through what remained of a small work desk in Chris's room. He went into the bathroom. The mirror in there had been smashed too. The contents of the makeup tray strewn here and there. On the medicine cabinet there were several smudges of blood. A small spatter on the wall.

"It's been deleted, erased. I can't find shit. Not even a skip in case numbers. Something stinks here."

"Something rotten in cop town? Say it ain't so."

"You want this or not? I'm doing you the favor."

Jim bit his lip. "Yeah. Sorry. Couldn't resist."

Miller grunted. "I asked a couple guys I trust. Neither of them had any recollection of her case. I stopped asking before I hit on the right person and made the situation worse. No need to tip off whoever made the file go away that someone is looking for it. This kind of shit is hard to do these days. Someone was working that case. And that someone had to agree to lose his memory."

Jim looked behind the bathroom door. More blood. A fingerprint.

"I got blood over here. Two separate places. Even a print." He saw Erica look up at him. Saw the fear in her eyes. "If I take the samples, it will be out of evidence."

"It will."

"You'll want it to be *in* at some point. I presume." Erica started his way. He held up his hand. She stopped. He wanted to be able to talk to her before she got in a twist. It was blood, but it was not enough to jump to any conclusions.

"I might."

"The door was unlocked when we got here. It won't be that way when we leave."

"I got a dead John Doe right this minute. Can't get there for a while, but I will. Bean, who's your client?"

Jim started to answer. He'd worked with this guy before. He seemed pretty straight up, but as much as he'd like to believe Detective Miller was the good cop in this scenario, deep down, Jim trusted very few people. Erica had taught him that. "Confidential. I'm not going to block your way here, Miller. I need the same answers you do. We'll play an easy tennis match. Back and forth."

"I'll call you."

"I'll answer."

He hung up. Changed his demeanor. Tried for reassuring. "It's just a couple little smears. No more than you'd get from a shaving cut."

She let out a sigh. She once again looked like she was going to ball up and cry. It was Chris's shit on the floor. Her baby sister. He needed to remember it was hard for civvies to see a room tossed. Seemed violent, invasive. It was just business to bad guys.

She nodded.

He wanted to reassure her. So she didn't cry. "Could be the guy cut himself breaking the mirror. Could be hers. We won't know for a while." He pulled a surgical glove from his case. Handed it to her. "Don't touch much. One of Las Vegas's finest is coming. Off case since the file has been hijacked. The less we disturb, the better."

She understood. Put it on her right hand. It was a little too big.

"I know you've never been here, but look around. See if there's something you know to be way out of place for her life. Anything. I'm going to check the fridge."

"What? You hungry?"

He smiled at her. "People put stuff on the fridge all the time. Schedules. Reminders. Numbers. Their whole lives. Don't you?"

She thought. Shook her head. "Not a thing. It's all in my phone."

He glanced back. She was leaning over Chris's desk. Most of its contents were on the floor. She squatted down and moved a few papers around, trying to touch as little as possible in the process. She held an envelope up and studied it.

"She drew this on everything." She tilted it so he could see from the counter. "She called it Crazy Child." It looked like a stick figure with a big head stuck on a body drawn of squares with flailing arms and legs. The thing almost looked like the art on the wall outside the window, kind of Aztec, like a cave painting or something.

"She started in high school, making fun of some guy. It stuck with her over the years. I never got a birthday card, Christmas card, nothing that didn't have Crazy Child on or in the envelope." Her hand trembled.

"She needs you to be strong now. Keep looking. I know it sounds harsh."

"You're right. No time for softness." She turned in a circle. "The condition of this apartment makes everything more urgent. How am I supposed to see anything in this mess?" She went farther into the bedroom. He couldn't see her, but he heard her. "What were they looking for?"

"I don't know, but my guess is they found it."

"What makes you think that?"

He joined her by the dresser. "The roommate's bedroom is intact. Four cabinets on the far end of the kitchen are unopened. They stopped. The only reason to stop looking is when you find what you're looking for."

She kept looking. Touching things lightly with the gloved hand as she passed. The jewelry box was opened, the contents strewn on the dresser. "Her diamond cross is here."

"Something of value left behind. So it's not a robbery, for sure."

She headed to the closet. Something shiny caught her eye from the far end tucked behind the winter coats no longer needed in the Vegas heat. Sequins. Lots of sequins.

"Chris is not a sequin kind of girl. More of a jeans and football jersey kind of girl." Erica pulled the garments out. Three of them. They each consisted of little more than a scrap or two of brightly sparkling fabric and there was a huge, feathered headdress hanging upside down from a strange-shaped hanger. "Are these showgirl costumes?"

"They could be. But my guess would more likely be stripper costumes. I think I remember hearing of a place that uses the showgirl theme for all its dancers." He didn't look at her or the garments as he spoke. His jaw was tight. Jim didn't like the idea of Chris in one of these outfits any more than Erica did.

"One of these is huge." She fingered the bottoms and held them up. "Three or four sizes too big for Chris."

He lifted his brows. "Nice catch. What about the other two?"

She dropped that one at her feet, adding to the mess, and checked the others. "These would probably fit. Do they mean anything?"

"I don't know. But it gives us another place to look."

Jim noticed her hands were shaking. She was having a hard time getting air into her lungs. She swayed like a tree in the wind.

She was falling. And he had no way to stop it.

"Korey."

10

SHE FAINTED. DEAD OUT in his arms. He'd managed to catch her but was not happy about laying her out on the floor with all the evidence, or on the bed with the shredded blanket and pillows. He carried her out to the walkway and down to one of the lounge chairs by the pool. There was a woman with a child at the other end. The mother eyed him.

"Fainted. You have any water?"

Typical mother, her scrutiny quickly turned to concern. She rushed over with the water. Her daughter followed a few feet behind, still leery of the big stranger and the unconscious woman. Until she got close. "Look, Mama. She looks just like Miss Chris." The child reached out and touched Erica's cut.

The woman pulled her child's hand away. Jim shook Erica lightly and tapped her cheek. "Erica. Wake up, sweetie." The endearment came out before he could stop it. *Fucking stop that.* He grinned at the little girl. Tapped Erica's cheek again.

"Is she Chris's sister?" the woman asked.

"Yes." He opened the bottled water the woman had contributed and poured some on his hand and flung the drops into Erica's face. She peeked at him under heavy lids, then jerked awake. She was shaking and pale.

"When was the last time you ate anything?"

She sat up, rubbed her cut and bruised forehead. "In Boston. Before I got on the plane, I guess." She took the bottle and took a drink.

"We need to get you some food." He turned to the woman. "Thanks for the water."

She smiled. "Anything for Chris. I have some Goldfish over there. I could make you a sandwich."

He didn't want to linger too much, but … She sent the child for the snacks. The little blonde happily skipped to the far end of the pool where their belongings were sitting under a bright red umbrella.

"When was the last time you saw Chris?" he asked the woman.

"Last week. She occasionally watches Beth for me. She's such a doll."

Erica sat up. "Did you see anyone hanging around her apartment in the last few days? Anyone that didn't belong?" He would have asked the question a little more subtly.

"No. Not that I can think of. Is Chris okay?"

Beth trotted up. "I seen a man I never seen before. A funny one."

"You're Beth?" Erica leaned forward. The girl nodded, handed her a little opened baggie of Goldfish. Erica thanked her and made a big show of eating some of what was no doubt the young girl's afternoon snack. They made a small bond there. He kept his mouth shut. If he needed to intervene, he would. Interviewing kids could be hard. Rapport and trust were important. Erica had it with this girl right off the bat.

"What man did you see?"

She looked to her mom, who looked a little hesitant.

"Chris is my baby sister. I'm looking for her. I could really use your help. My name is Erica Floyd."

"You look just alike her," the little girl chirped. "'Cept she's skinnier."

The mother smiled. A little embarrassed.

"Always has been." Erica took another drink. "And her hair is a little lighter. And she liked dolls more than me." Her color was getting better. Jim was trying to be small and unobtrusive as he sat behind Erica on the lawn chair. If he got up, his size might intimidate the little girl, and Erica seemed to be doing just fine.

"She plays with my dolls all the time!" The child was practically bouncing.

"I bet she does." She took another bite of the crackers and offered Beth a few. She happily took them. "Now. What was funny about the man?"

She nodded and finished chewing. Good manners and thoughtful. Jim was getting more confident of this witness testimony by the minute. "He had a bruised face just like you"—she grinned sheepishly—"and big yellow shoes."

"Good." Erica praised her. "Was he bigger than Mr. Bean here?"

She eyed him and put her thumb to her mouth. Tilted her head. "No. Not big-big like him. Big-tall. 'Cept skinnier."

Not Banks.

"Was he really thin, like the Pink Panther?" Jim asked.

The girl giggled. "Not that thin. No one's that thin!" She looked at Jim again. "Just not like Brutus either."

Her mom looked surprised at her answers. "When did you see this man, pumpkin?" Jim *was* surprised at her answers. He'd interviewed adult witnesses who were nowhere near this precise.

She put her hands behind her back and looked up at the nearest palm tree and wiggled one foot. Thoughtful. "After Big Bird."

"So you know what day you saw him?" Erica asked. Jim still hadn't moved from the chair. She leaned back, her shoulder pressed against his chest. He wanted to get up and step away, but that might ruin the girl's run. He held still, felt Erica's warm, distracting body.

"Yellow day. That's why I remembered his big yellow shoes. Brought to you by the color yellow and the number seven." She held up seven pudgy little fingers.

The mother shook her head. "I don't know. I don't watch them that closely. I'm usually doing my own homework at the time. I'm in graduate school. That's why Chris watches her for me occasionally."

"Something we can probably find out." The woman seemed to shrink back a bit at his statement. He was a big, scruffy man. He smiled at the girl. "You've done a really good job, Beth. Can I ask you one?" She didn't smile back him, but she nodded. "Did he have a friend with him?"

Again, she looked up. Thought. And then shook her head. "I don't think so."

"Thank you very much." Erica sat up and her weight left his chest. He was relieved. He wondered if she realized she'd even been there.

"We should get you something to eat," he said. She seemed to get his meaning. It was time to go. She wrapped up, giving her card to the woman. Praising Beth.

Time to change tactics.

————

Jim came out of the drugstore in the strip mall behind his neighborhood and tossed a bag into the backseat. "Sorry. Kid behind the counter was slow."

"I thought for a minute I was going through the fence."

"Good. You remember the plan." *She's probably going to need it.*

He pulled the car around the block and up next to the townhouse. He got out and she grabbed the bags between her feet on the floorboard.

"Don't spill that."

She gave him a sneer. "Maybe I should. It stinks." But she cradled the two white paper bags loaded with greasy things wrapped in even more white wax paper. He'd stopped at a local joint and ordered for the both of them. He was sure it wasn't her normal fare, but she needed protein and calories.

As soon as the door to his townhouse opened, Annie wrapped around his legs. She screeched up at him.

"Relax. I got it." He pulled a box from the drugstore bag. Cat food. She meowed happily if not a little sternly. Nearly tripping over the anxious cat, he made his way to the kitchen and poured a heaping pile into an empty bowl. He added water to the meal and she sat contentedly eating. Erica moved past them. The little hellcat did take a moment to give Erica the dick-eye as she took a seat at the table. He rubbed her head.

"Far neater here than the office," Erica chirped. "A little more like the man I remember. No dust. No clutter." She inspected the furniture. "Yet the space lacks any intimacy. Beige carpet, a nondescript brown couch, and a leather recliner. Pretty bland, Jim Bean."

She was right, and the blinds were all pulled down and closed tight, allowing no natural light in at all.

"Not one piece of artwork. No pictures."

"Just a place. The furniture was here when I moved in. Except the bed."

She sat at the little table as he pulled the first of the greasy bundles out of the bag and placed it in front of himself. Next were two gigantic orders of fries. Then he handed her the last bit of white waxed paper from the bag.

She opened it with a bit of a sneer on her face. A tidy little grilled chicken sandwich sat there. She lifted the top of the wheat bun to find avocado, sprouts, and pickles. Her mouth fell open.

"If you'd rather have the triple cardiac with bacon"—he shrugged—"we can switch."

"It's fine. It's more than fine. It's perfect. You remember. Maybe Jim Bean isn't such an asshole after all."

"Don't go thinking things like that. I just got the dieter special. Women always get that." He took a huge bite and stuffed several fries in his mouth.

She took another drink. "Have you lived here the whole time? Since Ohio?"

He stopped chewing. Meaning... *Have you been here since your life fell apart? Since we broke up?* He wanted to make a fist. Not think about it. Count to ten like the anger-management classes had taught him. Ten... nine... eight. "Most of it."

Before she could counter with anything else about his life, he stood and walked to the hall toward the office. Away from her. Seven... six... five...

He grabbed his laptop off his desk and marched back toward the kitchen and her. Four... three... two... He stopped. She was chewing. Trying to look apologetic. He took a deep breath. One...

He plopped the computer on the table and opened it. Still standing, he took another colossal bite of the burger, went to the fridge, and grabbed a beer. Better than counting all afternoon. "Want one?"

She glanced at the clock on the stove behind him. He knew it read four thirty p.m. "No. Thank you. Water?"

He opened the narrow pantry and pulled out an off-brand bottle of water. Annie jumped from the floor to the table to the counter just behind him. He tossed Erica the bottle and turned his attention to the cat. "Better, baby girl?" Yes. He was baby-talking the cat. He could feel Erica's gaze on his back as he petted Annie. "Her is a pretty girl." He gave her a final head pat and slid back into his chair and went to work on his computer search. Erica tried to hide her smile when he looked up, but she failed miserably.

He glared at her over his laptop screen. "What?"

"Nothing." Erica ate a few more of the fries and swallowed down half the water. She looked better. Her face glowed from her mirth.

After he hit the search icon, he took another bite, leaving only a small bit of the Triple Cardiac burger in his fingers. "Can you tell me how to get..."

She waited for him to finish. He didn't. He just looked at her as he typed a few more characters into the laptop to narrow his search.

"To get what?"

"You really are tired." So he sang, *"Can you tell me how to get, how to get to Sesame Street?"* It was off-key. He typed a bit more. "I would have thought we'd all remember that one."

He looked up and saw her grinning that big *I know you* grin. It made him frown.

"You can't hate me forever." Her eyes squeezed shut like the words were out before she had a chance to think through where this conversation would lead. Places she didn't want to go. That was for sure.

He didn't blink, didn't hesitate. "Oh. Yes, I can."

She sat there. He gave her a brutal accusing stare. He wasn't going to back down. It might not even be true, but it was better for his mental state if he believed it.

"Fine." She stood up and went to where the cat had perched on the back of the couch. She tried to pet his little Annie, but she hissed and ran away.

He chuckled. He liked that cat more and more.

He tried to ignore her as she made her way around the room. Picking up, inspecting, and putting down what little there was in the way of decorations in the room: a beer-bottle-sized vase from a Native American artist. Local made. It had the Southwest vibe to it. She thumbed through a book on the end table.

He pulled out his reading glasses. He looked up. Caught her eye. "Something to say?"

"Nope."

She peeked through the closed blinds facing the front of the townhouse.

"This past Monday was brought to you by the number seven and the color yellow."

She turned her attention back to him. "How did you find that?"

"Satellite network database."

She paused and went to look at the screen. "How did you even know they had satellite TV?"

"I saw the dish on the building."

"Nice. And you trust Beth's memory?"

He looked up at her. She had bent down to see the database. Their faces were close.

"For a ten-year-old … she carefully thought about the questions and related her answers back to something that mattered in her world. Doesn't get much better than that as far as witnesses go."

"The girl was probably closer to seven."

He shrugged. "Either way. We know the cops checked before the weekend and this tall skinny guy with big yellow shoes came Monday."

He turned to say something, leaned her way a little. He could smell the spicy sandwich on her lips. She was close enough he could kiss her with the slightest little effort. Just a tiny move.

Hate was a funny thing. He could hate her all he wanted but he still harbored some desire, some care for the woman, or he wouldn't be doing this. Not for the fact that Chris was someone he knew, if he was helping *her*. Fuck.

"How does that help us know where Chris is?"

He was not happy at his momentary step back into humanity. Not at all.

"Jim?" She stood there all smug at his loss of concentration. Dammit.

He thought hard about what she'd just asked. It took him a minute to clarify his thoughts. "It's just another piece." He Googled the address for the Social Services office. He needed to stay on track. "We have to paint a picture of what she was doing before she went missing and what's happened since. We need to talk to the chick in her office. The one who told the roommate that Chris had been out."

"It's almost five."

"She's a social worker. Too many cases, not enough time. And if Chris is not working her stack, this girl will be left to do even more." He slapped the laptop closed. "We probably have at least an hour or two before she heads home. It's the life of the civil servant."

When he got to the SUV he motioned Erica to the backseat. She frowned. "Am I banished?"

"No." He opened the driver's door so she could see the array of equipment in his work truck. He snapped the laptop into the cradle connected to the console.

"You really use all this? Looks like a cop car in here."

No sooner were the words out than a cop car pulled up. Not a LVMPD patrol car, but the dark blue unmarked cars detectives drive. The window lowered as the car stopped next to Jim.

Miller.

"Heading somewhere, Bean?"

"Evening ride down the Strip." No one went down the Strip intentionally unless they were a cab driver or a tourist.

"We need to talk."

Erica was in the SUV. She didn't move. Smart girl.

"Talk."

"Inside."

"I'm in a hurry, Miller. Places to go."

Miller put the car in park. He intended to stay. "You're suspected of murder. I suggest we go inside."

Well, shit.

11

AT LEAST THE SWAT team hadn't showed up this time. But there sat Erica. And the cops were accusing him of something he hadn't done. This was getting a little too routine.

Miller calmly followed him and Erica back into the side entrance of the townhouse. He led him into the kitchen. All three of them sat around Jim's little kitchen table. It felt much more crowded than it had earlier when it was just him and Erica.

Miller took out a notepad and addressed Erica. "You look amazingly like Chris Floyd. You wouldn't happen to be related to our missing girl, would you?"

She drew her brow, appraising him. Jim saw her fists ball. She then glanced to Jim. He gave her nothing to go on, wanted to see how she reacted to Detective Miller. "*Your* missing girl? Who exactly are you?"

Miller realized he had not identified himself. He flopped out his badge. "Detective Noah Miller. Jim here called me to help you out. He didn't bother to mention who his client was."

"I'll tell you who I am. *Your* missing girl is *my* baby sister. *Your* department has somehow decided her case file is gone and not one person is looking for her. So exactly how have you helped?" She raised an eyebrow at him.

He gave Jim a look of approval. As if Jim had something to do with her attitude. She'd had it as long as he'd known her.

"I took some blood samples at the apartment, had CSI go in to see what they could find. I got it all into the system on an unrelated case number without her name attached to it. Broke about six department rules to do so."

"In that case"—she held out her hand—"I'm Erica Floyd. Nice to meet you."

He shook her hand. "In that case, you're both suspected of murder. Seems you two are the last to have seen my dead guy."

"What?" Erica jumped up. "You're kidding!"

Jim wanted to laugh. So now she knew what it felt like to be falsely accused of something. "You kill someone before you ran into me?" He grinned at her.

"Not fucking funny."

"Hey. At least he didn't come in with the SWAT team and you're not in your boxers. You gonna cuff her, Miller?"

She narrowed her gaze. "You are an asshole."

Miller leaned back in his chair and crossed his arms. He was listening. Maybe hoping to gather a little evidence against him or Erica. Jim decided to leave his little bit of vengeance till later and steer this conversation his way.

"The John Doe from this morning?"

"Yep. ID'd pretty quick. Dealer's license. One Edmond Carver." He thumped his pad on his closed fist. "The auto shop owner behind Carver's house said you offered to paint his dumpster about twelve times to watch him."

Well, shit. "You're just guessing it's me." The owner never knew Jim's name or that he was a PI. But the cover was thin under the scrutiny of a murder case. Wouldn't take much for Miller to make this connection. "But yes. I spent the last week watching Edmond on behalf of his previous employer. The guy was a waste of space. Casino suspected him of filing a false workers' comp claim. They called it off this morning."

Jim pulled out his phone, punched a few buttons, and played the message for Miller. He nodded and took some notes.

"And why were you visiting such a fine young man, Miss Floyd?"

She looked at Jim, unsure what to say or do. "Do I need a lawyer?"

"If he really thought we killed Carver, we'd be cuffed and downtown. And Miller here wouldn't be behaving so politely."

She hesitated but nodded. "Chris had his name and number on her desk at work. I didn't have much else to go on since you guys snubbed me."

Miller opened the pad, flipped a few pages, scribbled some more. "When was that? What time were you there?"

She shook her head. It had been a long couple of days. She was getting pale. He was used to drug addicts, death, and crimes. She wasn't. "I left about two forty-five."

"And how'd you get that bump on your head?"

Her hand went there instinctively. Her gaze darted to Jim.

"She fell on the stairs." Miller didn't buy that for a moment, but he didn't push it either. "We left Carver's lovely house and had a nice afternoon at the Peppermint Pony."

Erica's eyes flew to him at the *we*. He smirked. Guess she hadn't realized he'd followed her there.

Jim wasn't looking to hide things from Miller, but he didn't want to bring up Banks at this point. Especially since Zant's name hadn't been mentioned yet. And Zant owned all kinds of people in this city. Police, politicians, other casino owners. No need for Miller to go rattling Zant's cage if the man wasn't involved.

So far, Banks was the only connection to Zant. And that didn't mean shit. Banks had his own game, his own network. As long as this all turned out to be small players, he was okay. The longer Jim could go under the radar with Zant, the better. Knocking Banks out was risky enough. Especially now that Edmond was dead. Mentioning him to the cops ... well. That could get him some cracked bones or worse.

"How'd Carver get it?"

"Two behind the ear. Clean. Professional."

"I don't carry. Even you know that."

"Yeah. People make exceptions." He shrugged. "Maybe you changed your mind. I heard you took a lesson or two." Cat and mouse. *I believe you, but I don't really have to. You could look good for this murder.* Miller tucked his little pad into his pocket. Looked at Erica. "The Peppermint Pony? Is that where Chris was supposedly moonlighting?"

"Who knows for sure? Everyone there has the same memory as the guys at the police station. No one's ever seen her."

He stood to leave, handed Erica his card. "Not surprising. For the record, I've worked with Chris. She's good people, does good things around here."

He didn't use the past tense. He was more confident than Jim at the moment. Or maybe he was just better with his bedside manner.

"I'll call Jim when I have any news from the CSI guys. But understand, this isn't TV. It could take a while."

"Thank you." Erica had paced to the refrigerator.

"Bean. Let's not forget our game. Like you said, easy volley, back and forth. I could have had you two picked up and questioned you in the station, taken all night about it. Return the favor. I want this cleaned up too."

Miller could have run them in. Probably should have. Instead, he'd delivered info to them personally. Jim took it as a warning. Things were getting hot. People were getting killed.

Miller let himself out the way he'd come in.

Erica walked to Jim. Tucked her head and fell against his chest and put her hands around his waist and held on like bandits would drag her away if she let go. He let her. His arms went loosely around her hips. She was subtly shaking. Maybe noiselessly crying.

He'd shoved his feelings deep into the pit of his stomach. This was not about him. Not about Gretchen Bates and what happened eight years ago. This was about a girl whose sister was mixed up in the unsavory underbelly of society, a place where death and drugs and disaster were the norm. He was familiar with the terrain, but women like Chris and Erica Floyd should never be.

She sucked in two really deep breaths. He felt her body stiffen. She stopped shaking. Slowly she pulled away from him.

"Sorry."

He shook his head. No need to get all mushy about it.

She wiped the dampness from her eyes and headed to the bathroom. He wasn't sure what to do with himself for a moment. Wasn't sure what to do about the case.

She came right back. Less than a minute. She looked better. No makeup smears. Not one sign of weakness. Game face on.

"Is it too late for Social Services?"

He glanced at the stove. Five thirty. "Maybe."

"But maybe not," she replied.

"Nothin' better to do."

———

The Social Services offices were indeed locked up for the night. Lights out. Nobody home. "Since this is the desert, I had imagined an abundance of sunlight in Vegas, but I guess late fall in Vegas is just like late fall in Boston. Dark at six."

"If you want longer daylight hours, go stand in a casino. Twenty-four hours a day of weird lighting that messes with your body clock." Jim pulled a bandanna from his back pocket, reached up, and wrapped it around the security light. "Keeps people playing." He then busted it with a swift swing of his elbow.

"What the hell are you doing?"

He frowned. "Going in."

"What?"

After another glance around the area, he got his pick kit out of his other pocket, selected the proper tools, and started in on the lock.

"Don't you need a warrant or something for that?"

"Cops get warrants." He pointed at his own face. "Not a cop."

"So you're a thief?" Erica chewed on a ragged nail. "Surely there was someone around to see this little caper."

"I'm not going to steal anything." He fiddled with the mechanism. The door unlocked with a low click. He pulled the glass door wide open and held his arm out. "Ladies first."

"Why? So if there's an alarm and cameras, I'm the one to get sent to the big house for it?"

"Big house?" He chuckled and went on in. "Have you been here before, when you visited?"

He knew she hadn't visited. She'd been unfamiliar with the apartment. Change of subject from his questionable activities.

"No."

He took a visual scan of the room. There was the doctor's-office-looking reception area where someone sat behind sliding glass windows and only opened them when clientele walked up. Given the types of people in the office, you probably needed to be buzzed in to get beyond that area.

The lights flipped on. A very little woman stood there with a very big handgun. She had the barrel trained right on Jim's belly button.

Erica squeaked. Her hands instinctively rose in surrender. She stole a glance at Jim. His hands were calmly at his sides.

He smiled at the woman. Kindness, as Double O always said, spreads thinner than honey. Whatever the fuck that meant. But it worked on people you needed to get information from or people who were pointing a .357 with a seven-inch barrel at your belt buckle.

The woman shoved the gun forward in threat. It shook hard in her hand. "I've called the police. You need to leave before they come. We don't have any money here."

"No need for the gun. We're not here to hurt anyone." Jim's voice was low in volume, but higher in tone than his usual tenor. Knew his size didn't make him look very nonthreatening, but he tried to sound it.

"Go on. Leave."

"We're trying to find Chris. Chris Floyd," he said, slowly, to make sure she got what he was saying through her fear. "This is her sister, Erica." He pointed causally to Erica. The gun swung in her direction. Erica whimpered and took a step back.

The woman squinted again. She took a step closer. Her stance eased but the gun was still dancing around, pointing about knee level.

"The situation with Chris is getting a little urgent."

The woman thankfully turned her attention and the weapon back to Jim at that. He gave her a weak smile. "We need to see her desk."

"Huh. You and half of Clark County." She looked back to Erica. The gun rose back to about stomach height. Erica squeezed her eyes closed as if she were about to be shot. She wasn't. Jim knew it. "What's her middle name? Chris's?"

Erica opened her eyes. "Chris's?" The woman nodded. Her eyebrows rose. Erica relaxed quickly as well, even snickered. "If you know, you know she'd be pissed that we were even talking about it."

She nodded.

"Edith. She hates it."

The woman seemed to relax a little more. Let the gun barrel fall to point at the ground. "And yours?"

"Oh. You know that too? Well, Momma did have a way with names. I'm Erica Madonna Floyd. Named just prior to the singer's big break, of course." She stepped forward, held out her hand. "I believe you're Karen Barnes. We spoke on the phone a few days ago."

The old battle-ax with the huge piece smiled. Her face seemed suddenly ten years younger. She tucked the gun into the pocket on her skirt. The handle hung out loosely, making Jim worry it would slip and drop to the ground. Maybe go off.

"We did." She shook her head and pushed her hair back. There were bags under her eyes, her face was drawn, and she looked exhausted. "That seems a while ago now. Things have been crazy here. Behind on cases, police in and out. We're all worried sick." Suddenly she looked down. "What am I thinking?" She let out a big sigh. "Forget about us, how are *you* doing, dear?" The little woman rushed up and proceeded to help Erica to the nearest reception room chair.

"I'm okay. Really. I just need to be doing something." Erica stood right back up. "This is Jim Bean. He's a private detective who's helping me. We really need to take a look through her things."

Karen looked at Jim. "You broke into my building."

"Sorry. Didn't do any permanent damage. Other than a lightbulb." He was still standing quietly, not interrupting.

"I reckon the state can afford that. Follow me." She headed toward a door leading farther into the offices. "But I don't know how much good this is going to do you. Police been here, FBI's been here." She held the door open for them to follow her in. "Can't imagine they missed too much."

"The FBI was here?" Erica turned to Jim. He shrugged at her. Still being quiet. Let these two start chatting. No telling what the woman might know that she didn't really know she knew. Happened all the time. Witnesses think they don't have information, but once they get comfortable, start chatting, clues fell out of their mouths like broken teeth.

"Man came out Tuesday morning. Was kind of a jerk if you ask me." She pushed through another door that opened into a large area of beige cubicles.

Jim moved in first. He ran his hands around the screen to the computer, under her keyboard, opened drawers, and felt for things hidden under them. Then he rummaged through her files.

Karen was chatting about how great a girl Chris was. Kept using the past tense. Erica cringed each time.

He interrupted. "Are these all her current cases? Could any be missing?"

"Oh. Well. The FBI agent took a few." She tilted her head. "Hard to know which ones. We have hundreds assigned to us at a time." She gestured to the desk and the small file drawer there. "The ones we keep out here are active, we're visiting, keeping track. They're getting current attention. But we each have hundreds"—she pointed to another door past the three rows of cubicles—"that are either dormant or closed. Back there. We reopen cases all the time, so we need them close."

"How about an electronic list that could be compared to the hard copies? So we can see which ones the FBI guy took?"

She laughed. "I see where you're going, Mr. Bean. It would take a few days to do that if I had full staff. I have one on maternity leave and Chris missing. That puts us pretty far behind. It would take forever to reconcile a list like that."

"I think she's missing because of something in one of those files. It's really important. I can have someone come help ..."

She stiffened. Jim knew what she was going to say.

"The information in those files is sensitive. Like physicians' records. You guys can't have access to them."

Jim stood. He stepped a little closer to the old woman. "You handed files to someone that is possibly mixed up in Chris's disappearance. Maybe even the kidnapper."

She put her hand to her chest. Narrowed her brow. "I most certainly did not."

"Did the agent have a subpoena?"

She backed up a step. "No."

"What was his name?"

"Um. Brown or something of the like."

Jim moved forward with each step she took back. "May I see his card?"

She scowled at him. "He didn't leave me a card."

"I'm sorry, Ms. Barnes, but you were duped. Agents come in pairs, generally. They always leave cards behind in case you think of something else, and they would not jeopardize a court case by taking your sensitive files without a court order."

"Oh dear."

Jim backed down now that he'd proven his point and she was duly guilt-ridden. "What did the agent look like?"

"He was in a dark suit. Had glasses with round black rims." Karen pulled out a chair from the cubicle directly behind Chris's. She sat. "He flashed a badge." She turned pleading eyes on Erica. "I'm so sorry if I made things worse."

"It's okay," Jim answered. She turned her attention back to him. "Badges are easy to get these days."

"Really? After 9/11, I would think it would be harder."

"I have one." He winked at Ms. Barnes. "I have a CIA badge too." He squatted down, got eye level with her. His voice softened again. He put his hand on her knee. "I really think the files are the key.

We can help." He looked at Erica. "Keep it just us and your people. We won't look at any files that aren't missing."

"I can't compromise this agency any further. I'll have my staff do it. It's for Chris, after all. But it'll take at least most of tomorrow to go through them all."

"That'll work." He stood. "Thank you, Ms. Barnes."

12

JIM GLANCED OVER TO see Erica was staring out as the bland part of Vegas rolled by outside the window. The working man's part of the city. No bright lights. No oversized monstrosity hotels. This was all drugstores, pizza places, and lube shops. Her head was pressed against the glass. Her hair hanging loose around her face. In the rearview mirror, Jim could see her pinching her bottom lip between her thumb and the knuckle on her index finger. They passed a particularly big Mexican *tienda* with flashing police lights in the parking lot and people loitering around to see what had happened. He cruised on.

"Four years of college Spanish and I only remember about four words." There was a long pause. "Chris speaks it fluently."

Two blocks passed before she started, but Jim knew what was coming. Confessions and remorse flow like the Nile when people are tired. Scared.

"We had a huge fight the last time we talked." Her position didn't change. Her face looked pale again, as if reality was draining the color from her cheeks.

Jim didn't answer. He didn't want to hear all this. But she needed to say it. So he would sit like a priest and listen even if he was in no position to offer her absolution.

"Two weeks ago. It was about her living way out here and us never seeing each other. She'd planned on coming to Boston. She canceled on me. I yelled. She yelled. I'd bought the tickets and changed my plans and ... you know. Nothing *really* significant. I made it seem that way. I just wanted to see her."

He didn't stop her, nor did he attempt to comfort her. One conversation can change everything. He remembered their last conversation—the last one before this week, anyway. That hadn't gone so well either. That had changed his life forever. He understood.

"I told her she was selfish." She let out a strained laugh that ended with her choking on irony. "Can you imagine me calling *her* selfish?"

He looked up to the mirror again. He shrugged before he returned his attention to the road. Chris was all about other people. Always had been. She was an activist on campus. Volunteering at the animal shelter. He remembered Erica complaining because Chris would spend the holidays at the food banks.

She sighed. "It was the last thing I said to her."

They sat in silence for a few minutes. More strip malls and neighborhoods rolled by as they passed through an inordinately large number of stoplights. He pulled up to the back of her hotel.

She leaned up toward the back of his seat, hung her arm over it so she was facing him. Back to business. But he could see how things were wearing on her. A dark circle was forming under the bruised eye socket. "So we wait to see what files the FBI guy took?" She made no move to leave his SUV.

"That's the next logical step." He looked back out the front window. "You need to change hotels. Call Adair. Pack your bag. He'll call you back once he's here at the hotel. Then do the express checkout on the TV. But wait until he's here."

She frowned. "You really think that's necessary?"

If Zant was involved, yes. He sighed. He didn't want to tell her about Zant. Too much to tell. Too many skeletons in that closet to open the door if he didn't have to. "After all you've seen today, you know we're in the middle of a cover-up. Maybe of Chris's disappearance, but I think it's likely something Chris found out. She stumbled onto something. She's gone because of that something. The thin man at your door this morning could also be our friend in the yellow shoes. If he is, they know where you are and that you're sticking your nose into their business."

She opened her mouth to argue but then thought better of it. She was smart enough to know he was right. "Where should I go?"

"One of the big ones in the middle of the Strip. Choose between Paris and the Bellagio, once you're on your way." Those were not owned by Andrew Zant. That didn't guarantee her safety, but it would make him sleep a little better tonight.

She nodded. "Shouldn't you come with me?"

"That'll just bring even more attention to you. I'll be close by. You be quick. Text me when you're settled." He'd know exactly where she was, but he didn't need her to know that. If she knew he intended to follow her every move, she'd blow his cover.

She nodded. Her eyes were sagging.

"Do not lay on that bed and fall asleep."

"Not if you think I might be in danger here."

"I do."

"Okay."

Ten minutes later Jim was positioned at a bank of slots nearest the elevator she'd likely come down. He'd dug in the back of his SUV and changed into white tennis shoes, a blue button-up sweater, and wire-framed glasses. He put a few quarters in the machine and then took out his phone and mimicked having a conversation with a lonely wife complaining about her gambling husband. "I'll be up in a little while, baby. Just a little while longer. I feel lucky."

The old guy a few machines down gave him an understanding head bob and went back to his own game.

Jim played the slots for the second time that day. This machine was not as high-tech as the one that had paid him off earlier. It clanked for real as he dropped the coins in the slot. He hit the button. It did its virtual spin. He glanced at the elevators as one set of doors opened and a group clamored out and headed for an evening on the strip.

No Erica.

Jim dropped his next coin on the ground. As he reached for it, he checked behind him. There was one of the doors that led to the bowels of the hotel. The kind that don't have handles or visible hinges. They have the wallpaper and trim on them, so at first glance they don't seem to be doors at all.

No movement. No security goons on the move.

He also gave the room a complete scan as he straightened. Nothing seemed out of place. After glancing at his watch, he dropped that coin into the slot.

Twenty minutes later she was still not down. He texted her. You go to sleep?

She replied. No. Adair just got here. Are you watching me?

He grimaced. If he didn't tell her, she would look for him when she came down. I'm watching everyone else. Just get in the cab and go. Don't look for me.

He's meeting me at the back. Where you dropped me off.

Smart girl.

He dropped another coin in the machine as he tucked the phone back in his pocket. Pushed the button. A bell rang.

Then another. Coins started dropping like rain into the metal till.

"Nice one." Three machines down, the geezer grinned.

Jim grabbed one of the oversized cups from the empty space next to him. As fast as he could, he loaded the coins in.

Erica emerged from the elevator as Jim moved, acting like he was going to the payout window. She traveled light—one slim black suitcase, carry-on sized, one black suit jacket, and a sleek handbag. She made no commotion coming off the elevator. No one had to step aside to let her and her luggage through.

She studied the far wall as she passed close by him. She didn't look his way. As if on a mission, she made straight for the back of the lobby, past registration, to the parking deck. All would look like a normal businesswoman here for a conference … if it wasn't for her black eye. Several people gave her the double take. She ignored it.

He meandered around more long banks of slots, heading in the general direction of the parking deck, carrying his cup, stopping to study the flashy displays, as if he was looking for the next hot machine. He found a spot with a straight shot where he could see her go all the way out. She'd made it down the hall, through the automatic doors. He saw Adair get out to greet her as she emerged.

Jim looked around again. No one seemed out of place, watching her or following her. But his intuition was twitching like mad. He'd learned the hard way to pay attention.

He dropped money in another slot. He smashed the button twice. The screen spun. No winner. He shook his head at the machine. She was away. He wanted to be close behind her, but he needed to linger if he was being watched. Dilemma. He often faced this kind of decision.

No cars had pulled out behind the taxi that he could see through the distant glass doors.

If they saw him watching her, maybe he had prevented her being followed. Maybe not. Maybe he was wrong this time. He played another machine, putting several dollars in before moving again. No one looked like hired help except the two men watching the card tables closer to the center of the casino floor. But this was Vegas. The eye in the sky missed little. He glanced up at the nearest camera. Had Zant's people watched her from the security room? If so, they were now watching him too. If Banks hadn't fingered him after the club incident, Zant would know he was involved with Erica by now.

He needed to linger a bit longer. Just in case. He did not want to be followed to her new location. The smell of bratwurst caught his attention. The sports bar was blaring the pregame for Thursday Night Football. He chose a high table near the door, back to the wall, and stood. A waitress in a costume cut so low it would make her mother blush commented on his cup of winnings.

His mind drifted to the night before and Erica as the waitress rattled off the long list of beers available on tap. Erica was still as beautiful as these young girls. He again wished he didn't know that.

The girl finished up her spiel. Jim knew that because she was no longer talking and now had that vacant uncaring look. She was waiting for his choice. "Just water." She frowned at him. "And one of those brats."

"Kraut?"

"Sure."

The game would be a good one tonight. He wouldn't get to see it. That was what DVRs were for. Erica's text came as he took the first bite from the dog. She was settled. The brat was cold and greasy anyway. He left the food on the table and the girl enough cash to cover the bill plus a decent tip.

He headed to the cash window. He had to wait behind two other winners. One held a cup as Jim did. The other had a paper printout in his hand.

It only took a moment for his turn for the next available teller. She took the cup with a bright, overwhite smile. There was much rattling and clanking as the mechanical sifter counted the coins. Something else intentional. The tinkling of money being won. The noise should have made him happy. He needed the money.

The machine quieted. The red LED readout said three hundred seventy-two dollars. Total winnings minus the nine dollars and twenty-five cents he'd fed the machine left him at three cents short of a thousand dollars for the day.

He didn't have luck like this.

Something was about to go very bad.

13

ERICA ANSWERED THE DOOR after verifying it was him with another text. Again. Smart girl. "You didn't say when or if you were coming tonight." She invited him in and then plopped her hands on her hips. "I tried to be anonymous and pay in cash at the desk. You know, and use a fake name?" She frowned. "I guess that's just for the movies. They required a credit card for incidentals and my ID." She closed and locked the door behind him.

Jim would have laughed at her agitation if he didn't find it so attractive.

"The woman was quite rude at my suggestion of it. What if I wanted to be in Vegas incognito?" She was so damned cute trying to be cunning. It was pissing him off. "Don't people come here to be crazy? What about all that *what happens in Vegas* crap?"

He looked around her room. It was almost as big as the first floor of his townhouse. A red silk couch with two matching chairs and fancy tables made a living area framed before a floor-to-ceiling window. The cozy area overlooked the Bellagio fountains. She'd paid for the view. There was a dining table for four with a bright chandelier twinkling above. He ran his finger over the marble wet bar across from the view. He could see the huge bed through an open door. Bright floral-laden bedding matched heavy daylight-blocking drapes that covered another window. Also with a view. Suite probably brought his monthly rent per night. Suddenly his winnings didn't seem so significant.

His life had added up to rent-to-own furniture and fast-food containers. If the place burned down today, all he had worth saving was Annie. Erica just dropped two grand on a hotel room.

He opened the bar. Fully stocked. "For anonymity, you go to a different kind of hotel. Not like this one. Not one you'd walk your expensive shoes into. Off the Strip. Not a chain. One story. No pool. The guy at the desk is happy to see your cash because there are no transaction fees for cash. That kind of place won't have incidentals to worry over."

"There are still cheap no-tell motels?"

At that he did laugh. "Yes." He settled down on the harder than expected cushioning of the couch. He bounced once or twice before he laid his laptop bag on the ornate glass-top coffee table with a clank. "Probably should have had you go to one of those. But they're not quite this nice."

"I ordered in, guessing you'd show up."

"See, incidentals."

"I know. I wouldn't have done it if I'd been able to pay cash. But my card had already been run. Room service charges won't make me any easier to find."

"Hungry again already?" He pulled out his computer.

"Wanted to take some more pain reliever. Need the food in my stomach."

He nodded. Made sense. He could always eat. You never know as a PI when you might get stuck watching someone or something for hours. Eat when you can. Pee when you can.

He typed into the search engine for the strip club, the one that used a showgirl theme. Two came up. One in Reno. The other, he'd heard about a few years back. But thought it was long gone. "Coyote Springs."

"What's that?"

He looked over the Googled articles for a moment. "A desert ghost town, basically. One of those communities that had been preplanned, presold, and then the recession hit, and nothing. There's a nice Jack Nicklaus golf course out there." That was what he'd remembered hearing about the place. "They planned several subdivisions, shopping, resorts, but they never built a single house. There was a hotel made for anonymity, and a strip club up there. About fifty miles north."

"Seems a long way for boobs."

"Golf and boobs." He skimmed another article. "Seems there's more to it than the recession. Lawyers and politicians involved. Builders and investors suing one another, embezzlement and theft."

"You think Chris got wound up in that?"

"Could be."

"She's a social worker. What would she be doing in that kind of investment deal? That's more my line of work."

There was a knock at the door. Erica jumped. "You answer it."

"Step into the bedroom," Jim ordered. She did as told. No argument.

Jim hated peepholes. Too dangerous. Never liked the thought of getting his eye shot out. Better to fling the door open and see what came through.

He did just that. Opened it wide and stepped behind it. Nothing came through. He looked through the crack between the door and the frame to see a small woman behind a large cart draped in red fabric. Two bottles of wine, two glasses topped the cart, along with flowers and covered plates. All the makings of a romantic evening.

"Room service." Her voice was timid. An empty doorway confused most people.

He stepped from behind the door. She jumped higher than Erica had. Jim was pretty sure she was no hit man. This was a clean hotel. Unless one of them had been followed, no one knew she was here. Cards can be traced, but it took a little time and good connections. Unlikely at this point, but possible.

"Sorry, sir." She hustled the cart close to the table. Cautiously, Erica came out of the bedroom when he signaled her. She signed for the food as the woman finished setting the table.

She thanked Erica with a huge smile. Tip was probably more than he usually spent on an entire meal. Maybe more than his usual dinner and lunch combined.

The waitress lifted the lids. Jim's stomach growled. She opened one of the two bottles swiftly. Practiced. "Would you like me to pour, sir?"

"Um ... No, thank you." He could manage to do that.

Just before backing out of the room, she bowed. "Call if you want us to clear, or you can leave it for housekeeping if you prefer your privacy for the evening."

Yes. Perfectly romantic. Great. He looked over to see Erica and her amused grin on the far side of the table. He suddenly felt like a trapped rat.

This kitchen was getting too hot. Might be time to get out.

She slid into the fancy French chair and held an empty glass out to him. This was as life should have been all along, all these years, the two of them, sitting at a table, with wine and good food. Sharing a meal like it was the most normal thing in the world for a couple to do. He found himself frozen in place, gripping the stiff wooden back of the chair in front of him. Muscles refused to move. If he sat and let it feel normal, then what?

He'd never have anything to offer a woman like Erica again. Any woman. His life was about scratching for survival. Month to month. And then there were those favors for Zant as well.

So he didn't date. Didn't make friends easily. Avoided any situation where his story would have to be told. Because he hated to have to defend his history, to feel the shame of being accused of such inflammatory things. Relationships meant sharing, and he certainly didn't want to get close enough to have to share. Didn't want to keep secrets either.

Erica let out a burp. A big, belly-rocking, echoing belch. At first he stood there staring at her as if her head had exploded. Not what he expected.

She turned pink. "Oops."

He laughed. "Nice."

She snatched the bottle off the table and poured a hearty glass of the red zin. Taking that and her platter, she moved over to one of the chairs and sat down to eat there. Casual, leaning over the coffee table like it was a working lunch or something.

"Can you toss me some silverware?"

He was still standing by the table, watching her. He gave her a questioning look.

"A knife. You know? I need to cut this steak."

So she hadn't planned seduction. For a second he felt a tinge of disappointment. But just for a second. He grabbed the rolled-up utensils and brought them to her. He also gathered his plate and returned one more time for the bottle and his glass. The tension in his body dissipated. He slipped back down in front of his laptop. Back to work.

"So now what?" she asked and took a huge bite of her filet.

He took a moment to savor his own. She'd ordered two identical plates. Filets, perfectly medium rare, lightly glazed in a dark wine sauce with shiitake mushrooms scattered about the plate. A mountain of garlic mashed potatoes was also topped with a puddle of the mushroom sauce. The rest of the plate was covered by asparagus.

"Lots of moving parts. Need to determine what's important and what might not matter to us."

"How do we manage that?"

"Easy." He took another big bite, stopped to chew for a moment. "This wasn't a cheap tab." He looked around the room. "And the digs, they set you back a few bills."

She didn't look up. "It's okay. I can afford it." Her voice was tight, angry. It made his hackles rise again. "And I can afford to do what we need to do to find her." He always knew she and Chris came from money. It shouldn't be a big surprise now. "I can pay your fees."

He took in a deep breath. He was letting her send his emotions all over the place. That had to stop. He went to his go-to feeling. Anger. "Don't you worry, sweet cheeks, you'll get a bill. But I meant that if *I* was going to find you, find out what you were up to, the easiest place to start is your money." He scooped up a pile of the potatoes and swallowed without chewing. "Always follow the money."

He stood. Carried his plate and napkin over to the table. Without a word he opened the second bottle and poured himself a hefty glass. "She had plenty of cash on hand. No abnormal deposits."

"You can hack her accounts? Really?"

"No. I saw her bank statement this morning, at her apartment. Called a connection at that bank. Asked a couple general questions. He just sent me an email. He didn't say anything that would put her identity in jeopardy. Just general info that would help us to know." He turned to look out the window. "But he said no red flags. Nothing but normal payroll deposits and no significant withdrawals in the last two months. If she was moonlighting, where did the money go? Stripping is fairly lucrative."

"I never thought it was about money for her. Must have been doing some of her own investigative work? Checking out the clubs for something?"

"Likely something to do with Coyote Springs."

"Why would Chris care about that? Big-money real estate wouldn't begin to be on her radar. All she cares about is abandoned children and battered women. I'd be surprised if she knew much about the finances of Coyote Springs at all."

She took the last swig from her glass and stood next to Jim. They stared in silence over the dancing waters of the fountains across the way. The colors changed along with the spray to music they couldn't hear.

He changed position slightly. He looked over at her. He was trapped between her and the couch. She started to back away, to give him some room, but his eyes found a scar on her neck. Erica was holding her breath.

He needed to get away. "You should move."

14

SHE WAS SO CLOSE he could smell her skin. His gaze fixed on the scar on her collarbone. He hadn't noticed it before. He knew the imperfection wasn't there eight years ago. It wasn't a minor scrape either. The mark was short but rather thick and ragged. Probably a deep cut.

Irrational anger bubbled through his body. He was furious not so much over the wound but the thought that someone might have hurt her. He hadn't been there to prevent it. Ridiculous.

All kinds of protective instincts stirred his blood. Had they been in a public place, instead of cooped up in that suite, someone might possibly be getting beat to a pulp right this instant. For no good reason other than he needed to release the baseless emotion pounding at his temples. He was still pissed as hell at her.

She nodded at his instruction to move and placed one foot back and eased her weight onto it as if she was frightened to go too fast.

Maybe she was sensing his anxiety, his arousal. Most likely it was his desire. He didn't care which, and she was too fucking slow.

Jim reached out and took her by the shoulders. Her eyes got big, like a squirrel in the road, unsure as to whether to make a go for the far side or to retreat.

He turned her just a hair to the left and pulled her heated body tight to his chest. His lips took hers as if they had a will of their own. She felt stiff, shocked. Well, too bad. So was he. His brain was screaming to him he that should take that stiffness as a statement of refusal and stop the madness that was about to ensue.

There was no pulling away from Erica's sweet mouth. Hot. Sensual. She tasted of wine.

Her body softened, molded against his. In the middle of his back, her fingers twisted into the fabric of his shirt, almost digging into his skin. She was pulling him closer. He was lost in her scent. Clean, lightly feminine, it was nothing he recognized.

He pulled away. Looked down past the soft fabric of that blouse, to the scar. He pressed his lips to that, hoping it would make up for something he couldn't name. Her head fell back, her grip on his back loosened. He kissed the top of her breast as he heard her breaths become ragged.

There was no turning back. He felt like a buck in rut. He scooped her up and took her to the bedroom. He dropped her on the bed a little rougher than he'd intended. She giggled as she recovered her balance and propped herself up on her elbows, kicked off her high-dollar black dress shoes.

"Clothes," she whispered. She wanted skin on skin. He stopped and nodded. They worked together. Then she was naked, laid before him like a buffet of sexual perfection.

She whimpered. "Jim."

His phone rang.

Jim froze. His eyes closed tight.

"Oh. God, no," she cursed.

What the fuck was he doing? It was like someone whacked him on the head and he suddenly remembered who and where he was. Like being awakened from a dream. He backed slowly down her body. He sat on the edge of the bed as the ringer went off again. He pulled the phone out of his jeans and tucked his feet back into them. He didn't look back at her. It blared again, a loud annoying sound like an antique car horn.

Dammit. All it took was one kiss and here he was crawling all over her like a cheap prom date.

He answered by the fourth annoying ring. A muddled deep voice was on the other end. Jim stood and tried to pull his pants over his not quite flaccid self as he did so. He had to bounce to get it in a position to get the zipper over it, and in the process the phone slipped from where it had been balanced between his ear and his shoulder.

It bounced on the bed and landed high between her legs. Erica hadn't moved. She was still lying there with her shirt off and her panties tugged down. Jim blushed as he picked it up. "Sorry."

This had to be the most awkward moment of his life. Well, maybe not. It was a woman he loved. Once loved.

He nodded to the phone, and then looked at her. "You know Chris's blood type?"

"A positive."

Jim repeated the information. Listened a little longer. The question brought the harsh reality of the day back to the forefront of his worries. Work. That was what he was all about.

He pulled his shirt over his head.

Erica was dressed and pouring the last of the wine into her glass when Jim hung up.

"Miller." He grunted and looked at the carpet.

"And?"

He looked her in the eye. Serious. Straight. "I'm sorry. I lost control there for a minute. My fault. It won't happen again." A totally weak apology, but it was all he had.

She gave him a slight nod and closed her eyes. Like she'd rather he just dropped it. That worked for him.

"I—it's been a strange couple of days." He fumbled for words.

"Yeah." She looked back at him with tears forming in her eyes. "Strange."

He nodded.

"What did Miller say?" Back on track. She recovered quick. No more tears. No complications.

"Three different blood types in Chris's apartment." He sat back down in front of his computer. "First one, O positive. Very common, but he had a hunch and ran it against Edmond Carver's." He looked at her. "Match."

"What?"

"The second, A positive. No sample to compare it to for Chris, but he assumes it's hers since it's her apartment. Good assumption, I believe."

Erica slid into the chair across the glass table from him. "Two blood types so far and one belongs to a dead guy?"

"The last was AB negative. Very rare. Tripped a memory for Miller. Another missing person, an older one that was his own case. Turns out the AB belongs to a twenty-year-old girl from Arizona. She's been missing for a few weeks. Reported by her roommate, who said this girl worked at yet another strip club."

15

THE LOGICAL CONCLUSION WAS to head to Coyote Springs. Jim had made a short but valiant argument for Erica to stay at the Paris, get some rest. Not a chance. She said she was scared to be alone. How could he argue with that? He was a chump. A protective chump. And the stakes kept getting bigger. He just had to keep a professional distance.

There'd been no conversation since they got in the car. The road was straight and dark. Not much to see since leaving Las Vegas. The terrain did a steady rise and fall. The rock formations that were a hearty display of red and gold in the daytime were merely looming dark shadows against a gray, cloudless night. He had his window down, needed the fresh air. Erica's hair was dancing in the breeze. She hadn't complained so he'd kept it open. The dashboard said it was fifty-six degrees out. It felt fresh, cool. Mind-clearing kind of weather. November in Nevada. He loved it.

They passed a closed gas station. Not one light burning. Not even a streetlight. No one cared to prevent an overnight robbery. Deserted, out of business.

She looked at her watch, then glanced up at the rearview mirror in time to catch him looking back. He turned his attention to the road. This was stupid. He was feeling like a schoolboy who got caught peeking in the girl's locker room. He should say something about it. Cut off this awkward feeling.

"So." She did it for him. Left the awkward moment in the hotel behind. "All this seems so random. We have a dead drug dealer who Chris helped out at some point in his miserable life." She held up a finger for each point. "A missing twenty-year-old stripper we know nothing about. Chris working as a stripper. A cop deleting case files. The Thin Man. The man in the yellow shoes. A searched apartment. Blood. Blood. Blood."

He glanced back up. Ten fingers. Back to work. Good. She'd failed to mention Banks cracking her head open. The bruise was a blackish purple around her eye, but the pain must be lessening since she didn't react to it or acknowledge it in her list. But he would leave that little detail out until he figured if Banks and Zant fit into this puzzle or not.

"Dirty cops, missing strippers, and dead drug dealers are all common in Vegas, sadly. It's likely the Thin Man and Yellow Shoes are the same guy. Different clothes and he doesn't look so thin anymore." She nodded when he looked up at the mirror to meet her eyes. "We just need to figure out what's tying that all together."

"Could this place be the connection? The development, not the club."

"Either. Both. That's why we're out here."

The first building to rise in the distance was a hotel on the west side of the road. He slowed the vehicle to a crawl as they passed. No other traffic at the moment to be disturbed.

"The anonymous type. Just as you described it." And it was. White stucco, stained orange several feet up from the foundation, one story, and spread out into two wings that mirrored each other off to either side of the small office. There was no lobby, no restaurant. A few lights were burning in small rooms. Two cars parked where they could see them. Could be more around back. Cheaters parked in the back. Dealers parked in the back. He wasn't looking for anyone in particular, so no need to check. Yet.

They went another mile and came upon the restaurant and the strip club. One on either side of the highway. The restaurant, on the west, was more diner than restaurant. It was small, built right on the road, glass front, maybe sixty feet long. Probably not more than fifteen tables and a long counter inside. It was well lit, and even at the late hour of ten p.m. on a weeknight, it had two cars parked in front, a few people he could see sitting at the counter.

Comparatively, the Showgirl seemed huge, like an edifice paying homage to the glory that was the stripping industry in Nevada. That building was well off the road and the metal structure rose three stories high. It had been strategically placed at an angle for perfect road-front advertising to those driving north from Vegas to the golf course and the planned community. Fresh clean paint said it was well kept. Black wrought iron held up a red canopy walkway that greeted *guests* for loading and unloading. A valet stood at the ready in khakis and black polo. On the roof, fifteen-foot-tall neon signs blinked to create the illusion of a dancing girl high-kicking to music Jim could not hear from the road. A nod to classic Vegas.

The joint was doing a good business too. Damned good for the remote location. There were probably twenty cars in the lot plus a few limos. Jim cruised by.

"Aren't we going in?"

"I looked over the layout of the community online. Full of computer-generated photos with happy families, schoolyards, and shopping centers. Sales video for pushing the dream. I want to see what's really out here." He drove on. "It'll be open till four a.m., at least. Best to let the girls make some money first. Then they're more likely to take some time to chat."

Past the club, there was little else to see. The golf club was less than three miles north, just off the main road. He'd read good things about it. Nicklaus designed it himself. It too was still well-maintained, popular, and tee times hard to get. It was the only reason this city was on the map at all. At this hour, though, the unimpressive clubhouse, which was a double-wide trailer rather than a country club, was dark. "It looks temporary. Part of the unfinished idea of the community."

"Seems sad," she said more to herself than to him. Her face matched the comment as it reflected off the glass of the window.

The rest of the town tour was short. Past the course there was a service road off to the east just before a sign reading *Thank You for Visiting Modern Coyote Springs*. A half mile or more down that road stood two more large metal buildings. Dark. Empty lots. Overgrown with scrub weeds. Several more streets had been cut in, but all were dead ends that led to nowhere and nothing. Six buildings were all that was left of the dream that was Coyote Springs.

He made a legal U-turn at the far end of what would have been a bustling community had it not been for investment scams and embezzlement.

———————

"Two times in as many days I'm going into a strip club." She shook her head as they started for the door. "Any particular reason we parked all the way out here?"

"Parking out here we walk by the row of hired cars."

And they soon did. Seven of them. All black or dark blue with heavily tinted windows. He studied each one as he went by. His brows rose at the third one from the end.

"What's with that one?"

"Private plates." He kept walking. "You still good with numbers?"

"Yes. I guess."

"Can you memorize that plate number?"

"Sure." She pulled out her phone and typed the license number into a notes app. "Done."

He laughed. "I sometimes forget to use my technology."

"Too much of a hard-ass. Always liked to do things the hard way. When you were in that criminology class, you used to say it was better working like the old guys. That you'd catch more details that way. Experience the case instead of recording it."

The fact she'd remembered what he'd said years ago momentarily stopped his progress. He remembered saying it. He didn't want to have that memory now. He looked past her to the door. A bouncer was off to the side smoking a cigarette, chatting on the phone. "Try not to piss off the locals this time."

Her hand drifted to her bruised brow. He returned to his path to the door.

A sharp-looking young man opened the door for them as they approached. "Have a nice evening, folks," he said with a smile as Erica stepped past him. Jim nodded and handed the kid a bill.

They stepped into the lobby area. It was much bigger and cleaner than the Peppermint Pony.

"You tipped him for opening the door?"

"Almost everyone in Vegas lives on tips." A very pretty girl stood inside a little coatroom. Not that it was often cold enough for coats in Vegas, but several suit jackets and a fur hung behind her.

"Welcome to the Showgirl." She flashed a brilliant smile. "Ladies' night tonight, so your lovely companion has no cover." She pushed her locks from her face with a slight flip of her head. She probably didn't even realize the flirty nature of the move. "For you, twenty-five."

Again, Jim reached in his wallet. He pulled out thirty dollars and handed the girl the cash. "Thanks," he said and turned to Erica, not waiting for his change. Another tip. He'd add it to her bill.

"Have a good evening," the girl chirped and she hit a button. A small click indicated a lock on the door leading to the main room had been released. Jim pushed it open and held it for Erica to enter first.

Locked for those coming in. Probably not for those going out. Jim noted the security cameras as well.

Erica's eyes got big when they entered the club. "This place is nothing like the Peppermint Pony."

Nope. There were two floors. The upper had a long open atrium with black iron railing wrapped around the dance floors. Two men were perched there watching the activities from above.

From behind a grand set of stairs, as if between floors, girls were dancing their way along a catwalk that curved down to the lower level, split, and led to various-sized stages. They were all dressed in the same type of elaborate costumes with large headdresses of flowers, feathers, and glitter. The bottoms were skimpy and there was no top at all. Just like the costumes they had found in Chris's apartment.

Jim took a moment to assess the room.

"What are you scanning for?"

"Exits. Bouncers that might be a threat. Cameras. Anything that might inhibit a speedy retreat."

"Do you always need an escape route?"

"Nope. But best to have one planned for the times you do."

They reached a bar. Its surface was bright and appeared to be slithering along like a neon snake as lights danced under the semi-opaque surface. The wall of liquor bottles behind it was equally opulent. Backlit bottles lined the thing from one end to the other, probably sixty feet, and then up at least fifteen gleaming rows high. Jim pulled a chrome-and-black stool out far enough for her to climb up.

Movement from the side caught Jim's attention. Mike Stands was making his way over. Mike was an older guy, very distinguished-looking in his black suit, white shirt, and neat black tie. "Jim Bean." Mike stuck out his hand. "What brings you out to the Springs?" He glanced at Erica. "Whatever it is, the company you keep has improved dramatically."

"Mike." Jim ignored his comment about Erica being *his* company. "I could ask you the same thing. Last I saw you was at the Rio."

"Zant bought this place a few months back. I got promoted. Front-of-the-house manager." He pulled on his jacket lapel as if to straighten the perfect coat.

Jim grunted, not happy that Zant owned this club as well. Didn't bode well. The evidence was piling up enough that Jim had to accept Zant was involved with Chris's disappearance. Maybe not directly, but...

A young girl, also dressed in all black, approached from behind the bar. "What can I get you?"

Jim ordered a Scotch. Erica asked for hot tea.

"I'm looking for info."

Mike indicated he was listening with a tilt of the head.

"You have any girls go missing lately?"

He shrugged. "Not that I noticed. Maybe some regular turnover. But I've only been up here a few weeks. Carl takes care of the girls. That would be back of the house."

The bartender slid Jim's drink in front of him and a large mug of hot water and a shiny tea caddy on the bar. Erica seemed overly excited about the tea. After looking at the selection, she chose one and dunked the bag into her mug.

Jim took a small sip. "Does the name Chris Floyd ring a bell?" He said it while the bartender was still there. The girl showed no reaction at all to hearing Chris's name.

Once she stepped away Mike leaned closer, lowered his voice. "Sorry. If you want to talk to one of the girls, wait a little bit. Two more songs and most of them will go back and change for individual performances.

"Thanks."

He leaned closer still. Gave Jim a stern look. "No trouble, Bean. Seriously. I can't afford to lose this gig. The old lady will kill me."

Jim raised his glass. Tipped it toward the guy. He didn't have any intention of making trouble. Never did. "I'll be on my best behavior. Just for you."

"Right." Mike straightened his tie again. Maybe he didn't trust Jim so much. He had no reason as far as Jim could think of, he hadn't busted up the Rio when Mike was running things. Not that he remembered anyway.

"The dressing rooms are behind the DJ booth. I mean it, Bean. No trouble and don't scare the girls."

16

JIM SMILED AS NICELY at Mike as he could. "I'll leave them all unscathed. Scout's honor."

Mike didn't look convinced. "I would bet my wife's boob job you were never a scout."

Oh but he had been. Eagle Scout, as a matter of fact, but that was all before. Regardless, Mike had little to worry over. Pissing off Banks yesterday had been stupid enough.

Jim turned to look out over the show. It was loud and Vegas-style gaudy, with the strippers all dressed in the coordinating costumes. The difference between the chicks here and real showgirls was that in about two minutes most of these girls would be buck naked and hanging around the scattered tables dancing up close and personal for tips. Showgirls stayed on the stage like it was theater. No table dancing.

"Enjoy your stay, Miss." Mike gave Erica a slight bow. "If you need anything, let me know. Anything at all. I'll be happy to arrange transportation for you if the need arises. You won't be the first date to abandon this one."

"Funny guy."

Jim watched Erica flash her gorgeous smile at Mike. "I'm fine. Thank you," she said.

He turned his attention to the rest of the room as Mike walked away. "Our time with the girls will be short."

She sipped her tea. "Okay."

"Mike will tell the back-of-the-house guy we're here, but he's giving us a little time. So when we get back there, pick one. I'll take a second. Maybe we'll get lucky."

She nodded. The song ended and another started. The girls moved around the room, changing tables, enticing money from different men. Four or five headed to the dressing room. "Let's go now."

Erica didn't question his decision. She got up and matched his pace to the DJ booth. Even that was big, and a half story up. They found the stairs behind it, passed the guy spinning the songs for the girls. The walls were black. The door to the dressing room was black. Without the bits of reflective tape on the corners and by the push plate, he'd have missed it.

He pushed in. It looked like a locker room. Several rows of wooden lockers were to the right. On the left was a bank of mirrors, well lit and with vanities in front for makeup. He headed that way. Pointed Erica toward the four women by the lockers.

There was one sitting alone in front of the mirrors. She was a little too old for this new shiny club. Big-money clubs were the playing field of the young. If she was working this room, she'd been around.

He set a twenty on the counter. "Just a question."

She looked down at the bill and started on her lipstick in the mirror.

"Chris Floyd?" He pulled out a picture. Held it up. "You seen her here?"

"Who's looking?" She looked at the pic and back to the money.

He set another twenty on top of it. "Jim Bean, PI from Vegas." He nodded at Erica across the room chatting with the other women. "Her sister's looking. No cops."

She finished her lips. Picked up some kind of black pencil and started in on her eyebrows. None of which was helping her cause, in Jim's opinion.

"Could be. But, sayin' so ain't worth the trouble for that."

"When?" He put another bill on the stack.

She put her hand on top of the stash and pulled it off the vanity. She folded it twice and tucked it in by her belly. Jim did his best not to notice any of it. "About three weeks ago. She was green. Real green. Then she weren't here anymore."

"You talk to her at all?"

The woman made an amused grunt. "Don't do no good to make friends around here. Specially with the green ones."

He glanced at Erica. She was pleading, just like she had been with Edmond Carver. The girls were giving her the same kind of pity-filled look. But none seemed to be talking.

The door slammed open. Another man in a suit came through. Was most likely Carl, back-of-the-house man. Carl was big. Not Banks big, but Jim didn't want any trouble. Time was up.

He smiled. Pressed another bill onto the counter. "So I'll bring the birthday boy Tuesday." It was loud enough for the big guy to hear and it covered her. "You'll take care of him?"

"You bet your ass I will." She scooped up the additional bill.

"Let's go, babe. I've got it all arranged." Erica had a pale face. But she came to his side and let him take her hand. "Great place you have here." Carl stepped out of the way as they passed. "We'll see you Tuesday."

He ushered her out. "The big girl," Erica said as they made their way back past the DJ booth.

"Not yet. We need to be out of here to keep the girls out of trouble." He made it straight for the door. It came open without needing to be buzzed from the inside.

He led her back toward the car. "Now tell me."

"I thought she might have fit the bigger costume. So I talked to her more directly. I showed her Chris's pictures. They all looked scared. But she almost cried. All of them denied seeing Chris, ever, said they were very sorry for me. But they've seen her, Korey. I know they have."

He didn't comment on the mention of his real name. She was starting to cry again.

"I figured that too. But the old girl didn't know where she'd gone. Said Chris was green."

"They didn't say they'd ever seen her, but you can tell when people are lying. Scared and lying." Erica was trying to slow down.

Jim nodded. Kept walking toward the car with his hand at her back. They were being watched, he was sure of that.

"She did tell me something strange just before we left. Once the guy came in."

"What?" He opened the back door to the SUV and let her in.

"She grabbed my hand and said the back of the place was hardly ever cleaned at night." He looked at her through the rearview as he started the truck. "She's saying there is something out back we should see, isn't she?"

"Sounds like it." He pulled out of the lot. Turned south.

"Then go back."

He looked out into the dark night, trying to see past the headlights. Go back? To snoop around a Zant property? When doing so might implicate Andrew Zant in a missing persons case? Actually, two missing persons cases... possibly a murder. Possibly three murders.

Not likely.

Zant owned Jim Bean at the moment.

17

ERICA'S VOICE WAS SO high she was almost screaming, the sound piercing his eardrums like ice picks. It'd gotten slowly higher the farther they'd made it away from the club. He got it: she was scared and sure the strippers had been telling her Chris was dead.

"You have to go back. Call Miller. Chris's body might be back there somewhere."

He'd kept his mouth shut. Wasn't sure what the fuck he was going to do. But he needed a moment to think. He pulled into the back parking lot of the Hotel Anonymous, stopped the car, and turned to face her in the seat.

"Look at me." She did. She was gripping her purse tightly. "Take a deep breath. They would not be so dumb to leave bodies out behind their club, on their own property, for days in the Nevada sun. Would they?" Jim made it a question on purpose. She'd have to think it through. Consider.

"No. I guess not."

"I need you to trust that I know what I'm doing. Give me a few hours."

She nodded but still looked like she was ready to shatter at the slightest touch or breeze.

"Can you do that? Trust me?"

She looked as if she was concentrating, trying to see his logic. He tried not to think back to Ohio and the last time he'd counted on her to trust him. And maybe this time she shouldn't. He wasn't sure of himself or his actions at this moment. She took a few more steadying breaths. "Yes. I will."

He wished now he'd worded the question differently. He didn't want her trust now. He no longer deserved it. He wasn't sure whose interest he would serve first if it came down to it—hers, Chris's, or his own. But she was making the decision to be strong, and *that* he needed. "Do you have the cash you were going to use to check in at the Paris with you?"

She nodded again.

He nodded to the no-tell motel, as she'd called it. "Go in. Check in. Two nights. Use another name. Say you lost your driver's license."

"Two?"

"More cash. Less reason to care about your missing license. Grease makes things work easier."

"Makes sense. What are you going to do?"

That was a good question. First, he needed to think for a minute without her in his grill. She'd been in his head for two days. He'd thought more about her and the past than he had this case. Hadn't taken it seriously enough. He needed to figure this thing out. Or … Maybe he'd just head for Florida. Not look back. Leave and not face this mess. He'd gotten good at that. Avoidance, the therapist had called it.

"What I'm trained to do. Relax. Watch cheap cable. Rest."

She stepped out of his truck.

"Erica."

She straightened, turned.

"If you don't hear from me by morning, you call Adair. Follow the plan. Get in your rental car. Fly home."

Because by morning, Jim might well be on his way to the Keys. The Showgirl being a Zant-owned establishment made it pretty clear the man was involved on some level with Chris. That meant Jim could *not* be involved. His cousin Alexis and her son would be put in danger if Andrew Zant found out Jim was nosing around after the girls in his clubs. Mike had seen him, and Banks most likely saw him too. He was in it up to his bloodshot eyeballs.

"Is it that bad?" She closed the back door and leaned on the hood looking at him. "You think she's dead and you want me out of the way?"

"It's bad. It's been bad all along, only I didn't see it. I figured Chris was shacking up with some bouncer, maybe just got hooked on something, got off track. I was wrong. They know who you are. *If* someone did kill Chris, you're now next. You're a target. I should have sent you home right away."

Her face was drawn, her eyes despondent. "If you don't show, I'll go home. But then what? Try the police again? Call the feds?"

"Noah Miller. No one else."

Jim put the car in gear before the conversation could go any deeper. No matter what, Miller would fix things. Finish the case or not. Jim could fill him in. Have Miller send a car for her and then Jim could get gone. Clear conscience.

"Fake name. Fake address," he reminded her.

She stepped back. He pulled out of the parking lot. South. He should go home, grab the cat and some clothes, and keep going.

He drove for twenty minutes.

Mentally he checked off a laundry list of things that could be behind the Showgirl. He slowed to a crawl.

Turned the car around.

And sat at a standstill in the middle of the road. Lights appeared in his rearview. Heading north. He had to accelerate.

Crap. He pulled over, slamming the shifter a little harder than he intended. The truck jerked to a stop. Jim Bean got out and paced around the deserted road. Dust from the passing car filled his nose.

Staying involved now would be committing a murder/suicide. Yep. This case would get him and Alexis dead. The deal had been clear. No loopholes for Jim Bean in the negotiations. Zant agreed to let Alexis leave Vegas and stay alive, but only if Jim agreed to owe him.

And he had paid. More than once. And not in ways Jim was too proud of.

But it hadn't been enough. How many favors was Alexis's life worth, really?

As many as Zant asked for.

Working a case that placed Zant into a position that might associate the casino owner with missing girls and a dead body? Well, that was no favor.

Jim hated it. Hated the thought of ever helping the cretin again, but Alexis and her son were safe. Their continuing safety depended on him.

And now so did Erica's. And Chris's.

He looked north. The sky was clear. Stars everywhere. How had he been cursed with this shit?

What was behind that bar that those strippers wanted Erica to see? Probably nothing. Probably used-up drug paraphernalia. Nothing that he would give a rat's ass about in the long run. He sighed. The mystery would kill him. What if it was Chris's body? Jim needed to know. The investigator in him couldn't walk away from that kind of tip. His goddamn curiosity. That and Erica Floyd were going to be the death of him.

He'd check it out and then decide what to do.

———

He killed the headlights as he pulled into the golf course. He crept passed the temporary clubhouse and followed the one-lane road to the maintenance shack, pulled behind that. He donned a lightweight black jacket, checked his digital camera for battery life, then checked his boot for his knife.

He determined the direction of the club by the direction of the low mountains in the distance. Jim started walking, trying not to think too much.

He was walking directly across the holes so he only got to get a look at about four of them. Golf. When was the last time he got to play golf? Never on a course like this. The course, what he could see of it, was beautiful. It was all he'd see of it. Out of his league, price-wise so he enjoyed the landscaping in the dark as he passed.

Eventually the lush, watered fairways and putting greens gave way to the rough Nevada landscape. He walked another mile after he came out the far side of the fifteenth hole and around a con-trived water hazard. There were no naturally occurring springs or random lakes out here. He glanced at his watch. Three a.m. The moon wasn't full, but there was enough light he would be noticed if someone was looking.

The back of that big metal building loomed not too far ahead. Maybe a half mile. The ground was rocky. No trees. Just scrub grass and rocks. And sand. He would have to go in low.

He started to crawl, military style, a few hundred yards out. His knees hurt by the time he'd made it to the back of the only real cover around. He studied the scene. Fucking dumpster behind the building was the only cover there. No outbuildings, no fence, no landscaping. He watched the camera mounted over the back entrance to the club for full a minute. It was stationary, pointed down, close to the door. Not really practical for capturing the back area. If it was on, it was only monitoring the door. Easy enough to maneuver around that.

This dumpster was not like the one he'd been painting over near Edmond Carver's place. This thing was industrial, eight feet tall, ten feet long with sliding doors at shoulder height that locked. Most had big locks. Maybe they could hide a body out here for days. He circled around as far as he could and still be out of camera range. One of the sliding doors was pushed all the way open. He peered inside with a mirror on a telescoping wand. Bottles. Paper. Cardboard. Food remnants. No bodies. No dead-man smell. Very little smell at all.

Beyond that, across the camera's purview and on the other side of the back entrance, was a table. A fancy one like you'd see in some-one's upscale back yard. Heavy iron and glass topped, it had a nice big umbrella and chairs with thick cushions. Next to it was a make-shift serving bar. No one was enjoying the outdoor seating at the moment, but Jim found it odd.

Expensive stuff for the unimpressive location, back of the house, view of the trash. Not the employees' smoking area. Maybe the strippers brought men out for outdoor entertainment at times. Maybe that was why the camera was focused on the door and not any of the area out back. Wouldn't want customers to fear being filmed. He snapped a picture of it and the big dumpster.

Behind the furniture, up against the building, was a stack of crates. Plastic crates with metal grating. To avoid the camera, he swung wide, back toward the golf course, and then came at the crates after a wide loop from the west. Dog crates. Big ones. Three stacks of them, four high. Was Chris investigating dogfights?

He snapped several pictures. Then saw one of the crates had a set of handcuffs attached, looped through the metal grate close to the bottom of the cage. Inside.

Dogs wouldn't need cuffs.

He leaned in closer. There were crumpled towels on the floor of the crate. One looked to have dried-up blood on it. But it was dark.

Several more pictures.

Nothing else out there to see.

Time to get the hell out.

18

HE KNEW IT WAS ERICA in that cheap chair as soon as his headlights shone down his alleyway. That plastic piece of shit was his sit-and-think-with-a-cigar chair. And she was in it. Instead of at the hotel. Where he had left her. Safe.

Her head slumped forward, her hands in her lap. He jammed on the brakes, worried she might be dead, left here by Zant as a warning. His heart bounced in his chest like it was bungee jumping. Only one way to know.

He eased forward. Her head popped to attention as he pulled close to his little garage door. Asleep. Relief washed over him. Anger. He wanted anger. "What the fuck are you doing here?" He slammed his door shut and marched up to her.

"I was going to ask you that very same question." She stood up to him. Nose to nose. She had to rise up on her toes to do it. "You're quitting, aren't you?" She looked so smug. Like she'd solved some great mystery. "I knew it. I stood in that shitty motel for all of about four minutes before I decided you were going to bolt on me.

"I called Adair. Like you said. 'Follow the plan.' But I have no intention of going home, *Jim Bean.*" She sank off her toes, but the venom was not subsiding with her height. "I sat in that cab straddled between mad and sad. Mad that you left me. Sad that we've come to this. I considered if I should just go back to my cushy room at the Paris and call Noah Miller. I considered going on without you, back to the Showgirl. Then I got scared. And then I got tired." She eased back, paced, and settled back in the plastic chair. "I'm heartsick with worry over my sister, all this craziness about strippers and bouncers—it's hard.

"I'm tired. I don't have the energy to fight with you. But there's no way I'm leaving Las Vegas until I know where my sister is."

He'd let her go on to get it out of her system. Little did she know how close he had come to bolting. But he hadn't. He'd given her one more opportunity. "I asked you to trust me. But obviously, you're incapable of that."

She sat in the chair and nodded, her whole body swaying with her head. "You're right. I *should have* trusted you back then. But I don't trust you now. I saw it in your face. You were done with me, with this. Something you figured out as soon as we walked in the Showgirl has you nervous. Did you even go back out there?"

He pushed past her and put his key in the door lock. "Did it occur to you that sitting your ass out here in the open was monumentally stupid? *You* are now a target."

"Another change of subject. You dodged again without answering a direct question."

"Not successfully."

Erica followed him in without invitation.

He spun on her in the narrow hallway. "Why are you here?"

"Why are *you* here?"

He scowled at her. "My house."

"I want to know what was back there. Was she back there?"

Jim let out an exasperated huff and made his way to the kitchen and tossed his keys on the counter. "No. She's not dead." The cat was winding in and out of his legs as he moved. He grabbed the cat food and filled Annie's bowl. Erica slid into one of his kitchen chairs, her hand on her chest, her eyes closed in relief. "I mean. I don't know that she's not dead. I just didn't learn anything more from that club. There were no bodies stacked up behind the building."

"Nothing? Those women were fairly insistent without coming right out and begging me to look back there."

"I don't know what I found. It didn't make any sense. I'm at a dead end." He leaned back against the kitchen counter, crossed his arms, doing his best to not look at her. Not give her the satisfaction of knowing he was considering leaving her on her own or in his tired state confessing the sins he committed in the name of Zant. She mimicked his position in the chair. Stubborn woman. "I need some sleep." Avoidance was one of his best attributes.

"I need to know if you're in this with me." She gave him her best business glare, locking her eyes on his, not giving him a chance to look away.

It didn't work. He laughed. "Just like I needed to know you were in it with me in Ohio?" He pushed away from the counter, cruised past her, heading toward the stairs. "I don't owe you shit." He stopped at the bottom, turned to face her again. "You show up here with your high-dollar suit and your sad eyes and you expect me to drop what little is left of my life, ignore my current clients, and put my ass on the line for you after you left me alone and rejected in a prison cell? And you're mad when I tell you I'm out of answers. That's priceless." He shoved his hands through his hair.

If he could piss her off maybe he could convince her to go back to Miller and let Jim off the hook. He decided a little downplaying was in order. "This is over my head, beyond my meager capabilities. I investigate cheaters, liars, and hacks. My biggest case this year was a car thief I helped a lawyer get off on a technicality. This is a murder case if just for Edmond Carver. Go back to Detective Miller and tell him everything you know. Let the proper authorities handle it. Leave me in peace."

He walked away.

"Lock up on your way out," he barked as his bedroom door slammed closed.

Jim watched her marching away from his house from his bedroom window. She'd stood silent in his kitchen for a good five minutes before she had decided he wasn't coming back out.

She made the turn safely to the spot where her car was tucked. She got in it, started it, and drove away with a tiny squeal of tires. She'd go to the Paris, sleep for a while, and then leave after talking with Miller again. He'd convince her that there was little she could do here but get hurt. Then the case would slowly disappear as Zant made any and all evidence of whatever he was up to go away. Erica would be in Boston and safe. As long as she wasn't here causing problems, Zant would forget about her.

Chris's fate was sealed. Nothing Jim did at this point would save her. She'd been gone too long. She was, sadly, a statistic. Jim putting himself, his cousin, and her son at risk wouldn't change that.

Erica was out of his life once again. And once again he felt a sucking emptiness in his chest.

The sun was peeking over the horizon as he glanced at his phone. Five a.m.

He went through the motions of showering before he crawled into his uncomfortable bed. Again. As he did every time he lay in it, he grumbled and thought to call tomorrow to order a different one from the furniture rental company. He drifted off with thoughts of dog crates in his head.

Jim Bean woke up exactly three hours later, sweating, twisted in his sheet, and wishing he was a different man. He'd dreamed of strippers, Banks, the Thin Man, and painting dumpsters, all with Erica Floyd looking on disapprovingly. He'd dreamed of Chris cuffed and cramped inside a dog crate.

He grabbed his phone and texted Double O.

COFFEE GIRL. 11:00?

Jim lay there and waited for a response.

It came two minutes later.

11:30 OKAY?

19

"GET DRESSED."

Erica yelped like a little girl and sat up, clutching her breasts. She looked at the clock. Nine thirty a.m. She shifted. Rubbed her eyes.

"How'd you find me? I was sure I did everything right. Extra tip. Fake name. Fake address. I didn't even go back to the Paris for clean clothes."

"There were only two rooms with a light left on. Reflects under the drapes in the window."

"And?"

He looked over to the cheap vanity that made up the back wall of the room. She'd left the light on over the tub, and the door separating the bath area from the vanity was pulled almost closed. A little light to find her way if she'd needed to pee. Not much. "You always leave the bathroom light on."

"So you had a fifty-fifty shot and broke in?"

He shrugged. She'd nailed him. "I was wrong the first time. Old guy. Snoring. Not you."

"I suppose that's better than young guy, heavily armed, and not amused."

He almost chuckled.

She shook her head, waved her hand. "Anyway. I meant this *hotel*. How did you know I drove back out here instead of the Paris?"

She was in her shirt and underwear. She indicated for him to turn around. He did. He heard her gather her clothes. Head to the bathroom.

He turned just in time to catch a glimpse of her ass. "You'd paid for the room. Made sense to come back out here." He was quiet for a moment. "I figure your plan was to go look around the Showgirl in the daylight." He knew her. That *was* her plan. "And I hope you thought it might be safer staying out here."

She came out of the bathroom, stopped at the sink, rinsed a washcloth, and wiped her face. She gathered her purse and put some lip balm on. "Two-fifty in cash for a couple-hour nap."

"Happens all the time in my line of work."

He led her wordlessly through the breezeway behind the office to the back parking lot. There was a nun entering as they exited the open area. Other than the clerk in the little office, she was the only person he'd seen at the hotel. The old woman was in full habit, big hat and all. Not so bad in November, but Jim figured that wool would be an absolute misery outside in a Vegas summer.

Jim opened the back door of the truck for Erica and plopped into the front. He was in his seat with the motor running by the time she was settled and buckled in.

"You're cranky."

"I'm here." They made eye contact through the rearview.

She nodded. He hadn't abandoned her to the police.

"What about my car?"

He glanced at the little yellow Fiat. "It's okay here. Maybe even better than in the city."

He drove in silence and at a high rate of speed.

"You look tired. Your brows are doing that scrunchy thing they used to do when you were pissed."

He didn't look at her.

"In business it pays not to ask questions you don't want the answer to ..." She stared out the window and watched the landscape for a moment. He knew what she wanted to ask. He wasn't sure he wanted to answer either.

"When you don't want to deal with the answers in a negotiation."

Maybe thirty more miles passed before curiosity got the best of her. "What was back there? Behind the club?"

"I told you I didn't find any bodies, but I don't know exactly what it is I did find. I said it before—this far out ... missing so long ... you have to know it's probably not positive."

She closed her eyes tight, gave a minuscule nod. "But knowing it and accepting my sister might be gone are two different things. I'll choose to keep my head in the sand for the time being. Thank you."

The landscape flew by in a blur. Jim blinked and Vegas appeared on the horizon, an island of glass and steel shimmering on a sea of sand. The themed megahotels shining in the sun were the epitome of life and vibrancy. His bones felt as heavy as steel rods, his mind as dull as river rocks. The sway of the car seemed to pull more than it should as he motored on.

Jim navigated back to Shalamar Avenue as if on autopilot.

"I need to go to the Paris and freshen up. I slept in these. I have no makeup and I need a toothbrush." She sounded as broken as he felt.

"Yeah, you do," he said as they parked in front of his condo.

"Funny man."

"But we have a meeting in ten minutes." He waited for her to get out, then indicated the direction of the café.

20

THE TRUTH WAS JIM *did* have a good idea what this was all pointing to. All the driving back and forth to Coyote Springs gave a man time to think, consider, add things up. It was new math. Bad math that gave him an idea what Chris was doing in the clubs and what had become of her. But he needed Oscar Olsen to confirm those suspicions, and Jim didn't have the balls to be the one to break it to Erica.

Coward?

Yes, sir.

He watched her face as the big man rolled into the parking lot and pulled himself off his bike. Oscar replaced his heavy flag-painted helmet with a ball cap with the American flag printed on it, turned backward.

Sandy showed up with the extra mug and menu. She glanced at Erica's bruised eyebrow. "You need anything for that?"

Erica smiled. "Some makeup to cover it up would be great. But it's fine. Looks worse than it is now."

Sandy poured her some more coffee. "He didn't do that, did he?" She tilted her head Jim's way.

"He probably wished he had by now, but no."

She filled Jim's mug too. "By special request"—she tilted her head toward the big man coming toward the door—"I was able to convince the boss man to order some real bacon. Well. Turkey bacon. But it's meat. You want some of it?"

"How'd he rate that kind of VIP treatment? I come here almost every day, offer you a real job, and all I ever get is that tofu shit?"

She shrugged. "He's not an ass."

"I'm downright sweet to you."

"He gives me kisses." She winked at Jim.

"I tip. You'd rather have kisses?"

She gave Jim that same look most women eventually gave him. The one he really didn't understand. Was it constipation or consternation? "Hardly."

She turned to go greet Oscar as he came in the door.

"She's certainly fond of him," Erica said. Her face said she was unconvinced by his appearance. *"He's* going to help?"

At times Oscar did look more like a criminal than most of the criminals he tracked down. The man was even taller than Jim. His hair was long and pulled back in a braid that hung past his shoulders. When he wasn't working as a bounty hunter, Oscar rode an ancient motorcycle that he'd cobbled together from nuts, sprockets, and odd parts. He lovingly referred to it as Franken-bike. Damn thing could outrun anything around and probably survive being run over by a tank.

Today Oscar's clothing choice was a sleeveless denim shirt—sleeves torn out, not cut; jeans faded by wear and time, not chemicals; and a thick leather choker that Jim was sure the man always wore. His chunky arms were a collage of tattoos. Some Jim knew the meaning behind, others he didn't.

"Best man I know," was all Jim said before Oscar stopped and gave Sandy her peck on the forehead and a giant smile.

A little huff escaped Erica. "Good enough for me."

Oscar dragged over a chair from a nearby table and spun it around backward at the end of the booth. He managed to ease into the seat with a genuine sort of coolness Jim did not possess. Oscar flashed Erica that perfect smile that had just melted the waitresses. Jim watched her respond. If he wanted to, Oscar could look like a giant lion on the verge of ripping someone to shreds, but once he turned on that charm, everyone flocked to him.

"*Hombre.*" He nodded to Jim.

Erica sat tall, stuck out her hand. "Erica Floyd."

Oscar shook it. "Erica." He crossed his arms over the top of the metal-backed chair. "I presume this is not about lightening my caseload."

Jim wished it were now more than ever. But he'd driven that broken road back out to Coyote Springs and brought Erica here for a reason. If he was right, if this was what he suspected, Double O would want in on it.

"I have a couple pictures I'd like you to take a look at." Jim brought the picture of the crate with the cuffs up on the screen, but didn't turn to share just yet.

Sandy had appeared to pour Oscar's coffee. She took everyone's order although it was unlikely anyone would be eating any of it once this discussion got underway.

Oscar's eyes lost some of their lightness as he glanced to Erica and back to the camera. Jim pushed it over to his longtime friend. "Found this out behind a strip club. What do you make of it?"

Oscar glanced at the camera for just an instant. He didn't need to study the photo. His eyes closed. He took in a long breath. Straightened his back. He looked at Erica. "Who are you?" His voice turned cold.

She blinked at his sudden change in demeanor and looked to Jim. He nodded. "Tell him what he wants to know."

Her gaze darted back to Oscar. She bit her lip. "My sister, Chris Floyd, works for the department of welfare here. She suddenly started working part-time in strip clubs. Now she's missing."

Oscar kept his expression blank. "Where?" He trained his glare directly on Jim. The lion was close to the surface now. That told Jim his conclusion was right.

"What is it, anyway?" Erica took the camera from the table, looked at the screen. "Dog crates?"

"People crates." Oscar's hand had a slight shake to it. He still looked at Jim as he said it. "Where was that taken?"

Erica answered. "The Showgirl in Coyote Springs."

"Have you told her?" Oscar pointed at the camera with an irritated flick of his wrist. "What that means?"

"Wasn't completely sure. Wanted to confirm my suspicions before going into it."

O looked down and slowly shook his head before he gave Jim a piercing look. "Better to hear it from me, huh?" Jim didn't have to answer. O's face softened. He suddenly looked older, much less threatening.

"My wife." He took a drink from his mug. "We were here on our first anniversary. Up on Freemont Street, downtown. We got ripped. Really ripped."

Erica was frozen in her seat. Jim saw her ball her hands slowly into fists to steel herself for the story that was coming. It was no fairytale with a happy ending. That was clear from the way Oscar pushed himself back into a stiff upright position. He was putting some distance between himself and Erica. "We were in a strip club. Thought it was cool. She was all proud of herself for doing it."

He looked right into Erica's eyes. "It was loud, dark, and late. I only lost sight of her for a minute. She was in line for the bathroom. There one second. Gone the next."

Erica was already tearing up. Jim felt helpless. She needed to know what they were facing. Needed to hear it from someone who'd experienced it or she would have trouble even believing it. Jim had when he first heard the story, but time had told him that people did horrific things. Still, Jim had never heard the account of the night directly from Oscar. Not like this.

"After months of badgering the police and selling off everything thing I owned, I moved here and started digging myself. I found a trail. A trail that led to Mexico, then to a man in South America. It's known as human trafficking in the media."

Erica's mouth opened. No words came out.

"They stole her, then sold her. We have a plague of it in this country. Both workers coming in and girls going out." He took his hat off, twisted the brim, and then placed it back on his head. "After more money, three years, and more than a couple busted heads, I got proof of where she had been taken and eventually … proof that she'd been killed." He swallowed hard. His hand went to the leather choker around his neck. A single, small gold ring was braided into it. He touched it gently.

Erica was trembling. Jim felt the urge to go to her. Hold her. No matter the past, this was not what anyone deserved to hear, to experience.

"I'm … I'm very sorry for you, Mr. Olsen, but are you suggesting Chris has been kidnapped and sold?"

He let out a long sigh. His face tightened back up. Business. "She worked for juvie?"

"Yes."

"She look anything like you?"

"Yes."

He took another drink, scratched his chin. "Is she the kind of woman who'd notice that she was losing girls from her client list and go looking for them?"

Erica didn't answer right away. The pieces were falling together for her. The same as they had for Jim driving that road. "Exactly that kind."

He nodded. "Sorry, lady. My guess is she found something that pointed to the clubs. The girls were going to work and not coming back. Your sister went looking."

Erica sat silent for a moment. Jim watched a range of emotions cross her face. Fear. Hurt. Anger.

He decided to do something. He couldn't just sit there any longer. He glanced to the waitress station a few feet from the back table they occupied. He got up and grabbed the coffeepot Sandy had left on the warmer. He slid in next to Erica, the vinyl creaking in objection to his weight. He refilled her cup. No need to reach out. Just wanted to be there if she needed.

"I knew she didn't start stripping for money or drugs." It was directed at him.

"You were right." Not that it helped, but he said it anyway.

"Is she gone?"

21

ERICA LOOKED LIKE SHE would shatter at any moment. The big bounty hunter had told his tale but had no reassurances to offer. Or didn't want to say it. Both he and Jim delivered bad news often enough. It was Jim's job to find out bad things about people and then deliver that news. He was glad he'd had O here.

"Is my sister dead?"

"Most likely." Oscar swallowed. "And if not, it might be better if she were. You don't need to know any more details." He shot Jim a look.

"Has to be really ugly based on the looks on your faces." She was searching for some hope. Jim had none.

"Bean, you need to let me handle this." O turned to Jim. "If you won't carry a weapon, I don't even want you on this one. We're talking South American drug lords and shit. Not a game for a guy used to chasing cheating husbands. I can't even trust you to be sober."

"I don't carry." Frankly, everyone was safer if Jim didn't have a gun. His real-life aim sucked no matter how much he practiced on the range. Probably would have never passed his FBI academy training years ago. But he was good with hand-to-hand, knives, street fighting. Easier being a brute. He could use his head too. Smarts got him out of more situations than brawn ever had.

O trained his big eyes on Erica. "And you need to be at home. Safe. With a guard preferably."

She glared right back. "I'm not going anywhere until I know exactly what happened to Chris. I will camp in that hotel, or buy a house next door to yours, if need be."

So she said the next part directly to Jim. "Whatever it takes, Korey. I will not walk away from her. I will not."

He cringed, but Oscar didn't flinch at her use of Jim's real name.

She made her point. "I realize I should have had the same conviction for you, years ago. It's too late for that. I won't make a mistake like that again. I'm going with my gut, and my gut says I need to be right here." She pointed a finger at Jim. "If you want out, fine. I'll hire someone else." She pointed at Oscar with her thumb. "Him, even. I'll call in the FBI. But I am not leaving her out there with that kind of vermin."

They all exchanged exasperated glares. Hung jury. No one giving in. Jim finally spoke to O. "I've known Erica for years. And as much as I'd like her to, she won't go home and wait by the phone. Not for me and not for you."

The trio sat in a silent stalemate. Erica inched forward, straightened, tried to look taller, stronger.

Oscar pulled that hat off, twisted the brim again. "If you're going to see this out, you have to know what we're dealing with. You have to be able to face it. You will never feel the same about anything ever again. Anything. This is the kind of shit that rips the spirit out of people. Destroys their belief that humans are generally good."

A bit of hair had fallen into her eyes as she looked down. She nodded but didn't look up. She was staring directly at the camera. Oscar didn't start immediately. Jim knew he was letting her process things for a moment.

It was a tactic Jim used in with clients and subjects all the time. Let the other party think through his options before you close on him. If she stayed, she was going to have to deal with how bad it could be for Chris. O wanted her to know that for sure.

"Even knowing that it's out there is going to change me. It already has. I still don't see a scenario where I abandon Chris." She picked up the camera. Advanced to the next picture. It was the one with the handcuffs. Her hand shook. They were giving her time to understand this. "Women have been in those crates? Like dogs?"

She advanced it again. Another shot of them. She zoomed it in. Sat taller. Stiffened. Zoomed it farther. She tilted the camera to Jim. The image was the last one he'd shot. There was a design drawn on the inside of that crate—a black-inked doodle against the plastic of the rear interior of the crate.

"It's her."

Oscar leaned over them, looming large. "What?"

"That symbol." She pointed to the marking on the screen. "Chris used it all the time as a kid. It was just a doodle for a long time, but then it became a signature of sorts."

He looked down. Erica had been excited by the revelation. Oscar was not.

"That means she was there."

"It does." Oscar's voice was low, controlled. "I'm going to say again that I think you need to go home. Let Jim, me, and the police take care of this."

She shook her head.

"Look, lady, I have years of pain and money wrapped up in this investigation. I'm close to proving some very nasty things about some pretty big names. Casino owners. Politicians."

Jim figured he meant Zant. He wanted to vomit. He was risking a lot for her, for Chris.

Oscar continued not knowing just how deep Jim had gotten in with Zant. "If you two do anything to jeopardize this case, I will kill you myself." He looked from Erica back to Jim. "You may be my friend, but I will not lose these guys again."

Erica interrupted. "I'll do what you say. Everything. I can help. If Chris left us a trail, I can follow it."

"You'll listen and understand for a minute. If you can still sit here after I'm done, I'll consider sharing with you."

Sandy walked up with the food. She placed the plates at the appropriate places. No one made any move toward them. She huffed. "It isn't all that bad. You've got real turkey bacon."

Erica mustered a pleasant enough face. "Thanks."

Oscar pushed his food away. His face had lost some color as he contemplated where to start. He pointed at the camera. "Those cages, they're for breaking the girls down. Destroying their will." He looked to make sure no one else was paying attention to the conversation. Satisfied, he continued.

"They are drugged, put in there naked, then abused beyond belief. *In* the crates. Starved. Left for days. Raped. All while being told that if they escape, if they don't do exactly as they are told, when they are told, their loved ones will be killed, or worse—captured and put through the very same thing."

He had to take a breath, to swallow to stop from tearing himself up. "It's done for days, sometimes weeks before they're shipped south in trucks to be sold like stolen electronics. Some, the prized women, are sold right here"—he tapped the table with his middle finger. The letter *L* tattooed on it—"in Vegas to Whales from overseas."

It was suddenly quiet. Erica wasn't breathing. She had to be imagining that happening to Chris. How could she not? He was. Chris, in one of those crates.

She tried to move, but Jim still sat beside her. It was a decent gesture at the time, he guessed, but now he could see his size was making her feel claustrophobic. She shoved at his arm. He moved, sliding out. "Erica…"

She crawled over him before he had made it out of the way. She stepped on Oscar's foot too. "Sorry." She looked down to check if he'd been hurt. His big black boots protected his toes from her. She let out an absurd, confused giggle. As if being concerned over his foot meant a hill of shit when her sister could be in a crate somewhere living out a nightmare.

"Erica."

"I just need some air. A minute to breathe."

She ran out the door.

O pushed his untouched plate farther away. "I have yet to figure out how people do this to other people. Her baby sister… She's going to need a friend."

Could he be a friend to her? After *she'd* been the first one to make Jim see how much people could hurt each other? Had he been tortured and raped in that cell? No. But his spirit had been broken.

He got up and followed her.

She was behind the building. On her knees, holding herself up with her hands. She stayed there, clawing at the rough gravel under her fingers.

She vomited. Her body tried to expel her agony, like a dragon sending fire and rage to burn the away the horror. But he knew the meager contents of her stomach had no such power. He drank way too much, far too often. Her stomach may have felt better for its effort, but nothing was going to rid her of the feeling of helplessness. Ever.

Erica learned things today she couldn't ever unlearn, couldn't recover from.

22

JIM PICKED HER UP and cradled her.

"I'm sorry." It was whispered against his chest. "I'll be fine."

Oscar loomed behind them, his tone tight, grim. "No, you won't. Unless we're wrong, you'll never be fine again. I know."

"Enough," Jim fired back at his friend. "She's got it, O. It's bad."

Erica tried to pull away. He held her. All these years of wishing she knew just how *he'd* felt back then, and now he'd cut off his fucking foot to keep her from living this pain.

"No way. I'm not going anywhere." She managed to wiggle and twist enough to get herself out of his grasp and to her feet. She wiped her chin on her sleeve. Her face was stern. White as a ghost, but unbending. "I don't scare that easy." She looked back at Jim as he stood. "Anymore."

His body was tired. His brain hurt. Now he wished she'd just let the past drop. Her pity and references made him feel like a heel. They faced much bigger problems. "Let's get you cleaned up." He put his hand on her lower back, urging her toward the townhouse. "And you need some rest."

"I'll square up inside," Oscar said. His voice had softened. "I have to drop a runner at the courthouse. He's locked up in my garage. I'll be over in a few hours. We'll compare notes. See what we have."

"You mean there's someone in your garage? Like as a hostage?"

"Relax, girlie. It's a holding cell. Human-sized, and this Jack had better get used to it. Gangbanger. Three strikes. He's out. Going in for life. I needed to get some backup before taking him in. I was hoping that's what Bean here was up to when he called." Oscar turned and headed back inside. "And I do want the fucker off my property. He stinks." He waved over his head. "Later."

Jim urged her all the way to the townhouse. Erica moved along like a robot. He led her in, straight up the stairs, past a protesting Annie and to his room. She sat on the bed looking at her own reflection in his window as Jim turned on the hot water.

He rummaged through his drawers, found a pair of sweatpants that would be big but keep her warm. He tossed them next to her. He dug out a black T-shirt. "Take a shower. Take a nap."

She nodded. Her eyes were red-rimmed, her face still pale. He was sick at the thought of Chris going through what Oscar had described; he knew Erica had to be experiencing an anguish he couldn't even imagine.

Jim always kept a distance from his clients. And like Oscar had said, most of his cases were domestic—abuse usually came in the form of cheating, dodging child support.

He didn't like being invested. Connected.

Sometimes he tracked down evidence for police for bigger cases. He'd seen some rough stuff, but it was distant, happened to someone else. There was no way to distance himself from this.

She got up and headed into the bathroom. "Where's your room key?"

She didn't turn. "In my purse. In the diner."

"I'll go get your things. Bring them back here."

She nodded again and closed the door on him.

———

Jim saw Banks trudging his way as soon as the polished glass elevator doors opened. Jim was wheeling her small suitcase. No way to avoid contact. He'd meant to get in, get her bag, and get out. Banks had to have been watching for her. Waiting.

The goon was cleaned up, wearing his good suit to mix with the upscale crowd at this hotel. His age-faded tattoos barely showed over the top of his white shirt collar. The small bandage behind his right ear could have come from anything. Jim could tell by the glint in Banks's eye that he hadn't been fooled by Jim's poor ninja skills. Toyota had probably given Jim up with the slightest bit of questioning. Say what you will, but those girls loved working for Big Banks.

"Let's go out back, shall we?"

Out back? Jim knew it was the one spot in the casino with no security cameras. Where fingers got broken and knees got busted. Not a chance he'd go willingly.

"Not sure I have time for that, Mr. Banks." Not for the meeting nor the medical recovery that it might require.

"Fine." Banks grinned. "No need to get worried, Bean. We'll have a friendly chat in the VIP lounge. Nothing major. I suggest you take my hospitality while it's being offered." The big guy didn't look the slightest bit upset. But then again, he now had the upper hand.

The VIP area was for big players, limited personnel in the area. Jim followed him behind the velvet rope. "You think it's okay for us to be here? Not one of your usual jobs."

The huge man smiled. "I have friends in all kinds of places. You have no idea how popular a guy I am."

Huh. Not good. That meant that Banks and/or Zant had connections with security in this hotel too. If Jim decided to make a move, they would swarm in and that *would* land him in an unsurveilled room. Better than out back, but still. No good options. He had to play it out. If he'd been really ready to hurt Jim, there would be no nice conversation in the casino.

"After you." Jim gestured.

Banks turned and walked to the back table. Jim was smart enough to follow.

They stopped in the far corner of a high rollers parlor that had yet to open for the night. The big-money men were still being impressed with golf and spa experiences all over the city. Wooed by the casinos with big-money lunches. They were sipping on wine that cost more than Jim's rent.

Banks made his way through the six oblong tables and came to a stop, leaning his big ass causally against the edge of the one closest to the wall. Even here, he fit in. No one questioned his authority to be in such a restricted area. He crossed his arms.

"We have an issue, you and me."

They did. Was it the same issue Jim was having? He suspected not. Banks sucked air between his front two teeth as if he had some ham stuck in there from breakfast. Jim kept his trap shut.

"I had a job to do. *Someone* got in the way of my successfully completing that assignment." He made the kissing sound again. He ran his tongue over his teeth, Jim saw it move like a fat slug under this his lip. "And now I have this headache and a long shift ahead of me."

"Hate you're not feeling well. Maybe you should see a doctor."

"I'm saying if this girl is a client, you'd be better off to let her find other assistance. Not only would that make my head feel better, but Zant will be happier with you."

"I'll send him some flowers. Flowers make everybody happy."

The moose closed his eyes for a moment. Took in a breath. He was trying to compose himself. Jim considered laying off the sarcasm.

Banks leaned in close. His breath was hot and stale, his face pockmarked and scarred—badly—the lumpy skin a glaring contrast to the sleek suit. Maybe he'd been beaten with some brass knuckles or something. Maybe more than once. Shit like that had to have hurt.

"You're a funny man, Bean." He pulled back, adjusted the jacket, and checked his button. "How about I say that I am aware of *your* personal obligations to Zant?"

Fudge.

He made that noise again and finally scraped a meaty finger between the teeth and came out with something. He flicked it to the floor. "You keep playing the tough guy. No skin off me. I was just trying to avoid a bigger mess." He shrugged. "Either way, I will fulfill *my* obligations. Cleanup is cleanup. Don't matter to me how messy things get first off."

Well. Shit. Banks did know about Alexis. His cousin was the reason he'd picked Vegas as a place to land. She welcomed him into her home. He had needed a quiet place to think over his future.

Jim never left, instead got his name changed and his life going on its crappy track. She had stuck with him through everything.

When she fell into her own problems, Jim had stuck his neck out. Made a deal with Zant. Alexis and her son were in hiding, deep hiding, and she was depending on him to keep his end of the agreement with Zant no matter how much he hated it.

The bitter bile of self-loathing churned in his stomach every time he thought about it. It'd been three years since he stood in Zant's office and sold his soul. Several "small favors" later, his tally card with Zant was nowhere near even. And one of those "small favors" could have landed Jim in trouble for evidence tampering or even worse. Zant hardly considered those jobs fair compensation for letting Alexis leave Vegas.

The question remained: did Zant actually know what was going on with Erica? Was he involved with Chris and the dog crates or was Banks the man in charge and using his knowledge of Alexis for his own game?

Banks didn't seem smart enough to be dealing with the kinds of people Oscar said were involved with the human trafficking ring. But he *was* dumb enough to be working for two masters. Maybe he had a second employer and Zant was not the ringleader. Always paid to consider all the angles.

Jim looked around the Paris. No one was worried about the pair of them in the high-rollers area. Jim looked down to his shoes and kicked the side of Erica's suitcase. Either way, it didn't matter if Zant or someone else was pulling Banks's strings at the moment. Banks was going to put the preverbal screws to Jim with his knowledge of Alexis. He wanted Jim to drop Erica as a client.

If Jim kept his nose in this mess, Banks and Zant would make sure Alexis's life was back on the line. If he walked away, went back to his shitty little agency, Erica was on her own.

An effective strategy Banks had there. If Erica Floyd was any client off the street, he'd just drop the case. But she wasn't just anybody.

Jim was truly and wholly fucked. "I'll see what I can do."

23

JIM HEARD OSCAR PULL the Franken-bike up beside the town-house. He gunned it once before shutting it down. So it didn't surprise Jim when the man entered the office. Without knocking. For such a big guy, he was quiet and moved like a trained athlete. He eased himself into Jim's chair. It creaked as Oscar spun toward the big board and stretched his legs. In that position, he took up most of the room.

Jim should have treated this situation with some seriousness from the beginning, but he'd been blinded by anger and hurt pride. Now he was charting it up. Pictures. Information. Working the board. The way he had learned in his investigative classes, the way he did most all his cases. But he'd cleared the board of his other cases for this one.

"So ... Korey. What the fuck is the deal with the chick?"

No way the bounty hunter missed Erica calling him by his real name. So here it went. He hadn't done this in years. Not once since he changed his name. Not since coming to Vegas.

"I changed my name. Six years ago." He hesitated. Felt sweat start to bead on his back. "Eight years ago, in Ohio, I was accused of sexual assault with a weapon." He watched Oscar's face. The cringe came. It always did, even though it was just a slight twitch of muscle under his dark skin. Even those who knew him, when he said the words aloud, they flinched like he'd thrown a punch. Everyone made *the face*.

"And kidnapping." It was *the face* that haunted his dreams. Almost as much as Erica's rejection.

It didn't matter that the charges were all dropped. Didn't matter that he had never done anything to begin with. The charges were so inflammatory. The words so distasteful. *Sexual assault.*

The mere combination of syllables frightened women. The idea of it angered men. Disgust always crossed once-friendly faces. Always would. That was why Alexis had urged him to come to Vegas, to start over. Everyone here had a past, but no one cared what it was. No one would have to know his.

"Holy shit, dude." Oscar sat up. The disgust fell away quick. After all, he was in the business. He knew the system well. Understood the ramifications of a false accusation.

"Falsely. Of course," Jim still felt the need to add. "But I'd have been better off if it had been murder charges."

Oscar nodded in agreement. "Hard to pick up the ladies with that out there, huh?"

Jim huffed. "Lost more than the ladies. I lost a bundle of money and my spot with the FBI. Not to mention my dignity." Somehow it felt good to say it again after all these years with no one to talk to about it. And Oscar would understand. He'd seen it happen as a bondsman. Every now and then the wrong guy did get arrested. "And the girl." Jim looked toward the front of the townhouse.

"Aren't too many times the wrong guy gets nailed, but it's hell when it happens. Sorry, man."

"After a year hanging out in Florida trying to *face it*, live past it, I decided to ditch that life. New place. New name." And by doing so he could bury unwanted feelings in the bright lights of the Strip and drink away the shame.

Oscar nodded. "A fresh start never hurt anyone."

But that wasn't what it had been. *A fresh start.* Nope. It had been running away, abandoning who he was. Letting that night eat away at his character and his self-image.

"The shame is the worst. When I'm sober and bored, I feel like ... It was all out of my hands." He held them up. Like he'd find something there. "It'd all been done *to* me. There was nothing I could grab a hold of, take responsibility for. Nothing I could fix. No way to change the outcome."

"I've seen it happen, of course. But I guess I never thought about later, what happens after the urgency of getting out of jail, getting charges dropped."

Oscar nodded for him to continue, letting him talk. He needed it.

"Yep. My name was eventually cleared. Took about a year. Charges dropped, record expunged. But you can't expunge the look people gave me when it came up. And it came up every time I met someone I hadn't known before or interviewed for a new job. Conversation is a glass ceiling when you carry around skeletons. Sooner or later, it had to come up. I felt compelled to tell people why my

155

apartment was a tiny hellhole. Why I was broke and working two or three jobs at a time to make ends meet."

O nodded. "Bail bonds and PIs ain't cheap or refundable. Neither are lawyers."

"Shit no." He shook his head, twisted the lid on the pen he was holding. "My life was a pile of crap in my eyes even if it wasn't to others." His pride and ego were busted. His career trashed. What did he have to offer anyone? But that was enough. Oscar didn't need more than that.

"Sucks, bro. The woman, Erica Floyd, was your girl?"

He gave Oscar a slow nod.

"And she came and found you when her sister turned up missing."

Jim looked at the board. To the picture of Edmond Carver. "Nope. I stumbled on her when she went looking for him." He pointed to the dead man.

Oscar chuckled. Slapped his knee. "Life sure has a way of sneaking up and sticking it to you, doesn't it?"

Jim saw the tattoo on Oscar's fingers. C-H-L-O-E. His late wife. The one who'd disappeared into the trafficking ring. Who'd lived and died by the horror Oscar had described to Erica in the diner. A horror beyond Jim's comprehension. "Maybe I need to keep things in better perspective, brother."

"Sometimes perspective is helpful. Sometimes it doesn't make a shit. Don't discount your own misery 'cause you're thinking it's easier than mine. Pain is pain. Loss is loss."

There was an awkward moment when Jim had no clue what to say. He glanced at his list on the board. It was missing lots of things. Things Oscar might know. "So who are the major players in the ring?"

Oscar turned his attention to the case as well. Sharing time was over. "Short list. Most are stupid and expendable, like your friend Carver likely was." He stood and paced to dingy windows that used to be part of the converted garage door. "There's a couple cops on the line, but I don't think they know what they're protecting. Just getting supplemental income to make things disappear. I do think we have a mayor who got his ass mixed up in it and can't get out." He turned back to face Jim. "I have some evidence that he's being blackmailed. Pictures with some of the girls."

Oscar studied him. Jim wondered what the big man was debating about telling him.

Eventually O spoke. "Andrew Zant is the main man, the connection to the out-of-country buyers. I can't prove shit yet, though. Bastard is like a new frying pan—slippery and hotter than hell. Their locations change, people change. I'm starting over at square one constantly. Anybody who might have a loose tongue dies before I can nail it down."

Jim knew that was coming. Knew he'd been fooling himself in the Paris when talking to Banks, hoping that freak wasn't involved. But this kind of weird-ass megalomaniac scheme had Andrew Zant's name written all over it. His palms were starting to sweat. No-man's-land. He was screwed no matter how he turned. Again.

O didn't know about Jim's self-made conflict of interest with Zant. He'd probably shut Jim out if he did. "They're taking them to Mexico in small groups. Not far over the border. Then someone from a European group gets them. It's run as a big entertainment company, very modern gangland. New faces every trip. New men. My guess is they don't live long enough to share their tale once they get to the final destination."

He leaned back in Jim's chair, stretched out. "I do have one guy in the FBI who throws me bones in exchange for whatever I gather."

Jim pinched the bridge of his nose as a headache bloomed behind his eyes. This was huge.

"I almost always lose them in Mexico. Small-town *federales* don't have the time or resources to help trace a few missing girls here and there. Too many drug operations to chase down in order to keep the politicians happy. On both sides of the border."

Jim nodded. He was still trying to figure a way out of a Zant-contrived death trap. No clear option jumped to mind.

"I have a few names. Not many faces. A Russian and two men from Dubai. But I know I can't touch them. Not enough resources, not enough firepower. No way I'm going overseas again. Can't make an impact there. I have to get Zant and the men here. I have to stop it on this end. In my back yard."

Dubai? Russia? It was all bigger than Jim imagined. The kind of thing he would be working on had he gone to the academy. The *exact* kind of thing he'd wanted to work on. But he was no agent. And there was no team. Nope. Korey Anders was now a washed-up PI with a drinking problem and major debt to the bad guy.

More shame.

Maybe he should come clean to Oscar about Alexis and his deal with Zant. Or better yet, he could just give Oscar all his intel and let the big bounty hunter chase down Chris and get his man. Jim could be left out of it. Alexis would be safe, everybody won. Sounded like a plan.

A chime rang out. Oscar's phone. He checked his text, frowned, and looked up at the board. "Share the rest, Bean."

Jim looked over to the board:

The instructions to stop surveilling Edmund Carver.

A dead Edmond Carver.

Cops deleting a case file.

The Thin Man.

Chris's tossed apartment.

The three blood types.

Missing twenty-two-year-old stripper.

The man in the yellow shoes.

A fake FBI agent.

Missing Social Services files.

And the picture of the dog crate with Chris's doodle inside.

24

A SLIGHT MOVEMENT DREW his attention to the hall. She was there, lurking in the shadows. Listening. How long?

"You didn't sleep much." Jim tossed the pen he'd been using to point at his board back on the desk.

She jumped. Stepped into the office. "It was enough." She was clean and in fresh clothes.

Had she heard him tell the tale to Oscar? Dammit. That was all he needed, her pity levels to be cranked up as high as her fear levels.

"Thanks for getting my things."

He nodded. Anger. He found that happy place again and could go with that. Better than the shame and the hurt.

Oscar leveled her a stern look. "I would like you to go home, hire a guard, and stay out of this mess."

Erica stood there and appeared to consider it. "With everything on that board, the bruise on my forehead, and the body count getting higher, it would be prudent."

"Good." O stood.

"But it's not what's going to happen."

He tucked his phone back in his pocket. "Okay, kids. I'll be on my way, then."

Jim couldn't believe his ears. "You're out?" He didn't want O to be out. Jim wanted himself to be out.

"Not worth it."

Her mouth dropped open. "What do you mean? My sister's not worth it?"

And now Jim had a pissed-off girl full of fear to deal with. Oh. Hell. No.

"Not at all. I've got a long time in on this, lady. I'm close to nailing the big players. You have no experience; therefore, you're dangerous to me. He"—Oscar indicated Jim with his thumb—"won't carry a gun. That adds up to two big liabilities." He moved toward the door. "I can't afford liabilities at this stage."

"I can fund it. All of it. Whatever you want."

That was rich. She was going to bargain with a man who'd lost his wife to the ring. Use him no matter his pain, his progress in the case. *Erica Floyd wants, she buys.*

"Sure, throw money at him, baby. That'll fix it."

Her snakelike glare was reward enough. She was pissed. But she refrained from getting into that battle with him at the moment. Her attention was back to her prey.

Oscar had hesitated. His body language changed. His thick brow twitched. Jim knew this much—if someone stopped to consider an offer, even for a second, they could be bought. He used that knowledge to get info all the time. All Erica needed was to bait her hook with the thick wiggly worm of cash. "You need equipment, man-power ... what?" She was beating the man with her skills, her brain.

O shook his head. "Doesn't matter. Your money can't reduce your riskiness."

Jim should shut this down. Toss her. Oscar had said she was a risk, and he was right. Jim knew that. But he wanted her out and he was not above nudging Oscar in the direction of the inevitable. "There's a chance Chris Floyd was leaving a trail. Breadcrumbs. She knew Erica would come looking for her."

"This chick left you, Bean." He grabbed the door. "You'd best re-member that, buddy."

"I have ten grand. In cash. Right now," Erica blurted.

Oscar stopped.

"I'll consider it a first donation to your cause. Stopping this insanity."

He turned slowly. Swallowed hard. "Your sister is more than likely dead, lady. Probably dumped in the desert. Never to be found."

She winced but nodded.

"If she's not dead and we find her, she may well wish she were."

At that, Erica shook. She balled her fists. "If she left us a trail, I'll find it."

"If they're all little doodles like that ... I can follow that on my own. Go home."

"I won't. Jim." She turned to him. "I'll give you the ten grand. We'll track her on our own." She nodded.

Jim couldn't hide his confusion. Was she trying to get him to help her suck in O or was she really thinking he would or could do this by himself? No way. He shook his head. Held out his hands.

"We'll get the info from Karen Barnes and then we'll track Edmond by his money." She looked back at Oscar. "I don't need you, Mr. Olsen. I don't need your permission to be in Las Vegas, or to look for my sister."

"If you get in the way... if you ruin my investigation..."

She stepped forward. "I won't if we all work together. And you'll have the funds you need to make this happen, to end it for good, to avenge your wife."

Bingo, thought Jim. He was hers.

Oscar scowled at her, as much of the lion as Jim had ever seen brewing beneath his surface. None of the charmer was lingering in that glare. He was being arm wrestled by a client and hated it. But he needed that cash. Wanted that trafficking ring busted.

"This is win-win for you," Erica kept on. "You get the cash backing. You get the legwork we've done. You get a couple extra eyes out there."

"This is not some bank deal. These people carry guns. Knives. They kill. They rape. Do you really want to be exposed to all that?"

"I wish there was another way. *I* noticed the size on the stripper costumes that led us to the Showgirl. *I* noticed the doodle on the crate. The chance is too high that you'll miss something Chris left behind, something *I* will see right away. I have to take the risk. So do you."

"Son of a bitch." He shoved one of the office chairs and then pointed at Jim. "She's your responsibility. If you still don't want to carry a gun, so be it. But you're playing babysitter. You better not let her fuck this up."

Exit stage left, thank you very much. This was Jim's escape hatch, and he was going through. "No way." He shook his head. "You two go right on without me."

Erica spun on him, gaping like a fish.

"I don't need any of this shit." Relief washed over him. Erica would get good help, his thumb out of the pie would make Zant happy, and Alexis wouldn't be put in danger. "I told you from the beginning that someone else would be better for this job. And now you've found him and used your *money* to retain a better man. You don't *need* me anymore. I'll sit right here with my cat and my Scotch, thank you very much."

Oscar interrupted. "Oh no you don't, Bean. You're not dumping your problem on me."

"You're right. I'm not. My problem seems to be giving you a *huge* amount of cash and is leaving me. Just as I asked her to do two days ago."

Erica seemed shocked. "You want out … still? After all you've seen, you can just walk away from this, from Chris?"

"I told you, I am an asshole." He plopped right into his chair. "Why you doubted it, I have no clue. You now have more qualified help than I could ever be." He looked at Oscar. "You have a set of eyes that has a personal connection with your target. I am not needed."

She looked at Oscar. He looked as dumbfounded as she. He shook it off quicker. "So be it. She's less a risk than your drunk ass."

That would piss him off if it weren't true. As it was, he intended to drink. A lot. "You can take her to one of your safe houses. I'll call you if I hear from Miller."

"Grab your belongings." Oscar looked at her for a moment while she stood speechless. She seemed completely unsure how things had gotten so out of her control. "Now. We have things to do."

"Fine." She looked down at Jim, her eyes spears of hate hurling his way. "Why should I be so surprised? So hurt? I deserve it. But Chris does not." She nodded to Oscar, flung her visual daggers at Jim once more, then headed upstairs.

———————

After a shower, a restless nap, and a beer, Jim eased into his recliner. Yes, he was an asshole, but he'd managed to find her help and keep his cousin alive. He was out of it. He'd let Banks know that in the morning. Zant would know shortly thereafter. Alexis would continue to live her life with her little boy. He couldn't have planned it better if he'd tried.

Of course, he had tried to plan a way out, but like with most things he touched these days, he'd failed. But now he was no longer between the rock and the hard place of choosing between Alexis or Erica. That had been a losing hand. Time to fold, check out. *Vamos.*

But Oscar Olsen had saved the day. Someday Jim would tell the big lug just how grateful he was for the unwanted heroism. Right now he wanted to watch something with a ball and big men smashing into one another. He flipped through the channels. Not much. He'd recorded last weekend's games. He knew the outcomes, but he only wanted the noise anyway. He took a big bite of delivery pizza. Annie showed up. He tossed her a mushroom slice. She slapped at it a few times before taking off with it like it was a prize.

He looked over at the table. Wished Erica were sitting there. Cursed himself. He could not start that. He might need something stronger than beer. The Scotch was all in his office.

His phone buzzed. He was half afraid to look at it.

Ely. His tech guy. He was still working on Jim's last intact case, the rich lady with the cheating husband who'd called the other day. He hadn't called her back. "Yeah."

"I need you to see something. You home?"

"I am."

"I'll be right there." The phone went dead.

Ely lived in a converted commercial building about three blocks down the road. Usually delivered his info in person. Got his money directly that way, Jim figured.

Ely walked right in just like Oscar had. Maybe it was time to up his security. He could start with locking the door.

Ely was pretty old for a tech guy. Most were young, right out of college, but Ely was a Vietnam vet. A strange man with a lot of stories he held close to the vest. He was smart, talented, and had been doing this kind of thing since he got out of the army. Cash only. Jim thought he might even live completely off the grid. He created metal sculptures and oil paintings and sold them off the street and online.

Most of the time, Jim was sure Ely was stoned, but once Jim had seen him in action, he'd quit using anyone else for getting his equipment or ghosting computers. This guy could build a tracking device from scratch or crack into a bank's system if needed. Not that he'd ask the man for such a thing, but Jim had no doubt Ely could do it.

Ely helped himself to the fridge. Grabbed one of the beers and plopped down on the couch. He pulled out his laptop, flipped it open, and fired it up. "You're not going to believe this shit, dude."

"Hello, Ely. Welcome. Have a beer. Grab a seat."

"Yeah." He slid forward and started typing. "You'll be buying me more than a beer in about thirty seconds."

A distraction stronger than football. The night might be looking up. "What'd this prick do?"

"Weird-o. And I don't say that too often. Shit, I ain't cracked all the encryption, but from what I've seen so far, dude is into some nasty shit."

Jim sat forward. It was good to have something productive to work on. Something not about Erica or Chris or dog crates. "Why would a dry cleaner need encryption? Encryption *you* can't crack."

"Tat. Tat. Tat. I didn't say *can't*." He wagged a long skinny finger with a silver ring at the knuckle at Jim. "I said I haven't ... yet." He took a long swig of beer and grabbed a slice, shoving a large portion of it into his mouth. "I will. But you—know—shit's—spensive." It was garbled. Jim got the gist. A lot of time and money went into hiding something on that hard drive.

Ely typed some more with a half a slice of pizza hanging from his mouth. He took another bite and wiped his hands on his jeans before touching the keyboard. "So. Mr. Gregory Lake. Fifty-two. Married plus three. Owns a dozen dry cleaners in two states, Nevada and Utah. Primary investment is in an electronics manufacturer in California but has some other small holdings, spent last Christmas in Disney World with the family, pays his bills on time, plays a mean game of golf, graduated cum laude from USC, and has an excellent credit rating. His bank account and cash investments add up to about six and a half mil."

He took another bite. Spoke with his mouth full. "And it appears the guy has a rape fetish."

Jim closed his eyes. "Rape?"

Ely went on. "Seriously fucked-up dude. He has about thirty rape videos on here." Meaning the hard drive they had copied from

Mr. Lake's desktop computer. With the permission of Mrs. Lake, of course. "I glanced at a few. Looked too real for me to even watch long enough to decide if they're snuff vids or not. Most had some kind of opening credits, so I figure they're actors and legit. But in the same folder was a file labeled with a date, no name. It was an image file, not a video. I opened that one. It was the ugly fucker himself with some Asian girl who looked none too happy to be there."

"Christ."

He steepled his hands as if in prayer, tapped his index fingers together. "Oh it gets better, J-Man." Leisurely, Ely took another drink. Building the anticipation, Jim suspected. Ely loved this shit. The reveal of information he'd spent brain cells and time to mine from hard drives. Juicy things thought long deleted.

At the moment, Jim was about to punch the man for making him wait.

"Or worse, I guess. Then I found the encrypted stuff. Hacked at it for hours. When I finally got it open, there were several more pics and a couple videos. All dated, not titled. All of them are this dude forcing himself on some poor chick."

"He's raped that many girls and not gotten caught? Not even accused?" After the last day or so, Jim was ready to forget the word *rape*. Life was brutal with its allocation of irony. "This guy is a millionaire, public figure even, and he hasn't been charged with anything? Nothing like that in his record, right?"

"Nope. I can't stand to watch long enough to tell if they're pros just going along with his weird fetish or if it's real. Some of the chicks look pretty fucked up. One was even tied inside a dog crate when he did her."

Jim's head dropped to his chest. A fucking dog crate. What was the chance that was a coincidence? Fucking none. Oscar would be happy with this information.

"I think we need to turn this over to the cops, dude. Mrs. Client will get her share in the divorce, no question of that at all. May not need to even fight it at this point. Just let him get busted and then divorce him once he's doing time. Take it all. She deserves it."

Jim looked up and shook his head at Ely. "How much more is there?"

"Hard to tell, exactly. Not too much."

"Sit right where you are and keep going. Have all the pizza you want. You want the Scotch?"

25

"BRING IT ON." Ely grabbed the pizza box and his laptop. "But we have to slide over to my place. The drive is still decoding. There's more buried deeper. Want to see what else this sick fuck is doing."

Jim went and got the bottle. "You able to drink and crack a hard drive?"

One graying eyebrow rose. "I think I could manage for a bit." He passed Jim in the hall on the way out. "The work part of the day is done, dude. The software is cranking away. Matter of patience now."

It took about four minutes to drive to Ely's place. Jim followed him as he scooted along on his homemade motorized tricycle. A small motor that looked like he'd ripped it off the back of a boat was welded into the frame. He had a large car headlight bolted on the front and the rear sported two oversized wheels. The ridiculous thing was painted to look like a cheetah. Ely's silhouette was similarly laughable as he managed to carry the pizza box above his head like a waiter. Somehow he was able to balance the box and steer the trike contraption at the same time. Jim had offered to put it in the truck. Ely seemed reluctant to let go of the pie.

Ely lived in a Vegas rarity: architecture that was older than a college student. He'd rescued the building from destruction. It was a large old law firm. Ely gutted it, but left the catwalk library upstairs. It was still full of fifty-year-old books for the most part, but the closest section of shelving had been emptied of the boring law tomes and was filled with comics, graphic novels, and art books.

He'd welded several species of huge metal birds he'd created to the iron railing that overlooked the main room. Some of the creatures were low-hanging, and their angry expressions were a little unsettling to Jim at times. When the light hit them just right, he felt like some of Ely's nightmares were watching him move around the room as if he were the next bit of roadkill they might pick to pieces. Hell, there was probably a camera mounted in more than one of them.

On the first floor, under the library walkway, was the tech area. The long wall full of servers, monitors, and four separate workstations with blinking lights and whirling fans was Ely's temple. The man stopped in front of the second station with Jim looming over his shoulder. The program working on the encryption was humming away. Only half the progress had been made according to the blue bar on the screen. It was going, that was all Ely would say. "Relax, dude. You'll make yourself old in a damned hurry. Quit churning about things you can't control. It's all about the chill. That's how we survive this life we live. Believe me. I've seen it all. Done it all." He slid the pizza box onto the bar.

The rest of the space was a long room that had been offices, but the walls had been removed long ago. Across from the tech wall, in the middle of the open room, he'd added a small, wall-less kitchen. Retro, as if he'd pried it from a house in the sixties and plopped it in the center of the open room. Table, long bar, and lighting, and lower cabinets. He pulled some beer out of his fridge that also looked recycled from the sixties. Small and burnt orange.

"I came crawling out of hell with a smile on my face. If you hold too tight to the wheel of life, stop it from spinning, it *all* stops. And life is not about the *all stop*."

Jim had no clue what that meant. Ely had been in Vietnam, in the thick of the nasty part of that war. Had been captured. Two years a POW. Jim had no way to understand the hellish things he'd lived through. The thought made Jim reflect again on his own situation with some perspective. Yes, his life had taken a major turn. No, it was not what he had wanted or felt he deserved. But shit. Ely hadn't run from his anger or pain. He'd become an eccentric dude with giant metal fowl in his living room. Jim looked around the ridiculous house. The sculptures, retro-designed furniture. He'd been changed. Affected. But he was rolling with those changes.

Ely reached under a cabinet and pulled out a tray. It was covered in weed. Lots of weed. Enough to send them both to prison for years. There were three very distinct piles. "Good. Better. Best." Ely smiled like he'd delivered a Christmas pie. "I suggest the best, dude."

Jim declined it all. "Why even have the good and better?"

The man tilted his balding head, cocked an eyebrow. "Customer relations."

"More than I need to know." Jim paced to the far end of the room, back near the monitor with the unmoving progress bar. He didn't want the contact high as Ely lit up. He needed to think. It was curious that suddenly the life of the ugly Mr. Lake was colliding with his.

His phone vibrated in this pocket. The same unknown number from before. "Miller?"

"I need to see you. Now." The detective was as short and as curt as usual.

"I'm in the middle of something. Can you come to me?" Jim watched Ely fire the end of a blunt the size of a Cuban cigar and changed his mind. "Never mind. That's a bad idea. What's the problem?"

"You're under suspicion. No. That's not entirely true. You're the prime suspect for the Carver case now."

That meant he was *the* suspect. The *only* suspect in Edmond Carver's shooting. An APB would likely already be issued. His house was about to be swarmed. Maybe the SWAT team. He was going to be arrested on sight. Charged. Thrown in a holding cell. Questioned.

Just as he had been in Ohio. Accused of something he did not do.

"On what basis?" His chest was getting tight. His vision blurred. The room closing in on him. He tried for deep breaths.

"Gun has your prints. That and the witnesses placing you at the scene. It all points to you. The captain's so excited I thought he was going to cream himself in the briefing. One day I want to know what you did to make him so happy to see you burn."

"You know I'm not carrying, Miller. You can't like me for this?" he asked Miller.

"Holding out for now. You have a narrow window, Bean." There was a long silence. "Don't make me regret this."

Jim nodded. Miller couldn't see him, but that didn't matter. It didn't need to be verbalized. Miller hung up without a response.

He turned to Ely. "I have an issue."

"You *are* an issue. I need to find a way to get you to relax, to enjoy life. You could benefit from smiling. Smiling brings clarity."

"How's this for clarity? I'm being accused of murder. The cops are looking for me right now." Jim watched Ely's face. Sure enough, being accused of murder brought less disgust and rage than being accused of sexual assault.

"Hard to smile about that, J-Man."

But he found himself doing just that. "You know. You're right." He did feel better once he let some of the rage go. "How do you feel about a little aiding and abetting this evening?"

Ely took another long toke off the blunt. "All kinds of productive today. I love productive."

"You're on your own if you're caught. The mess on that hard drive is deeper than you know. This accusation puts me in the wind. Not only from Vegas PD, but Zant as well. It's deep. You can bow out now and I'll understand."

Ely stalked closer. He was medium, somewhat lean, and probably more dangerous than Oscar and Banks combined. What kinds of skills did one acquire in a life like his? In jungle-fighting survival conditions most would perish under? "I just told you, dude, no room for the *all stop*." He tapped his index fingers together. "What's the precious?"

Jim found himself smiling again. Maybe he'd gotten a contact high after all. It didn't change anything. He wasn't giving in. Or giving up. *All go.* "I need everything off the board and two files from my desk."

"That all? You'd think you could offer me a challenge every now and then, J-Man." On his path to the door, Ely plucked a black backpack from under the stairs. Jim hadn't even noticed it sitting there, ready.

"Two folders from the desk. Should be right on top. The Lakes file and one marked *Fucking Bitch*."

"Back in thirteen minutes."

Jim looked at his watch. Ely slid into the night.

26

SEVENTEEN MINUTES LATER ELY returned carefully cradling that pack.

Jim looked at his watch. "Four minutes off." The pack meowed.

"Grabbed up Annie. She was being coy." He pulled the fussing feline out. "Didn't want the pigs to let her out or hurt her when they pulled their Stormtrooper act." He cooed at her. Patted her head. She calmed some. "They're down the end of your street. I'm assuming you'll need a new front door when they leave. I unlocked it, but they were gearing up like they're gonna face zombies, man. Doubt they'll check it first."

Again, Jim fought the urge to let the past and his anger overwhelm him. Annie leaped from Ely's arms to his. She clung to his shoulder, digging in with her claws. He inhaled her kitty scent. Petted down her soft back fur. "I really like that damned door. Just painted it blue."

"Blue's a soothing color, man. Maybe they'll try it first." Ely shrugged.

"And miss the rush of the battering ram?"

Annie had calmed enough to realize where she was and that no monsters were getting her. She hopped down. Her fluffy tail twitched as she made her way toward a bowl of water Ely set out. "Easy, baby cakes. I won't leave you hanging." She circled Ely's feet, purring. He pulled out another bowl. This one had a lid. He snapped it off.

"You buy her better food than I do."

"I like her better than you."

That wasn't really true, but at times it may have seemed that way to Annie. The little minx sometimes was here as much as at home. Ely would come get her when Jim got stuck on surveillance longer than expected. Which was almost always. But those trips were made in a carrier not a backpack. She loved sleeping up on the shelves in the library overlooking the huge open room below. The giant metal birds didn't intimidate her at all. As a fact, she found that the eagle's wide body made a nice high perch.

The console with the progress bar made a dinging sound. Loud and shrill like a tacky wind-up kitchen timer.

"Your code has been broken, sir." Ely bowed before Jim and then sauntered to the keyboard. Jim read over his shoulder as he typed a series of commands. The file structure opened up. "Thought you could fool ol' Ely, did ya?" He scanned. "More videos. Lots more. And a couple more text files." He looked back to Jim. "You want to look at any of these? Just so you know what I'm talking about?"

Not really, but what if ..."Same as before?"

"Yeah. Dates. Not titled."

"What's the latest?"

"Little more than a week ago. Maybe the day before I ghosted the hard drive."

Shit. He riffled through the stuff Ely had rescued from his board. Tossed a picture of Chris in front of Ely. "See if that one's her." He couldn't look.

Ely clicked the file. A video player opened. The sounds and the picture came right up. No music. No credits. The girl was screaming. Jim couldn't stop himself. He glanced at it with held breath. She was young, blonde. Not Chris. The man was large. Hairy and bald. Mr. Lake. Two other men were in the room. He couldn't see their faces. One looked thin, in those ridiculous skinny jeans the young kids were wearing. The Thin Man?

"Fast-forward it. See if you can get that guy's face. Any of them for that matter."

"If I have to." Jim half squinted as the video rolled past. Even in fast pace, it was clear how bad this was for this poor girl.

Jim felt his stomach roll. He had to swallow down disgust and anger. This time it wasn't over his own life and emotions. It was her fate that was making him sick.

"Nothing," Ely said. "The camera angle doesn't change."

"Close it." He went to the Scotch bottle and poured himself a shot. Then one for Ely. He needed several good breaths even after a slug of the strong liquor. He prayed to a god he didn't believe in that he never had to witness anything like that again. Knowing was bad enough. "What else is there?"

"Calendar file." Ely clicked it. Jim made his way back over the terminal. Set the glass down. Ely had pulled a rolling stool over and sat. "Dates marked as meetings. Five sets of four, each close together. January third, sixth, tenth, and fifteenth. March nineteenth, twenty-first, twenty-sixth, thirtieth. And so on." He typed a few more things. "Printing."

Jim liked to see things on paper. Made it easier to visualize, to connect the dots, and Ely knew it. He went to the printer and pulled the sheet off. Started spreading out the items from the board.

Four separate dates in five separate months. January, March, June, August, and just last week, November. "How many of the videos? Do the file dates match?"

"Twenty videos." There was a moment while Ely checked. "Yeppers. Each one falls between the dates in the file."

He looked back through his meager notes. Again wishing he'd taken this more seriously at the time. He was missing something. Something big. "They're luring four girls a month. Taking them from the strip clubs, alleys, and escort services—doesn't really matter, does it? Who would notice that in the sea of lost girls in Vegas?" He rubbed his forehead. "Chris, that's who. She must have seen a pattern in her client lists. She got nosy." It was logical. "Can you find me a number for Karen Barnes? Here in Vegas. Works for Social Services?"

"Sure." Ely slid his chair down the wall of geek with a squeak that made Jim shudder. New terminal. Keys rattled. Screens popped up. Within a minute he read a number to Jim. He dialed.

"Karen Barnes." She sounded older on the phone than she had in person.

"Hi, Ms. Barnes. Jim Bean. We met yesterday, with Erica Floyd."

"Yes. You broke into my building."

"Yes. I did."

"I was going to be calling you soon. We're just finishing up with these files."

"Good."

"We found a couple unusual things here, Mr. Bean. I think I need to let the police in on this."

"You're one hundred percent correct. After we get off the phone I want you to do just that."

"Oh." She'd expected him to argue. He was not. This was over his head, but he was in too deep to run now. Oscar and Erica needed all this information. But so did Miller. He would just have to decipher it before anyone else to prevent Zant from getting to Alexis. Unlikely. But there were twenty girls on those tapes. Even Alexis would have his head for walking away from this shit.

"What'd you find?"

"A hidden stash."

"Stash?"

"Yes. A box that was made to look like two large case files. Hidden folders. It was labeled with Erica Floyd's name. Of course her name isn't in our system." She spoke to someone off the phone. "Sorry. Still had a last few things to account for. I have to say, I wish Chris had said something to me about this. Maybe the police as well."

"Oh?"

"She had the files pulled for fifteen young women. All hidden in that box. No activity on them as of late. Some well over a year old. Most were active, getting benefits, and then suddenly nothing."

"What does that tell you?" He got a pencil from the terminal Ely was currently working on.

"Well. If you were so desperate that you were working with Social Services or forced to work with us, getting benefits and food stamps, you don't just stop showing up one day. It's a lengthy process. You have to check in and be clean before you get your checks. These girls all went inactive, *suddenly*. No closed cases. They simply quit asking for the checks."

"And no one noticed."

"Chris must have, or someone she was working with did. She has dated notes with information from a 'source.' No name, just 'source.'" He heard her shuffle some paper. "Then there seems to be ten missing files. That was trickier to figure. But I got mad, Mr. Bean. Broke a few rules. Brought in some help I trust."

Ten missing files. The rest could have been at Chris's apartment. Maybe that was what the man in the yellow shoes found there.

Chris was not in a video. He wasn't sure if that was good or bad. If they kept her, she would be brutalized but alive. If they just considered her a threat, she'd be lizard bait in the desert.

"Could you recognize that FBI agent? If I had a picture?"

"I most certainly could. That has miffed me more than you can imagine. I don't appreciate being lied to. It happens in this business enough from the clientele. It's worse having someone come in here and pretend to be the authorities. Pretend to be helping Chris."

"I understand. One more favor, Ms. Barnes. I know you guys worked late to do this. You've been so helpful, I hate to ask it."

"It's for Chris, right?" She sounded tired but resolute.

"Yes. It is. I'm going to bring you some pictures. See if you can ID the FBI agent. Also, can I get you to fax me the names of the girls … and the last date they got their benefits?"

"I'm not sure if that is legal."

"First names only is fine. I'm trying to piece together a timeline. The same one Chris was trying to piece together."

"I … I guess that would be all right."

"Great. Right after that, I want you to call Detective Noah Miller. No one else on the department. You tell him everything you told me."

"Okay."

27

"**NEITHER ONE OF THEM** is answering text or calls."

Ely took another bite of the pizza. Chewed for a second. "I'll look up Double O."

He rolled his little doctor's stool to the next keyboard and monitor down the bank of humming equipment and typed in a few things. A map appeared. Several blinking dots appeared. A few green, a couple red. One enlarged as he scrolled over it. *Double O.*

The blip was at the southern edge of the city. "How the hell do you have that?"

"It pays to have someone know where you are occasionally, J-Man. I call it Ely's Lost and Found Service." He tapped his index fingers again. "Tracking technology. Hard-to-get stuff. We've used it on a couple of O's roundups. Some of the skips he chases are pretty bad boys. Like our buddy Lake." He looked up at Jim. "You need to be in on this too."

"You want me to wear a tracker? No, thanks."

"Nah. Not that much drama needed. It's your phone signal. Kind of illegal shit, but it works as long as you have it turned on anyway. You might as well let ol' Ely babysit your mean ass. It ain't perfect, but O's alerted me more than once to keep an eye on his flashing dot. Gives me check-ins on a regular basis and a text to let me know he's homeward bound. If he were to miss a check-in, I'd call in the cavalry and send it to his last known."

Not a bad idea, really. "How much will that set me back?"

"For now. For this one"—he looked at the screen with the files and videos still displayed—"let's call it a favor."

"Count me in."

He clicked some more. A new green blip came on the screen to indicate *J-Man*.

"How about Erica? Can we do the same if I give you her phone number?"

"Supposed to have her permission, you know?"

"I'm giving you her permission."

"Works for me. What's her 4-1-1?"

Within a few seconds Jim watched a second green dot light up down south a short distance from Oscar's.

"Where is that exactly?"

Ely zoomed in. Changed his view to satellite. The Vegas terrain filled in the screen. Dirt. Sand. Roads. "Looks like a ranch. Maybe a horse stable. O is right there. She's back in the edge of that subdivision." He pointed to the blip that was representative of Erica. "Maybe he left her in the car while he checks something out."

"Maybe." Jim patted Annie on her head as he gathered his stuff and headed out. "Call me if they move."

"Roger that." Ely gave him a weak, loose salute as Jim closed the door.

28

THE AIR FELT THICK, tense. Considering there had been at least one person in the background of the phone conversation with Karen Barnes, Jim expected cars, noise … something as he approached the Social Services building. The front was still dark from the broken light bulb. The area *felt* deserted.

He opened the door and slowly entered the reception area. No activity. The room smelled of old dirty carpet and only a single dim light glowed against the sliding glass reception windows. He pushed through the door to the back. On the contrary, the cubicle area was lit. Bright. Yet empty.

With a smooth, soundless motion Jim popped open his blade. He eased toward the far door, the one that led to where Karen Barnes had indicated all the paper records were stored. A watery cough came from ahead. He could see no one around the room. But that was a sound he'd heard before. A racketing precursor to death. He followed the sound.

It led him to a cubicle near the door to the records room. Karen Barnes lay on the floor. She was on her side with one leg rotated awkwardly under her body. A large-caliber round had knocked her backward. Her head was bleeding from the desk's attempt to break her fall.

"F—" She gasped. "I—"

"Dammit!"

"Lan ... guage," she whispered, tried to smile.

Jim knelt as he pulled out his phone. He dialed Miller. He didn't give the man a chance to speak. "Social Services. Ambulance. Bullet wound." He hung up.

She was holding the wound just below her chest.

"The FBI guy?"

She nodded. Still struggling to get air in her lungs as they filled with her blood.

With a bloody finger she pointed to a scrap of paper under the desk. Jim got it. It was the list of girls and the dates. He put that in his pocket and pulled out the picture of Lake. He'd planned to do a photo lineup to make sure of her testimony, but she was fading, her breath getting shallow and slow.

She took the photo in her bloodstained fingers. As her hand jerked and shook, Karen Barnes nodded. Made a serious effort to look him in the eye. Willing him to know she was sure. Jim took her hand, gave her a small smile. He held tight to her cold palm as she fought for her last few breaths. Held her as she passed from this world trying to save other young girls.

He was frozen, motionless, gripping her hand tighter than he needed. Could he have been here sooner? He liked the lady. She'd worked hard for other people her whole life. Even dying for Chris Floyd.

Would she have helped had she known the stakes were so high? He remembered the steel in her voice when she said she'd gotten mad. He wanted to believe a woman who served others as her life's work was not lost in vain.

Her death stare was directly on him. Appraising. Could he finish where she'd failed? He didn't like the odds.

Where were the others? He quickly looked around. No one else there, dead or alive. She must have sent everyone home as soon as she'd hung up their call. Lake must have been waiting for just that. Her alone.

Jim glanced around the building one more quick time. No boxes of files. Lake clearly took all the evidence with him. Jim was lucky Karen managed to toss that list of names under the desk.

His phone vibrated.

Text from Ely. GIRLFRIEND ON THE MOVE. TO THE RANCH, TOWARD O.

It was time to leave anyway. Miller would be here soon, and Jim was a fugitive. Noah Miller may have tipped him off to that fact, but he wouldn't let Jim just walk away from another body.

Jim headed south. He was a good driver, knew all the back roads, and that old Taurus was faster than it looked. Reckoned he'd be on the ranch in ten minutes.

Lake had gone back to Karen's office for a reason. He must have suspected she might find the same pattern Chris had. He took the files and notes Chris had gathered, but he couldn't continue to kill off every Social Services clerk in Vegas, could he? No turning back for him. Death sentence now.

The image of Karen lying dead was burned into Jim's retinas. Churned in his gut. Senseless.

This new scenario drastically lowered the probability that Chris was alive. Why keep her alive and kill the old woman in the office?

Chris was dead. Dumped somewhere. Sweaty palms gripped the wheel tighter. He pushed the throttle a little farther to the floor. Blew through a stoplight.

He didn't slow until he hit the clean little subdivision below Blue Diamond Road. The neighborhood was upper middle-class. Yards were landscaped with stone, sand, yuccas, and cacti. Houses neatly painted stucco in sage, muted brown, and creamy beige. Lots of iron-work fencing and porch rails. Lots of lights. A very cheery, pleasant place to be by all outward appearances. Jim knew outward appearances were deceiving.

He scanned the houses as he passed. He wasn't looking for something specific, but maybe something would jump out at him. He was bad with a gun, but his eyes saw everything.

He slowed as the neighborhood and the paved road came to an end. Beyond the dark smooth pavement was a gravel path that wound back behind the subdivision. There were scrub bushes and a few short palms scattered along the way next to a fence and a metal gate.

He found O's Escalade and cut the lights as he rolled past. The ranch gate was a mile down the gravel road. He pulled off the path, drove his car to the left, and killed the engine.

He pulled his night-vision goggles from under the seat. Erica was inside that fence somewhere. He opened the trunk and gathered the necessities. Vest, two M84 flashbangs, handcuffs, some zip ties, and wire cutters. He shoved his slapjack into his back pocket. The thing was basically a small leather billy club stuffed with lead. Very intimidating and very effective with lots of stopping power.

A slow scan revealed a small horse ranch, just as Ely had said. House, barn, outbuildings, a couple trucks, and an old tractor, all in need of a paint job.

Everything looked asleep. Nothing moving. Maybe nothing alive. The thought panicked him. He considered starting the car back up and driving right up to the door.

But O was good. He'd see evidence of a struggle if O had been taken down. So Jim scanned again. Looking for the spots where he'd take up to check the place out if he'd been the one to go up to take a peek. He found two good spots. One by the tractor, one by the barn. But if there were animals in the barn, the buttheads might give him away.

He scanned again. It was like the night before Christmas out there. He didn't see O. He didn't see Erica. He didn't see a dog or a freaking cat. Nothing was moving. Not even a mouse.

So Jim eased his way through the dark to the tractor to get a better look.

And there she was.

29

WITH HIS GOGGLES ON he found Erica easily as he took up a spot behind the tractor. She had made it to the odd-shaped blue building between the barn and the house.

She moved along all bent down and tippy-toed like she was in the movies. Her can of pepper spray was out, ready to spray. She held it with two hands like a loaded gun. He wanted to chuckle at her timid bravery, but he smelled the stench of bad luck in the air as strong as the horse manure.

She peeked around the corner at the main house. He glanced that way too. One more check for trouble before he made his way to her location. There was a good deal of open real estate between them.

Nothing moving. Nothing making any sound outside the regular night song of insects. The aging porch was flooded with light. There seemed to be a light on in the kitchen as well, but he saw no one moving around. She jumped when a horse nickered in the distance.

It sounded muffled, so Jim couldn't tell if he was in the barn behind her or the pasture beyond.

Dammit. She turned back and headed around the oblong building. *Why can't she just get scared and stay put?* Through his goggles he could see that instead of windows, the rectangles on the rounded front of the building were wooden panels. The third panel was a door. He knew that because she pulled the door slightly ajar and stuck her fool head in. All the way! She was going to get herself and probably him and O killed. *Where the fuck is O?*

She closed the door and turned to see a tall man in a cowboy hat looking down at her from the yard. Fuck. Jim had been so focused on what Erica was doing that he hadn't even noticed the man. She yelped and turned. Too late. She was a trapped rat with nowhere to go. The man easily caught her as she tried to get past him.

"Well, you just saved me a lot of trouble." His voice carried across the empty night air. He wasn't concerned over being heard now that he'd grabbed her arm. Instead of fighting this guy like she had Banks, Erica stilled. Her eyes widened as if she had seen a ghost.

It happened. Sudden surprise and fright could momentarily stop all clear thinking. Jim counted on it more times than he could remember. Erica seemed to stare at the guy for about ten seconds before she remembered she was packing pepper spray. She started to raise it, but the guy beat her to the punch and pointed a shiny gun barrel in her face. "Go ahead. Spray. I don't need to see you to hit you from this close."

What the hell was she doing out here? Jim should have kept her with him.

The man dragged her toward the porch. She stumbled but was in no position to put up much of a fight with a gun barrel jammed into her ribs. She missed the bottom step and tripped. He yanked on her. She yelped again. Loud. Jim guessed she was hoping that O would come bursting on the scene with guns a blazing. Jim kind of had the same hope.

"Hush up." He wrenched her to the door. Jim took the opportunity to get closer.

Cowboy pushed open the front door with his foot and shoved Erica through it. She tumbled into a dimly lit living room with an old woven carpet on the floor. Jim evaluated what he could see. Large room. One guy on a couch to the right. Kitchen behind. Maybe a stairway, not sure if it went up or down. The roofline was low and the terrain rolled slightly downhill behind the house. Jim guessed down. Cowboy inside the doorway. Rest unknown.

While everyone was concentrating on Erica as she tried to get her balance on her hands and knees, Jim used the cover to move up closer, ducking behind a watering trough. He knelt, looked over the edge near the pump. It was clean, smelled of fresh oil. The guy had left the door open. Nice of him.

"What the hell?" A very tall, very thin man in a black suit stepped from the unknown area to the left of the front door. Not a cowboy. The asshole was the Thin Man from the hotel. "Where'd you find her?"

"By the storage building."

"Here?"

"What the fuck other storage building would I mean? I needed to take a leak, not go to town."

"How'd she get here?"

"I reckon she drove."

"Dumbass. Must be with the bounty hunter."

They'd found O, then. Jim hoped he was alive.

Time to act. They were confused—he needed to make that confusion into chaos, panic. He was outgunned. Not a new situation to him, but with Erica in there, he was more than eager to even up the odds. No time to consider and evaluate.

He pulled a flashbang from the vest, popped the pin, counted to ten, and then tossed. It sailed through the door and fell slightly to the side of the room, toward the unknown behind the door and as far from Erica as possible. But since she was on the ground, she saw it first. Watched it with huge eyes as it rolled past her. She must have thought it a live grenade. It tumbled at first, then rolled slowly, coming to a rocking stop past her toward the kitchen, between the Thin Man and Couch Guy.

They didn't have time to decide its origin or contemplate its risks.

Erica fell all the way to the ground, tucked into ball, and covered her head.

Jim was on the way in as it exploded a second later.

On the porch he turned away, felt the enormous clap of the explosion. He closed his eyes to the two ultrabright flashes that blasted through the small room and covered his ears. Jim turned immediately, his slapjack in his left hand, his knife in his right. He only had seconds to keep the upper hand.

Acrid smoke filled the room before anyone had a chance to look up to see him coming. Someone shouted, "Get up—" Jim's knife penetrated his throat before he could speak another word. Cowboy down.

Stumbling footsteps and cursing behind him. He turned, the slapjack crashing onto the man's face as he tried to get up off the floor holding his eyes. Couch Guy down.

Now the unknown. How many were there in the house and where had the Thin Man gone? Recon *before* was the usual operating procedure, but he was not leaving Erica with these cretins for even a few minutes.

A groan came from his feet. Footsteps echoed from behind. He knocked Couch Guy on the floor a second time with the slapjack as he turned and faced the stairway.

Erica was coughing behind him. With some effort she did a sort of crab crawl for the door. He could see she'd closed her eyes to protect from the burn of the smoke and scrambled as fast and as low as she could toward the night. He had no clue what was out there. He needed her to stay close.

He grabbed her leg, pulled her back. His lungs were burning from holding his breath. She kicked with her free foot and caught his chest. "Erica."

She kept struggling, unable to hear him from the temporary deafening effect of the flashbang. He tried to tighten his grip, but not enough to hurt her. A shot fired downstairs.

The room fell silent. She stilled.

Two more pops. There was a yell and a gurgle and the unmistakable sound of a body hitting the ground very close to him. More footsteps. More shouting. Jim hoped it was O shooting.

Erica started to wiggle and kick in a panic. This time she connected with a solid boot-heel to Jim's head. His grip on her foot fell away and she scrambled up to make her break for the door. "Erica."

It did no good. She was going. He raced, caught her by the back of her shirt, lifted her all the way to her feet. Another gunshot rang out. She screamed, hearing that, and reached for her boot.

He held to her shirt even when he was jerked from behind. Another bad guy. "Erica!" His louder voice did no good. Her ears *would* still be ringing. She was pulling away from him.

He punched the guy in the throat with a quick jab, the end of the slapjack crushing his windpipe. He wobbled back, but the man had no intention of giving up. He lumbered forward, arms out like a half-drunken Frankenstein's monster. Another blow landed. Same locale. No air for him. Maybe some blood in the trachea. Frankie went down. It was not the Thin Man.

Jim saw Oscar at the top of the stairs, two guns drawn. Standing still. All threats eliminated. Erica struggled one last time. Jim yanked her to his chest. Her eyes were closed tight, tears streaming, but she managed well enough to aim that damned sprayer dead to rights. Pressed the nozzle. Jim let go. She ran.

A stinging, swarming cloud of hell sucked his face off his skull. His eyes sealed shut by involuntary muscle spasms compliments of the capsicum. Angry ducts streamed acrid tears down his cheeks.

"Erica," O shouted, "it's Oscar!"

Jim tripped off the porch to find the water trough through bleary slits of stinging lids and memory. The cold stale water did little to rinse the oily concoction from his face. But it was better than nothing. He assumed O would clear the area of hostiles.

O patted him on the back. "Nice job."

Jim nodded, not opening his eyes. "We clear?"

"Lost one when the craziness started, but the rest are down."

"Get her."

Jim heard him walking away. Calling her name. He knew O would still be armed and ready to defend. He dunked his whole head in the water. Tried to open his eyes.

"You okay? Hurt?" O was talking to her, not Jim. His voice was calm, low, soothing. Asshole. They were moving closer.

"I should have stayed. Listened to you and stayed at the truck. I could have gotten you killed." She sounded panicked.

"It's okay. You're okay."

"I'm shaking. Shit. Thank you." She sounded weak.

"You better thank Jim, not me."

"What?"

Jim raised his head and tried to look over. He saw blurs of human shapes. Waved.

"Asshole saved both our asses. I'll never live that down." Oscar chuckled. "But that pansy squeal when you nailed him right there at the end, I guess I can make fun of that for a while. Sounded like a little girl."

"*He* saved our asses? How could that be?"

"You didn't know?"

Jim could tell she was leaning forward, resting her hands on her thighs. Fighting for air.

"Know what?"

"I walked into an ambush out by the barn. They had me downstairs. I broke loose when the flashbang went off." He tossed his head to the right. "Jim came after us. Without him, we would both be in trouble."

Jim had to bend back over the water and continue the effort to scrub the pepper oil from his melting corneas. He cursed. Loudly. Hopefully she'd feel like shit.

"All right, kids." Oscar spoke to them both as they huddled by the three prisoners. "We have a procedure for rescued girls. Not only from this situation, but any we get off the streets or out of the clubs.

Not that we've had many success stories lately. But we get them occasionally."

"They're holding girls here?" Jim asked.

"Two. In the basement. Pretty much passed out right now. We need to take them to Sister Nora at St. Agnes Catholic Church. She'll help."

"Won't they need a hospital?" Erica was still shaking a little.

"She'll take care of what they need. We don't want them in the system for several reasons. Mainly, these girls have seen faces. Faces of men who will find them. Kill them. The hospitals are not safe. Sister Nora will get them out of the city and out of the cycle for good."

Erica rushed past Jim as Oscar spoke. She wanted to go to the girls. He understood that, but...

"Wait!" Jim wiped his still-unfocused and half-dissolved eyes on the tail of his shirt. "We need to make sure there's no more surprises lurking around this house. We're missing a player." The stubborn woman was already on her way into the basement. Ignoring him completely.

But Oscar caught her. "They're alive. Drugged, battered, but alive. God help them from here on out, but they're out of the skin game."

Jim needed Oscar to know what he'd found out with Ely. "Karen Barnes is dead." That stopped both of them. He had their attention finally.

Couch Guy was on the ground. He grunted. "My eyes. Jesus. I need some water."

Jim kicked the man hard in the ribs. "Now you need Percocet. Shut the fuck up."

The man cursed, rolling around making even more noise.

"Nice, Bean. Make him even worse. How's he gonna talk with no air in his diaphragm?" Oscar pointed the gun at man on the floor. "I can make it so you need the coroner."

That shut him up. Jim pulled some tie wraps from his pack and tied the guy up. He jerked his arms behind his back. O had plugged the man who'd come up the stairs in the shoulder, close to his neck. He wasn't moving around or complaining. He was alive and seemed to have the desire to stay that way. He got tied from the front. "Keep still or I'll twist that arm around back and make this shit hurt."

He nodded.

The cowboy who'd taken the knife to the throat was dead. No need for the zip tie. Erica was staring at him. Nothing Jim could do about it.

"We'll need to call Miller to come clean this up. But he's busy at the moment with Karen, I'm sure."

Erica was still staring at the slit throat. More likely she was looking at all the blood pooled on the floor under his head. Jim tried to ignore the pain on her face. He wanted to say that this would be the worst she'd see, but was afraid they'd just gotten started, and the ugliness on the floor before them was likely just the beginning. He concentrated on delivering the evidence to Oscar as he trussed up the men.

"I identified one of your big players. He was a subject I was investigating for adultery. Ely cracked the man's hard drive. All kinds of nasty shit hidden behind some heavy-duty encryption. We found him on video *with* a bunch of girls. There's some other files Ely is still trying to decipher. Bank records maybe.

"Then I called Karen Barnes. She'd found a pattern. Chris must have too. Matched the dates on the videos we have. Four girls at a time. Five times a year."

They heard an engine start up. They all rushed to the porch since the men on the floor were no longer a danger. An older-model truck pulled out from behind another one of the outbuildings, probably a garage, and headed for the main gate, passing behind the house. Out of range for Oscar's handgun.

"The guy from the hotel. The Thin Man." Erica looked at Jim. "I saw him. I'm sure of it. That has to be him because he's not here." She gestured toward the men on the floor.

Oscar twisted his cap backward on his head. "Dammit. I'll get him. You guys take the girls to Sister Nora."

Jim grabbed his keys and tossed them to his friend. "The Taurus is right outside the gate."

Oscar ran pretty fast for a big guy. The truck broke through the front gate and hit the road well ahead of the bounty hunter. No matter. Jim knew O would eventually catch the guy. That was what he did. Hunted. Once he had you in his sights, you were property of Double O.

Jim walked to the kitchen and turned the water on full blast and doused his face once more, opening his eyes, shaking his head. It was better. Still stung like a mother. His nose was running and his chest felt tight. Dang, she'd gotten a straight shot at him.

"Sorry." Her face was scrunched up as if she was experiencing the burn with him. "I had no idea you were here."

"No. You didn't."

She nodded. "I didn't see you but ..." She looked at the floor. "Even if I had, I may have shot you with it anyway for dumping me on Oscar like that."

"Don't blame you." From her perspective, he deserved it, since she didn't know anything about Zant and Alexis. It was time to tell her. But those girls down in that basement needed to come first. "I'm here now. I'm not going anywhere."

She looked skeptical. "Okay."

He nodded. "Okay."

"We should ... we should check them?"

He blew his nose on his sleeve. "How about you go get the Escalade? I'll do a first check."

For an instant he thought she might agree. That she'd want to run and hide from this disgusting truth about humanity. But he knew she was the kind of person who would want to help those girls. He understood the swing of feelings. "If it helps, I don't think either of them is Chris. If these are the girls from the list ... from the videos ... Ely checked them. Chris wasn't on them." He took her shoulders, made her look him in the eye. "Any of them."

Her shoulders dropped as if she was relieved, but her face still looked like she'd lost everything. Drawn and tired. She was searching the walls for something. Anything. That wasn't going to help her. The room was a mess. Two men were tied up and groaning. Another was dead in a pool of cooling blood. The scene was a lot for a banker from Boston to take in.

Jim stepped over the dead body and headed for the stairs to the basement. The scene was going to be hard to see for him as well. Maybe he *should* shield her and deal with it. She stepped up next to him.

"Maybe you should go—"

"I need to do this. Not you. Last thing these women want to see is another scary-looking man." She sneered at him.

"I'm not scary!"

"Right now you are." He looked at himself in the reflection of a window. She was right. His shirt was torn, his eyes red and running, and his lip had managed to get busted in the mêlée. He was a mess.

He wasn't sure which was worse: how badly he'd scare the girls or how badly the state of the girls was going to *scar* Erica.

30

JIM HAD TO TEXT MILLER. *Meanwhile back at the ranch ...*

He included the street address from his phone's GPS and a quick sorry.

"We *may* have half an hour before cops get here." Erica acknowledged him as he tossed his torn, pepper-spray-covered plaid shirt in the trash. That left him in a black tee. He rinsed his eyes one more time and used the water to rinse his head as well before they headed downstairs.

"That's better. I guess." She touched his busted lip. He'd lost the urge to pull away from her at every opportunity.

Jim led the way with Erica tight on his heels. He hesitated about halfway down. O had to have eliminated his targets down here.

"More bodies." And he'd seen snippets of those videos. "The girls. They could be the worst thing you've ever seen," he whispered. "Worse than the bodies or anything you could imagine."

She put her hand on his back. "They need us, Korey. These poor women need us to be strong and to be human. No matter how bad it is in there, we have to make it better. That's what Chris was trying to do."

She was right. But thinking that was one thing; seeing the broken lives left in the wake by the horrors people inflict on others could change your life. He knew. Saw it in his business all the time. Marriages, families, lives broken and torn by greed and lust. The stories some guy told you he heard about from some other guy. Usually there were six degrees of separation to buffer from the atrocity. But this? This was the stuff of movies and late-night news stories. All live action.

Erica was holding strong. She had been sheltered from this kind of shit and here she was. Most people would have crumbled long before now in this situation. She was still standing tall, still telling him what to do.

"Keep it soft, quiet. Move slow," she whispered. Erica Floyd, all grown up, impressed the shit out of him.

Whether he liked it or not, she was bringing back a hint of his humanity; even in the middle of this fucked-up situation, she'd managed to find something left of Korey Anders. He nodded. She gave him a little squeeze.

He put his game face on and moved down the rest of the flight of stairs like a tiger hunting prey, slow, deliberate, and aware of every sound and scent in the place. The men upstairs, the remnants of the flashbang. At the base of the stairs he stepped in, knife drawn and at the ready. Dead guy at the bottom.

Jim scanned from one end to the other of a large open room with a set of sliding glass doors. In the middle. Walk-out basement. A closed interior door was all the way on the far end. No other escape routes or danger spots.

The only occupants were two very young women and another dead guy. A brunette on a small sofa looking out the sliding glass doors. She was naked, old bruises peppered her skin, her hair dirty and matted. No concern about the death around her.

The second was lying on a dirty mattress on the floor near the far wall. Also nude, on her side, and facing away from them. The poor girl's skin was pale, very pale, her short hair very blonde. The marks on her body stood out bright and angry. Her thighs were covered in deep lash marks. Jim felt ill. But at least they weren't in the cages.

Erica's sharp intake of breath must have mirrored his own. She started for the girl on the couch. Neither had responded when Jim and Erica entered the room.

Jim stopped Erica's attempt to pass him by and tilted his head at the closed door. She understood he needed to check it first, but let her anxiousness be known with an angry scowl that told him to hustle. She wanted to get to the girls. "I know," he mouthed as he moved off, trying to be smooth and slow, as she'd instructed. He turned the knob. Not locked. He peeked in. Big closet. Some linen. Cleaning supplies. Three dog crates.

At his signal, Erica eased onto the couch next to the girl. Her attention swung from the unknown object in the distance to Erica. Her brows drew, she looked a little confused, but quickly laid back and opened herself up as if Erica was there to have her way with her. Frail hands fell to her breasts as if to display them. "How may I please you?" Her words were practiced, her smile forced.

Jim closed his eyes. Swallowed his anger. If this was Zant's doing—and everything seemed to be pointing that direction—Jim would be the one to make that man pay. How had he let himself be manipulated, basically owned, by a man who could order things like this done, partake in it himself? The horrible thing he'd done to get his cousin out of Zant's clutches was nothing compared to knowing what Zant had done to these girls. Directly or indirectly. By not putting a stop to Zant before now, he was partially responsible for that girl's condition.

"No. Sweetie." Erica pushed her thin legs together. Tried to give her a simple smile. "Sit up here with me for a minute."

She needed help to sit up. Her head lolled back and then flopped to the side as Erica pulled her back into a sitting position. Certainly drugged. Erica eased her against her chest. Held her there, pushed her hair back out of her eyes. "What's your name?"

"Lola."

"That's pretty. Where do you live, Lola?"

"I don't know." She looked up at Erica with heavy eyes. "Do you?" Her left eye was healing from a nasty blow, much worse than the one on Erica's face. The lingering bruise was green and brown and yellow, like a bad sixties painting. There were a few others on her body at different stages of healing, but most had to be days old. They were letting them heal up as much as possible before taking them to the next stage. That eye was probably still rather sore. Jim figured the girl was too drugged to care at the moment.

"We'll find out. Okay?"

Lola didn't answer. She let Erica rock her. Closed her eyes.

"What's your friend's name?" Erica was still talking in a low, soft motherly voice.

Lola fought to raise her head and look over at the mattress. "Oh." There was a moment's hesitation. "That's Lola too."

The girl snaked her arms around Erica and rested her face on Erica's chest. Jim could see her body tremble from ten feet away. "But I was the first Lola. I'm better trained." She looked up to Erica again.

Big fat tears poured from her eyes. "Take me with you. I'll be real good. Do just what you say to. I swear it."

Erica looked at him over the trembling girl's head as she held her. The once laughing green eyes that Jim had loved so much as a younger man were now filled with loathsome anger. He was witness to a moment that would forever change the woman before him. He'd never again get to see her as carefree and light as she had been back in Ohio. Before he was changed, before this changed her. She was silently pleading with him to do something. To fix this. He couldn't. Life happened to a person. That was the lesson he'd learned long ago. He looked down, wishing it were different.

When he met her gaze again, Erica bit her lip to stop its tremble. He watched as she steeled herself. As she hardened to this world. "Find them some clothes. Take 'em off those bastards up there if you have to."

A job. Action was good. "Yes, ma'am."

———

He made his way past the two living suspects upstairs, not caring if they got help anytime soon or not. As a matter of fact, while Erica was soothing the girls ... He grabbed the guy bleeding badly from his neck and jerked him pretty hard. Jim was standing over him. Holding his shirt. "That looks like it hurts."

"Fuck you."

"You like that kind of thing?" Jim turned him a little to the side and pretended to check out the man's ass. "Huh." Never in a million years of forced celibacy, but this guy didn't know that. "I think I will." He yanked him up and dragged his body over to the couch and dropped him, facedown. He landed with his chest on the cushions and his ass facing Bean. Jim kicked his feet apart. All the movement had to hurt. The guy had to think about getting violated … just like the girls downstairs …

"Oh fuck this." The man struggled. Jim ground his knee into the dude's back. He wiggled the guy's huge wallet around, the god-awful chain jingled against his side as Bean got it from the pocket. The stupid ass would think Jim was trying to cop a feel.

Cash. Not much. Not one credit card. "No ID?" He grabbed the guy's spiked hair and turned his head. The bleeding increased. "What's your name, sweetheart?"

"Fuck you."

Jim dropped his head—well, slammed his head—to the cushion. The guy curled as best he could around the front of the couch. He was all but crying.

The other one, the one still on the floor, moaned. That one was no use. His jaw was shattered. Jim felt it when the slapjack connected with his narrow face. No way he was talking. Not for eight to ten weeks, anyway.

"Who is the thin man that headed out?"

"I don't know."

"You don't know?" Jim put his thumb over the bullet hole. Little bit of pressure. Amazing how little it takes when a guy knows you're willing. "Good thing my friend uses a small caliber, dude. Would have hated to have had you lose your head."

That had to hurt too. The poor man was probably just baby-sitting the girls. Easy money. Money to keep this pathetic ranch running. Or money for drugs. Or prostitutes. Or video games. Right now the guy was wishing he'd found other employment. Jim pushed just a hairsbreadth harder, his thumb poked inside the ragged wound. Cursing turned to quiet, still crying.

"We call him Earl. Don't know nobody's real names. Honest." He was shaking. About to hit his threshold.

"Who was coming to pick up the girls?"

"I swear. I don't know. Earl was in charge. I was just supposed to make sure the girls stayed in the house. That's all."

"How long?"

"Saturday night." He tried to pull away from the pressure. Jim applied more. "Just till Saturday. And someone was gonna take them." His feet started to twitch and wriggle. His breathing was fast and shallow. Jim should keep at him till the little fuck's heart exploded.

"Where from there?"

He shook his head in a short, brisk movement. He knew Jim wouldn't like that answer, but Jim was danged sure it was the truth. Nothing like pushing on a gunshot wound to bring the honesty out in a man.

"Clean clothes somewhere?"

Jim let go of his neck, his body relaxed. "What?"

————————

"I was hoping you'd leave those assholes naked and scared like the girls were."

"Considered doing that. Believe me, they're not happy. Miller will be here soon. If we want to get them to that nun, we need to move it."

"Okay."

"Can you manage while I go get the Escalade?"

Erica barked out a laugh that made Lola jump. "No. I can't manage this. Not the whole of the thing, but yes, I can manage to get them dressed." She looked at the two lying there listless. "Kind of like the end of the night at one of the old house parties. Back in college."

Back when you still loved me. He thought it. She left the words unspoken but he saw her face. She was looking for comfort. He wasn't capable of that at the moment. Too much anger. Disgust.

"Minus the injuries and the abuse." He handed her the knife. "Keep this close."

"Like I'm going to do anything with it."

"You will or you won't. I would suggest you do if needed." He turned for the steps. "I'll pull it around the back to the sliding glass." He tossed her the clothes, turned away. Faced the wall, but there was a velvet Elvis print on the wall. Strange to see the King reflecting this reality, so he turned back.

She inspected the jeans for size and eyed the girls. Both pairs were going to be huge. She found a length of cording around the ancient green drapes pushed off to one side of the glass doors. Used his knife to cut it down to the size of two belts.

"Lola, sweetie." The brunette opened her eyes again. She took a moment to remember Erica. "Can you put these jeans on for me? We need to go."

Her eyes got big. She sprang up to a sitting position. "Oh. No. No, we can't go nowhere. Earl. He'll get real mad again." She looked over at the blonde Lola. "We stay here and as we were born." She nodded. "Just like we're told."

Jim felt ill. He remembered what Oscar had said at one point. These girls may wish they had died once they sobered up, realized what had been done to them. How would they ever find a way to function in the real world again? They'd been brainwashed, conditioned to want to be good for their captors. Beaten down so badly that they'd lost all sense of self.

Erica turned the girl so she was looking her directly in the eye. She wanted to make sure Lola believed the next thing she said. "Remember, you're mine now. I bought you from Earl." Erica let that lie set for just a second. "And not just you, but Lola too."

That Lola's face scrunched. It looked angry in the reflection, but Jim knew she was trying to think through the drugs. Believe what she heard.

"But I need to call her something different so I can keep you two straight. What should we call her?" Erica situated the jeans at Lola's feet like she was a child. Turned her attention to something productive. *Nice work.* The young woman stepped into them and tentatively stood. The pants were gaping around her hips and waist. Erica quickly rolled up the legs so she wouldn't trip on them and then laced the cording around the belt loops and tied it snug.

"Connie. I think her name should be Connie."

"Okay." Erica grabbed the other pants. "Let's get Connie dressed so we can go get some food."

"Food?" Lola was waking up a little more. "What ... what kind of food?"

"What would you like?"

"Anything but oatmeal and bologna."

Jim wondered how long they'd been fed that particular diet.

"How about a cheeseburger?"

She nodded again, with even more vigor. But when she stood to assist Erica with Connie, Lola lost her balance and wilted to the bed. Her eyes fluttered with the effort it was costing her to remain coherent. "I'm ..."

"It's okay, Lola." She patted her gently on the shoulder. Jim waited to be called to help but Erica was able to move Connie. The tiny, young girl couldn't weigh much more than a case of glass-bottled beer.

She rolled the blonde onto her back and Erica gasped. Jim spun to check the room for threats, but apparently it was the bruised state of the girl's face and chest that had Erica shaking. That and the welts on her thighs. The poor girl must have fought them hard. How could this happen to a child not more than nineteen or twenty? In this country, for fuck's sake.

Erica took in several breaths. Jim clenched his teeth and willed himself not to march up those stairs and rip those bastards up there to shreds with his bare hands. He could do it and never lose an instant's sleep over it.

"I want to help," Lola said. She looked to be concentrating on being stable. Maybe realizing now that leaving with Erica would be better than staying here with Earl and his friends.

Erica handed Lola the shirt. "Get this on first."

Erica worked the jeans over Connie's feet as Lola fought the T-shirt. She got the jeans almost all the way up before Lola had managed the shirt. But she'd gotten her bare chest covered and seemed quite proud of the accomplishment. "Did it." She gave Erica a braces-straightened-perfect grin.

"You did. Now. When I lift Connie's hips, you tug up her pants."

Lola smiled. "Okay." And she positioned her angle to be optimal. Erica lifted. Lola pulled, shimmied that denim, and once she worked the waistband past Connie's hips, they slid right up. Erica tied them off with the other length of cord. She heard one the men holler from upstairs. It was muted through the closed door.

Lola froze. Her body shook. "Earl might catch us." She backed away.

The fear in Lola's eyes was contagious. Jim felt it wafting through the room. They were dressed. He felt like he could get back into the conversation. "Look at me. Earl's dead. You're coming with Erica. Do you understand?" It was a lie, but he'd make it a truth as soon as he got the chance.

"Dead?" Lola bit her lower lip and fingered the fabric on the shirt. She'd only glance at him, her dead gaze clinging to Erica. "Go with you." She nodded.

Connie's torso was so frail-looking as Erica eased her up and managed to work the shirt over her arms and head.

"No shoes, but at least they're not naked," she said to him. Lola was inspecting the shirt carefully. Jim wondered when was the last time she'd been allowed clothes.

31

LIKE MOST BUILDINGS IN Las Vegas, the church looked practically new and somewhat plain. There was a large stucco archway out front with little in the way of design. Two women (one in nuns' clothing) and a young man in a collar were waiting under it.

"Are you sure about this?" Erica was between the girls in the back with an arm holding each one close. He didn't think blonde had lifted her head the entire trip. "Her pulse is going strong and her breathing seems okay, but she's still out. This one may need a doctor, not a priest."

As they pulled right up to the trio, Jim realized the man wasn't wearing a collar but a black shirt buttoned up high to give the impression of a collar. "Don't think she's getting a priest either."

He eased down the window. A very short older nun stepped toward the truck. The beige dress and black fabric veil covering her hair did more to make her look fragile than the sullen face and wrinkled eyes. Erica also lowered the back window as far as it would go.

"Mr. Olsen said you'd be arriving soon. You're even early. Excellent." She had to step up on the running boards to stick her head in. "The girls are unconscious?"

Erica started to speak, but Lola raised her head. "Are we getting cheeseburgers?"

"Yes, dear," the nun answered. "As soon as we get you safe."

"I'm with Erica." She leaned her head back onto Erica's shoulder. "I'm safe."

"Good." The nun stepped back down so the young man could open the door.

On Erica's other side, Connie snuggled closer. It was the first voluntary movement he'd seen her make. The nun looked at Erica. "I'm Sister Nora." She indicated the pair with her. "This is Tricia and Keith. They'll get them checked out and out of the state as soon as possible. We have doctors and a psychiatrist ready to greet them by the time they are aware what's going on."

He could see Erica was reluctant to let go of the girls. How could she trust anyone? A lesson Jim had learned years ago. Trust no one. Still, he tried to reassure her. "She is a nun and this is a church."

"Since when does that mean anything?"

Sister Nora coughed.

"I'm sorry. They've just been through so much. I feel like I need to be the one to make sure they're safe."

"You have, dear heart. This is a very well-organized rescue service. Much like an underground railroad. I would usually not even let you two be around for this part of the mission, but Mr. Olsen assured me you would not leak our location or our identities."

Before Erica could argue or disagree, Tricia came around the far side of the truck. With little effort she pulled Connie out of Erica's arms and heaved the young girl over her shoulder in a fireman's carry.

"Hey! Careful. She's bruised all over."

"Thanks," the woman said.

"Thanks?" Erica glared at Jim in the mirror.

"How about we help them in?"

She nodded and tightened her arm around Lola to help her out of the car. Jim was sure Erica was going to keep hold of the girl, as if by carrying Lola, she could follow Connie and see for herself what was going on in this church. Jim had his curiosity as well. He'd let her participate for a few more minutes and then get her the hell out of this. In his mind, the less Erica was involved with the girls, the less impact it would have on her psyche.

"That's fine." The nun turned. "Keith, get the door." She turned back to Erica. Miss..."

"Floyd."

The nun narrowed her gaze at Erica. "Well." The nun hesitated. Scrutinized. "Interesting. Miss Floyd, help bring the other one in. But get at it. Narrow window for the Lord's work tonight. The short notice made for lots of scrambling. Things had to come together quickly to get these two out of here safely. We're used to it, but it can be a feat."

Erica eased Lola through the doors with Keith's help. She was getting more and more coherent but walking on her own was still asking a bit much. Being kept in those crates for long periods at a time could be causing muscle atrophy. That, more than the drugs, may be the problem.

"Is this a church?" Lola asked as they passed through the big wooden double doors.

"It is."

She went stiff for a moment, gripped Erica's shoulder and arms where she held on. "Are we being punished?"

"No. Why would you be punished?" Erica asked. Jim wasn't sure he wanted to hear that answer.

"Cause we deserve it."

"You deserve no such thing, young lady." The nun appeared before them, popping out from behind a column as if from nowhere. Erica jumped. "You deserve love and respect. You are a beautiful child of God."

Lola's head lolled a little as she tried to focus on the nun. "You're cute." She looked back to Erica. "I'm a possession. A dog. To be treated as such and be happy for it."

Jim felt his stomach churn. He couldn't get the thought of the bruises and welts on the girls' bodies out of his mind. The nun rushed past and opened a door to a dorm room. It housed two little beds, a dresser, and an open door to a bathroom. Tricia and Keith were arranging Connie on the bed. Taking the baggy jeans off. Erica started to protest. They'd just gotten them in those clothes.

"You need not worry. Tricia is a trauma nurse. Keith is an EMT. Both will be with them until they get to the next step. You've done an amazing thing." She put her hand on Erica's arm. "Bless you both. But we need room to work and we are in a bit of a time crunch." Sister Nora was herding them out of the room as she spoke.

Erica looked panicked as Tricia took Lola from under her arm and settled her on the bed. Erica hugged herself and took a timid step in Lola's direction. "Wait. Wait."

They all looked at Erica, waiting for her to elaborate on her protest. She stammered, "What happens next?"

The two started moving again. Doing their assigned tasks. Keith brought clean scrubs from a cabinet in the corner. Tricia was checking Connie's wounds, cleaning the welts and cuts on her.

"We have a network of sorts. Like I mentioned. Sort of an underground railroad. Gets them out of this city." A pointy nose exaggerated the movement as she shook her head. "Vegas feeds on poor girls like this. We get them out of it for good. They'll be placed into a rehab facility under new names. When they are ready, they will be moved into a halfway house of sorts. If they're ever able to support themselves, they'll be given new jobs, new lives, so they don't fall back into the prostitution cycle. It's a sad fact of girls that have been through this kind of reconditioning. "

She gave Erica a grave look after an abrupt glance past her. "In these cases, it's complicated. The mental abuse is often worse than the physical. They've been tortured. Broken. Much the same way prisoners of war are broken to give up information. Only they were tortured in order to give up their sense of self." She clasped her hands in front of her, straightened. Dismissive. "They will get plenty of counseling. I promise you that. You have delivered them into the hands of the Lord."

Tricia read off a blood pressure number for Connie. It sounded low. "The process of rebuilding their confidence and personality needs to start as abruptly as the deconstruction did."

Sister Nora placed her body between Erica and the girls and lifted a stern hand to direct Jim and Erica out of the room like children. "You have nothing to fear for them here." The sister turned back to the activity in the little dorm. "Tricia will make sure they are fit for their journey."

Given all the scandals involving priests over the years, Jim wasn't so sure, but the nun was very nearly pushing them out of the building. Erica glanced back in there one more time. Keith was listening to Lola's breathing with a stethoscope.

They would be fine.

Jim was well aware that Erica was clinging to Lola because in all this, they had come no closer to finding Chris. Erica had to worry that Chris was possibly in this same condition. Already sold to someone as a sex slave. Jim suspected that Chris was dead, though he wasn't in a hurry to prove that fact.

Lola waved at them over the EMT trying to treat her wounds.

"We need to let these people do their jobs."

Erica stepped back. They were in the hall. Sister Nora pulled the door closed behind them.

"How many girls have you gotten out?" Erica sounded a little shaky again.

"Of prostitution and drug abuse … close to a hundred. Rescued from the skin game … four."

Jim pushed his hands through his hair. "Including these two?"

"No. Oscar did manage to rescue two about three years ago. And then last year a pair were found along the highway and taken to the hospital. Had managed to escape on their own. Tricia was on duty and brought them to the network. We've learned a great deal of what to do and not to do." She looked at Erica. "We've studied and prepped for this moment. I assure you they will get the best care possible."

"Can they ever go home?" Jim asked the question. He had wondered that on the way over as she'd held the girls. How could they ever get past such a thing? He probably shouldn't have put that question in Erica's head. But he wanted to know if this would be close to a happy ending. It was better than if they hadn't been pulled from that ranch, but...

The nun looked down and back at him. "Odds are they'll not want to."

He nodded. Understood.

Erica swallowed. She shuddered. "Is there a restroom I can use?"

"Of course. This way." The nun headed through a set of double doors, deeper into the church.

Jim touched Erica's arm. "You okay?"

"No easy answer to that one." She gave him a halfhearted shrug. The small gesture seemed to suck the last of her energy. "I have to be. Chris needs me to be."

Without thought, he touched her cheek. There was no room for the hate or anger he'd felt for her over the last three days. Maybe he was even more exhausted than she. She lingered a second to feel his touch. He didn't pull away. He felt pity for her. For having to let the girls go. For not knowing what had happened or was happening to her sister.

The nun continued her mission to the restrooms. Square heels on low sensible shoes curtly clomped on the tile as she marched to her destination. He and Erica had to rush to catch up, once again making Jim feel like a schoolchild chasing his teacher. His head hurt, and his mind was stuck on what had become of Chris in attempting to help these girls. At least they had accomplished that much for Chris. These girls would be safe. If she'd given her life to that cause, she had helped Erica accomplish the rescue. Maybe in time Erica would find some peace in that knowledge. But peace was hard to come by.

The nun made several turns before stopping before a large wooden door with heavy metal fixtures tarnished black with time.

"This is the staff area. We have to meet a deadline. I must leave you. You can find your way out?"

He nodded. "Thanks."

The nun gave them a little bow. Erica returned the formal gesture. "You assist in a dangerous mission, Erica. Know that the Lord is with you in your battle."

The room was a lounge. Several connected rooms, actually. Restroom, shower, kitchen area, and a cot in the corner under a small window that seemed overly high up the wall. So high, a black metal cross on a pedestal was displayed on a shelf over the cot and yet still under the window. It was as if this part of the building was much older. She looked at the emblem for Christianity for a long moment.

"That's not comforting, it's just pissing me off more. Where was the Lord when those girls were snatched out of their lives and forced into slavery?" They turned back to get Sister Nora's reaction to her harsh question.

The nun was gone.

"Figures." Jim grabbed a water out of the fridge and took a swig. He offered her one. She refused and made her way to the large white basin that was the kitchen sink and splashed water over her face. She used a paper towel to wipe away the sweat and grime from the altercation at the ranch.

She dried her face and spun to him. "A shootout. How is that even possible?" She looked down to shaking hands. "Last week these hands penned the sale of a string of television stations to a movie star and now I'm chasing down drug dealers and slavers."

He could see that blood still hid under her nails. She washed them again. He knew the rest of her felt stained from the situation as well. "You'll need a long hot shower, maybe two, before you feel clean."

Her gaze darted toward the door marked *Women* at the end of a short hall.

"Oscar may need help chasing down the Thin Man. We need to finish up and go. Let me take quick break."

He felt the need to follow. She left the door to the ladies' area open, maybe not wanting to be alone. He took another long drink of the cold water. Considered washing his still-stinging eyes again. But it wouldn't help. He knew the chemical irritation had to work itself out. Time.

"Great. You'd think in a church the rest room would be better provisioned than the strip clubs, but no. This is Vegas," she yelled from the room. It echoed in the large lounge area. "Peeing on myself would be the perfect end to a hell of a day."

He heard her moving. Probably changing stalls. Muttering. Probably cursing even in the church.

"Jim." It was loud and clear. "Holy crap. Come here."

He rushed over to the door but slowed. The small room had another sink. Hand-washing size. Aged yellow tile. Two stalls. She was in the second one. Door shoved open. Buttoning her pants up.

She pointed up at the door. There was a poster advertising vacation bible school taped to the center of it, eye level for a visitor's reading pleasure. *Kingdom Rock: Where kids stand strong for God.*

The poster had a cartoon of a castle, a lion, a giant oak tree, and a very familiar-looking black doodle. She reached out and ran her fingers over the drawing of the Crazy Child. Her delicate finger traced the ridges left from the ink pen as Chris had scribbled it over a perfect blue sky.

"She's been here. Maybe helping with the network? It would make sense."

Jim remembered Sister Nora's parting words, *a dangerous mission.* She'd called her Erica. "How did the nun know your first name?"

32

THEY'D SPLIT UP TO search the building for any other signs that Chris had been here. The nun, the girls, and the two helpers were gone. Through a small window they watched as a vaguely marked ambulance pulled away.

Jim tucked his phone back in his pocket. Ely had happily agreed to house he and Erica for the night. It would do. But one night was all Jim was willing to stay since he was still a fugitive. No need to bring that kind of pressure down on his friend. Even though he was sure the murder charges would play themselves out, right now things were dicey. Lots of dead bodies around.

He had to laugh at that. Eight years earlier his confidence had been high that those ridiculous rape charges wouldn't stick. They had. Maybe just for a few months, but they had done their damage. Now, he might be in even more danger of facing time for a crime he didn't commit. Not to mention he was crossing Andrew Zant, and that was bad for one's longevity. He wasn't sure which was the lesser evil—jail or death by Banks.

He needed a way to link the Thin Man and the disgusting Mr. Lake directly to the all-powerful Andrew Zant, and he needed to find it quick. Alexis and her son wouldn't be safe until then. Jim looked all around the sanctuary. Nothing. Without any reasoning or forethought, he dropped to his knees just below an oversized statue of the Virgin Mary.

Surely she wouldn't mind his Baptist upbringing. The alabaster likeness stood quiet, with open arms and a kind face, welcoming. Jim Bean had no faith. Alone in that jail cell, he'd asked God to set everything straight. He'd sat and he'd waited for someone to open that door. *Knowing* they would come in and tell him it was just a big mistake. Apologize. Shake his hand. Send him on his way.

Four days he waited for someone to realize that mistake.

After two nights, they tossed him into the general population. Holiday weekend.

He closed his eyes to the rest.

He'd been scared to death. Angry. Lost. Hurt.

No one answered *that* prayer; why would he get help now?

"Just keep Alexis and that baby safe for me." He looked at Mary. "I'll figure out the rest."

How he was going to nail one of the most power-hungry egomaniacs in the country was beyond him. Men like Zant lived above the law in giant penthouses with armed guards. Everyone did what Zant said because everyone was afraid of the crazy shit he'd do if they went against him. It was a wonder Oscar was still alive after chasing the man and his trafficking ring for this long.

But like Oscar, there was no turning back for Jim this time. No-where to run. No longer was his pain or his pathetic life a good enough reason to bury his head in the sand. A life he deemed ruined by his time in a cell and a derailed career path. Small stakes compared to what women faced daily.

Lola. This was about *all* the Lolas.

Above him, the Virgin Mary watched over him with nonjudgmental features. She had no divine influence here. That lady was all about comfort and support. In this world you had to work your own shit out.

And what he was facing was the fact that he'd really let himself fall. He thought of the younger girl, Connie, with bruises around her mouth and welts on her thighs. It was disturbing. Made him want to spit nails. Jim Bean wanted to kill for those girls. But the hardest thing—no, the most ironic thing—for him to face was that for the first time in ages, Jim Bean considered himself a lucky man.

Yes. He'd lost his career, his reputation, and his girl. And hadn't *he* made a shit storm out of his life after that?

What might have happened if he'd stayed in Ohio and fought for his reputation, his life, and his girl? What if—

Erica burst through the doors before he could go down that path. "Nothing else in the activity rooms. I couldn't get into the offices. That hall is locked. Fucking locked behind us when we left the lounge."

He looked to the Virgin Mary with a cringe and whispered a silent prayer: *Keep her safe too.* To Erica he said, "Well. I see you still have a profound respect for the church."

"I'm serious."

Pain shot through his knees as he got up off the floor. "Yeah?" He rubbed them, hoping to alleviate the burn.

She looked around and realized where they were. "Sorry," she said to the statue, but her glare snapped back to Jim. "Chris was here, in this building. My guess is that she didn't write on that wall just to pass the time in the john. It's part of a trail she's leaving."

"I agree." His instinct was to hide out for a day or two, rest, regroup. The girls were safe. Flush out Lake. But it was time to go against his instincts and do the hard thing.

Erica followed as he made his way back to the double doors to the lounge room and the offices. The church offices. His weight hit the door and pressed on the metal bar that would release the latch. It was locked.

"You're right, locks from that side."

"Break in." She was demanding. "Sister Nora knew who I was and didn't say anything."

His internal clock was ticking. "We're in a church. That part's not public. Likely to have an alarm." Her lip was trembling. She was exhausted. "Besides, we're already putting this network at risk. People with lots of resources will be looking for them, and us. We need to go. If they find us here, Sister Nora won't be able to help any more of these girls."

"Jim." It was a plea. Her eyes were filling with tears again.

"I'd love to, but we don't have the tools or the time. The longer we're here tonight, the more likely we'll be spotted. That big shiny Escalade is not exactly inconspicuous."

She started to protest. He wanted to do what she asked, but not now. "We'll be back. I promise. It will be better to question the sister anyway." It would be hard, though. The woman was used to hiding evidence, protecting that network. She was fighting for God. "The likelihood she left something about Chris laying around her office is nil. We'll come in the morning and ask her. Right now we need to get back to searching for Lake and the Thin Man. Those are the clues that will lead us to Chris. Think about it. The nun doesn't have her. The bad guys do."

At least he hoped they still had her.

She clenched her fists at her side. He saw the moment she decided she agreed with him. "Fine. But first thing tomorrow, we come back."

———————

Detective Miller was leaning on Jim's car when they pulled Oscar's Escalade to the curb outside Ely's place.

"Is this trouble?" Erica asked. Her voice sounded like that of a lounge singer who'd smoked too much for too long. She needed food and sleep. Might could use a snort of his Scotch.

"I don't think so. Plainclothes." Miller was dressed in jeans, a white tee, and a thin jacket. Warm for a jacket even in November. Still loaded with weapons, he presumed. Jim opened the door. Let his leg hang out. He displayed no hurry to meet him, no fear that the detective was there.

Even for a man younger than Jim, Miller's eyes were thick with dark circles, his face scruffy like that of a man who'd been at work for days. "Time for some sharing," Jim said to Erica.

She lingered in the truck when he got out.

Miller walked to meet Jim halfway, his hand out in greeting. Jim took it. "I've been removed from duty as of this evening. IA investigation into supposed missing narcotics."

"Internal Affairs? That can get sticky. Must be some heavy hitters involved to make a frame job that big roll through the channels." It was not especially helpful to have his one connection inside the police force now on the *outside*.

"Seems the case." He nodded at Erica. "Miss Floyd." She started walking toward with them without an invitation.

Jim looked around. "Do you have a tail?"

He shook his head. "Wouldn't bring you heat, man."

They rounded the corner a few hundred feet from Ely's door.

"I need some food and a shower. I'll go back to the Paris and order room service if I don't get both soon. And hell on you to try to stop me."

Miller looked taken aback, but Jim didn't care. She had the right to be grumpy at this point.

"You'll get both here." Jim slowed before a narrow alleyway. "Not so sure my host is going to be all too happy with you crashing his party, Miller."

"Ely'll be cool. Damned smart old man. He tosses us a bone every now and then. Finds evidence before we know we have a crime. I was coming to see him to get intel on where your ass might be. All points up, cops all over Vegas looking for you, and I pull right up to your car on a coincidence."

Jim nodded. "Gotta love the lucky break."

"Not sure anything about you is lucky, Bean."

Erica was walking behind them like a zombie, but Miller's quip made her laugh out loud. They both turned to look at her. She shrugged. "He's right."

He was.

Jim led them into the alley, behind a building, and up to a dark little door. He knocked. Oscar opened it after a short silent wait.

Erica perked right up at the sight of the big bounty hunter. "You got him?"

He looked at the ground, not her. Shook his head. "He seemed to vanish. Ely's trying to track the truck."

Jim put his hand on her back. She moved because he pushed her forward. He was tired too. His bones felt like old Pick-up Stix, brittle and thin.

"Oh. Look who's joined us," Oscar said loud enough for Ely to hear. "Detective Miller." Oscar moved back, holding the door open.

The detective hung back. "Give him time to get his *things* in order. I don't like surprising people. Not why I'm here."

Ely must have been close enough to hear the entire conversation. Or maybe he could just hear that well. Either way he yelled from inside, "Nothing to stash, my good officer. Nothing to worry your little badge over."

"You guys can take your time all you want." Erica, however, took Oscar's invite and walked past them all.

"Miss Erica." Ely gave her a little bow, much like the nun had done. "I am at your disposal. *Mi casa es su casa.*"

"Thank you." She fell into his overstuffed couch like a drunk girl late in the evening. She closed her eyes. Jim grabbed a water bottle and handed it to her.

Annie trotted past all the men and leaped on the couch. She gingerly made her way to Erica's side. She sniffed her for a moment before turning a circle and snuggling down against Erica's right hip.

"Traitor," Jim remarked and headed over to the bank of equipment where Ely had returned to his post and started typing away.

It was time to share. He pulled out the charts for Miller and Double O. Putting it up on the wall made it a board game, like none of the players were real humans with families. He was marking off players as dead or unknown.

Erica sat up when Miller started talking about Karen Barnes.

"Large caliber. Nothing could have put that back together again," he said.

Jim looked at the board. Five dead bodies in three days. Two were the cretins at the ranch, but a dead man was a dead man.

"Is there any way I could get a shower? Some clean clothes? And away from hearing all this right now?"

They all stopped and turned their attention to her. The other three looked as if they'd forgotten she was sitting right there. Jim had not.

"Sorry about that." Oscar rubbed his face. "We have to take a step away from the reality of crimes like this. They call it a professional distance. We treat the crime like it's something else, someone else, to keep our emotions from tainting evidence. Keeps perspective sharp."

And he should know better than most. His wife was one of those girls. How did he do it?

"I get it. I ... I just can't do it. At least not right now." She looked at Ely. "Shower?"

"Yes, ma'am." He hustled toward the stairs at the far end of the room. "The door at the end of the library shelves"—he pointed up—"is the guest suite. Big shower with great pressure and nice soft bed." He glanced around. "I'll see what I can rustle up for you to wear. And don't be afraid of the dragon."

"Dragon?" She looked at Jim.

Jim shrugged his ignorance. "Given the metal birds on the railing, it doesn't surprise me to hear there're dragons in the guest suite."

33

ONLY FIVE MINUTES LATER Erica came down the stairs like a girl on fire. Only this girl was clad in a too-small towel, her hair dripping water and soap like she'd jumped out of the shower and was running from something. All four men stopped and put their trigger fingers near their favored weapons. Jim braced for her to fall, slipping on the metal and concrete steps like a six-year-old on ice skates. He had an instant vision of broken bones and stitches.

But somehow, she made it safely to the bottom. Not one of them had changed position as she slid into the room and over to the seating area.

"My phone." She grabbed the phone off the end table and tapped on it a few times.

She looked directly at him. "Paper. I need paper." She was waving her hand at him as if to fan him. Rushing him. He'd seen her do that before when she was excited. But Ely was the first to break his stance and move. He rushed to the kitchen area and grabbed a notepad from a drawer. She followed him over to the counter as he passed.

"Shaun." She barely gave this Shaun on the other end of the line time to answer. "Last year. Maybe the summer before, we passed on a big one. Lionbridge. Consortium, I think. Look it up."

She paced, still holding the towel with one hand, the phone with the other. "I know you're busy, but I need it *now*." Her voice was smooth but laced with a serious undertone that told this Shaun character this had better be his priority at the moment. "Please," she added as an afterthought.

She looked back to the men standing in the room. "It's too much to be coincidence. The names of the two men you guys were talking about tingled at the back of my mind. Zant sounded familiar. And Lake. I knew those names. And Neal." She turned and paced a few more feet and then turned back to them. "Andrew Zant. Gregory Lake. Neal. Something…Neal. Had to be a couple of summers ago. The Lionbridge Consortium."

Nobody answered her, because none of them knew what she was up to. Her attention swung back to the call. The towel almost fell.

"Great." She nodded. "Players?" She tapped the pad with the pencil. "Gregory Lake." As she said the name, she made eye contact with Jim. "Andrew Zant. And *Thomason* Neal. I couldn't remember the last one's name. That's it."

Jim couldn't believe his ears. What did Erica—a Boston banker— have to do with Zant? And who was the third guy?

"Remind me of the details." She was quiet as she listened and took notes, her hair dripping soapy water on the pad as she wrote. "Shit." She looked down. "The name of the Nevada development?"

Erica looked back up at Jim. She bit her lip. "Coyote Springs." She repeated the info back to the men in the room. "Thanks, Shaun. Sorry to have interrupted you. I owe you one." She hung up and set the phone down on the counter.

She looked back up to the four of them and resituated the towel. "Who are these men?" she said as she brandished the pad.

"Vegas heavy hitters. Casino owners, businessmen," Oscar answered.

"Is Andrew Zant the one you suspect is behind this trafficking ring?"

Jim came over to glance at the notepad. "What do you have to do with Zant?" He may have sounded madder than he intended, but …

She shook her head, took a deep breath, resituated the towel to prevent it falling. "My bank facilitates large transactions, big development deals, corporate buyouts, foreclosures of major industrial sites, and such. *Big*-money deals that need the backing of lots of cash. Sometimes short term, sometimes long."

Ely slid up to sit on the countertop. Oscar and Miller closed in to be able to hear her as well.

She pushed her wet hair off her face. "My job is to look over the deals and evaluate the risks and rewards. My employees look into the people involved, their assets and liabilities. With all that, I determine on behalf of the bank if a project is a healthy investment. Or not."

Oscar groaned. "I see where this is going."

"Yeah." Erica nodded. "I said no to Lionbridge. If they didn't find other funding—and given the state of Coyote Springs, I'd say they didn't—my *no* cost them a bunch of cash they'd put out to start up the projects. Not only Coyote Springs, but two more similar developments were started in New Mexico." She was starting to shake.

He didn't care if it was the situation or the room temperature. Jim grabbed her, pulled her to his chest. "What if this is all about me?" she said. "What if he took Chris because of me?"

He didn't want to talk. Didn't want anyone else to either. He needed to think this out. Maybe it was coincidence.

Ely was the one to break the silence. "How much?"

She pulled away. More like pushed him away. It was that buzz of nerves and tension that made a person want to pace, to move as if they could shake off whatever horrible thing was pushing adrenaline thought their veins with the movement.

If Zant had been after *Erica* all along, that changed the game. Changed everything. They'd been lucky. Really lucky. In the Peppermint Pony. At the ranch.

She moved back to the couch, to where Annie was stretched out on the arm. She ran trembling fingers along her fur. "A hundred and eighty-eight million … plus or minus."

"You can cost people that much money in one deal?" Oscar whistled.

"Sometimes they came to us because they're already overextended on a project. We can afford to bear the risk, pull them out of the hole until income can equalize. Sometimes we do. For a hefty interest rate, of course. These guys were upside down in a drowning project package. The economy had turned, and the housing market with it. It looked bad. Too bad to risk. I said no."

"Since the man's killed people over a few hundred bucks before, I'd say there's more than a good chance this *is* about you, honey." O lowered himself into the chair and stretched his legs out.

Jim eased beside her. "Seems rather elaborate. To kidnap the sister, lure Erica here."

"Ha." Ely jumped down from the counter. "Think about it. A megalomaniac like Zant wouldn't see it as elaborate at all. The opposite, dude. He had Erica researched, stumbled on her sister living right here in Vegas, and found out she worked for Social Services. You said this girl had notes about an unnamed source? He couldn't have planned it any better. A welcome boon. Haven't you ever seen a Bond movie? The more money infects a villain, the more he wants to see the reach of his power, the more elaborate his schemes get. Andrew Zant is full up with power and greed. He thinks there's nothing he can't do or get away with. The man is torturing and selling humans to show his power."

"The crazy bastard has been selling girls to other crazy bastards in Asia and the Middle East for years. How much more evidence do you need that he's psycho?" Oscar was right.

Miller piped up. "If he's got that much money and power, why go to a bank for help at all? Casinos are full of cash."

"A casino's cash is monitored constantly by the gaming board," Erica said. "His business, the hotel, is just like any other corporation and is not cash-based. Corporate money is all on paper, electronic, these days. He couldn't cover all that red ink with casino money. Gambling regulators would notice." She resituated the towel again. "And the other partners. All their assets were tied up too." She looked down at her feet. "I should get dressed."

"You should be in a safe house. Now." Miller pulled out a cell phone. "I have a friend in Henderson. Retired L.A. cop." He looked at Jim. "No real connection to me through the force. He was a friend of my dad's. I've known him most of my life. I'd trust him with my own wife. He'll take care of her until we can work this out."

"You don't have a wife." Jim watched Erica's face. She wanted to protest. He could see it brewing. But she was so worn out he didn't think she had it in her.

Miller rolled his eyes. "You know what I was getting at. It's the best we have."

Oscar nodded his agreement. "Dragging her around with us is making her an easy get. We've been lucky to keep her alive this long."

"Do I get a say?" She looked at him. Her damp hair was a mess, her eye blackened from the blow.

"Not this time. We need to know you're safe to make this play out right. You're the target."

"But what about helping track Chris? What about talking to the nun?"

Oscar stood. "We won't be tracking her anymore." He straightened the shirt tucked into his jeans. "It's time to take off the head of the snake."

34

JIM BEAN STOOD AT the door and considered exactly what to say to Erica. After seeing those girls, realizing the danger his cousin was in, and worrying over Chris, his perception of the world was wavering, changing. He'd made a deal with the devil himself apparently. And even though Alexis was alive, she'd always be living in fear of Andrew Zant.

The past, his arrest—it had all seemed to be so big at the time. His hurt and the loss of Erica's love was the driving emotion behind his anger, even if he hadn't admitted that to himself. Anger at Erica was gone. Things were dicey now. He needed to tell her so much. Let her know how he felt. How deep he was in with Zant no matter how ashamed of it he was. Before he had a chance to gather his thoughts, solidify his intentions with this visit, the door opened.

She was startled by his unexpected appearance in the doorway of Ely's guest suite. She took a large jump back. She was nervous. Frazzled. The decision to send her into hiding was a good one.

"Sorry."

She nodded. "I wasn't expecting you right there."

"I know." He wanted to go in, but she was already coming out. "Can I say something?" He stepped just inside the door. "Talk for a minute?"

She shrugged. "Sure. I guess." She stepped back again, giving him plenty of room. She'd been that way since they were last in her room at the Paris.

He pushed the door closed behind him. "I wanted to tell you that I'm"—what was he?—"not really sorry. Because things happened the way they happened and I felt the way I felt. I was pissed. But more than that, I was hurt."

She looked at her feet, her face soft with remorse. That was not what he had intended. He didn't want her to feel that anymore.

"What I mean is, I'm okay. I should have been okay a long time ago. Okay with you."

She tilted her head and scrunched up her nose. He was making no sense. He was no good at this shit. Why didn't he just keep his mouth closed? He was a man of action, not blathering monologues. He put his hands on her shoulders, pulled her closer, and kissed her hard. Let the emotion he was trying to convey speak through action.

She fell against him. Her arms traced around his body and held him tight, nails tugging at his shirt. That was what the hell he meant to say.

Time was very short. Reluctantly, he broke off the kiss and let her go. Not that he wanted to. He wanted to hold her, feel her heat, her warmth along his body.

"So you're not mad at me anymore?" She pressed the back of his hand to her lips. Those eyes, even red-rimmed from the last few days of stress, no sleep, and crying were laced with a hint of relief.

He wasn't.

There was a knock at the door. "Guys. It's time to go." The door opened. Miller stood there looking sheepish. "I got a heads-up from a friend. The boys in blue are heading this way. We have to go now. If they take us, they take her, and I don't think the station is a safe place for her when I don't know who's under Zant's thumb."

"Look." Jim grabbed her hand. "I don't know what's going down from here on out, but I need you to trust me."

She nodded. His stomach clinched. Would she? Should she?

"Whatever you hear. You have to know that I am the man I used to be. Can you do that?"

She nodded. "I will."

"Good."

She sniffed. "You sound like you're not planning on seeing me again."

Miller coughed. "No time, kids. Need to go. Now. All of us." He held his hand out to Erica. "You're with me."

"Go." Jim pushed her toward the detective. "Keep her safe."

Miller sucked in a deep breath. "That's the plan."

"Jim ..."

———

Jim followed from a safe distance. Ely had really set them up—earpieces, mics, a tracer on the car. Jim felt like an agent. Like he was part of a team.

"Any chance we can get my bag from O's place?" He could hear Erica through Miller's mic, but she was muffled by ambient noise in the car.

"Sorry. We go straight to the safe house. Do not pass Go. Do not collect two hundred dollars." On the contrary, Miller's voice was crisp, clear.

Hers was tight. "Fine."

"With any luck, this is over by morning."

The car got quiet. Jim knew what she was thinking. Would that mean they'd find Chris? Dead or alive? Or tortured and broken? She was probably drowning in guilt and self-blame. But this was not her fault.

"Was all the double secret agent stuff really necessary? I hate not knowing what's going on with Jim and Oscar."

"Yeah. For your protection and theirs." Jim glanced in the rearview for about the twentieth time since they'd pulled away from Ely's house. Miller said the journey to the safe house was about thirty minutes taking the back roads.

Miller took the anticipated left turn.

"Jim was worried I'd get antsy and do something stupid, wasn't he?"

"Maybe just a little bit. But it's procedure for us in this circumstance. You just chillax with my friend Archie and get some rest."

"Chillax? Doubtful."

Jim knew that was not her style. Never was. And no way she would ever relax after what she'd seen. "So they'll contact me, let me know what's going on?"

"Yes, dear," Miller cooed sarcastically. Jim chuckled, knowing her face was mangled in irritation.

They hit a red light, rolled to a stop, Jim's car three lengths behind. He read a sign a grungy old man in tattered clothing clung to like a shield. It was tilted almost sideways, the lettering uneven and blocky. *Homeless. Hungry. Humble before God.* That was a new one.

A motorcycle pulled up next to Erica's window, blocking Jim's view of the homeless dude. The rider was covered head to toe in black leather with bright yellow accents and a shiny black helmet. The bike was all black. Only his boots stood out as shiny and loud. Screaming yellow. Hot in the sun, all that leather. The helmet turned to face down into the car. Jim couldn't see features or eyes through the tint. The unseen scrutiny made him uncomfortable.

Miller pulled off. The bike did too. It stayed parallel with them, matching their speed in the right lane. Jim passed one car, trying to get closer. The bike was right at her window. "You have a visitor," Jim said into his transmitter.

"Uninvited. Hate that," Miller quipped.

Jim saw the gleam of the gun. Saw Erica's head turn when it caught her eye as the biker steadied his aim on the front of Miller's car and fired.

"The man in the yellow shoes!" Erica yelled. Only they were motorcycle *boots*, not shoes.

In response, Miller floored it. The sedan lurched forward, but the bike easily caught up.

"Down!" Jim could see Miller wave her toward the floorboard. He could do nothing from his position to help her.

A second shot exploded.

Jim nailed the gas pedal, lurched the car to the right, onto the curb, the sidewalk. Rows of shelving were in the way. T-shirts, sunscreen, hats, and other Vegas necessities. In the movie car chases,

drivers blow right through that kind of blockade. In real life, innocent bystanders are shopping, loitering, chatting with loved ones, or
sipping coffee among them. He stood on the brake. Jim pull back on
the roadway to pass the tow truck in front of him. Movie chases were
cool. Real life sucked.

A block up he saw Miller slam on the brakes, spin the wheel.
An abrupt direction change. Through his in-ear mic, he heard Erica
scream again, her fear echoing in Jim's head. He heard the *ooof* of
expelled air as she collided with the passenger door.

"Fuck." Miller zigged the car again. With a thunderous explosion,
the back glass shattered. "Shit. They're behind us too. Where's a cop
when you need one?"

Jim passed two more cars and got closer. He swung hard right
and saw a glimpse of the motorcycle. Miller's swerving action made
the bike lean off to the right to avoid getting run down by the sedan's
front fender. The rider was still able to fire off a shot.

Then Miller hollered, "Hit!" He must have lost hold of the steering wheel. Jim watched the physics of motion, the car careening into
a sideways slide. In only an instant, the sedan jerked back, indicat-
ing that Miller had regained the wheel. Jim gripped his own steering
wheel. Sped up.

"You okay?" Jim passed another car. Only one truck left to get by
before he could take out the bike. The truck seemed to be keeping
pace. Not good. Probably with the bike. Would make sense.

"You're bleeding!" Erica was screeching. Panicked.

"I'm fine. Get back down. Now."

Jim was able to see her head disappear into the well of the passenger floorboard.

"How bad?" Jim asked into the mic.

"Not bad enough." The motorcycle reappeared on the driver's side, driving on the wrong side of the road. He fired again. This time the front driver's-side tire blew.

When the rim bit the pavement, the car jerked to the left like a train had hit it, sent them flying down a city street. Miller's hands flew up, above his head.

Jim watched in horror as the car started to flip. Time seemed to come to a complete standstill. This time the movies had it right. That slow-motion shit they love to show on the big screen was playing very real in his head.

The sedan careened over to its roof. Jim then realized the back end of a truck was too close. It had slammed on its brakes. Jim's front end connected with the truck's solid, stationary oversized bumper. His airbag didn't deploy. It was turned off. His head bounced forward, then back, tearing at the muscles in his neck. Like a wet noodle, Jim was wrenched and his head slammed something hard.

Things were flying around inside the car. A notebook. An empty coffee cup. He tried to concentrate and watch Miller's car as it continued its roll.

Twenty yards away, Miller's car shook and tumbled over again and skittered to a stop. It rocked back and forth several times.

Jim's dash had collapsed onto his lap. He struggled through his cloudy vision to move. Trapped. The door jammed. The shifter pressed into his ribs prevented his getting out the window.

Miller had been sucked through his window by the momentum of the roll. Jim could just see his legs past the wreckage. "Miller?"

He tugged again, and pain shot through his thigh. He didn't feel blood but there was pressure. He hoped it wasn't broken. The bike swung back around. Approached slowly. People flooded out of close-by businesses.

It looked like Erica was hanging in the car by the belt. It rocked slightly. Jim saw her struggling to push herself up to check for Miller.

The man in the yellow boots got off his bike. Jim wished for a gun, any gun right now. Even if he missed, it would make enough commotion for the ass to back off. Biker boy grabbed Erica by the hair. Jim's blood boiled. He pushed with all his strength against the dash. Fragments of plastic broke, but nothing eliminated the pressure that had him trapped.

She screamed again. This time he heard it across the broken road. It was as if that was the only sound in the universe. He saw the glass falling from his windshield, knew there should be creaking of twisted metal, but all he could hear was the biker pulling Erica from Miller's car.

Jim saw him put something over her mouth. White cloth. Had to be chloroform. "No!"

This couldn't happen. It was the middle of a Saturday, on the streets of Las Vegas. People were around. A car wreck attracted attention.

35

JIM'S HEAD THROBBED LIKE he was inside a bass drum. The stupid off-brand aspirin Adair had wasn't helping. At least the cabbie was close and was able to get him out of the scene of the wreck in a hurry.

It wasn't long after that goon dragged Erica away that he heard the sirens. He had no choice but to run as soon as he managed to work himself free.

Jim was leaving a trail of bodies and wreckage the slowest of detectives could follow, and the LVPD was not staffed with dimwits. If Miller had bought it in that rollover, Jim would probably take the rap for that as well. Not making friends these days.

He should go get his stash of cash and IDs he kept for just such emergencies and hightail it out of the state. Maybe out of the country.

He sighed. Instead, Jim Bean shoved a fiver into the same slot machine he'd won on two days ago. Sullivan's Fortune. He pulled the arm. Looked around. The drums spun. Lights flashed.

He looked up at the expensive car above the bank of machines. Pretentious.

The bells rang.

The false sounds of coins echoed far and wide in the casino, reminding other players to hold out a bit longer, feed the machines.

Winner? How was that even possible? His luck sucked. No way he wanted to waste any on the slots now. This wasn't why he was here.

It was early in the afternoon and only hardy slot players were scattered about. One skinny old lady looked away from her own machine long enough to nod at his windfall. He returned it. Glanced at his watch. Shouldn't be long now.

The ticket spit out.

Three hundred sixty-two dollars and seventy-eight cents. That couldn't be right. He added that to the winnings from Thursday and it made an even thousand. One large. He needed to look around on the far side of the casino floor as well.

He'd walk right up to the cash window. One more blatant sweep should do it. He strode boldly down the middle of the casino making faces at the various security cameras, following the hideous design of the carpet as it led him toward the higher-dollar machines and the poker and blackjack tables. He stopped and ordered a soda from a middle-aged woman in a top and shorts that were too young and too tight for her. He then slowed to watch a rather lovely young blonde winning at craps.

The cash box was dead ahead. He glanced behind him. Still not being followed. *Dammit.*

Only one other person cashing in chips. He was first in the line.

The old guy behind the glass was pleasant enough and congratulatory. Jim was suspicious.

He looked past the old dude and saw a reflection of Banks heading his way in the polished glass behind the teller. *About damned time.*

"Let's go, shall we?"

"After you." Jim gestured as he tucked his winnings into this pocket.

Banks turned and walked away. Jim followed.

"Through there." He nodded his big head toward an inconspicuous door.

Jim needed to calm down and do what he did best. His plan had been to go see Zant. He needed to be with the big guy to get answers he needed. "Zant want to see me?"

"Nope." That had been the point of this little field trip. Jim wanted to see Zant and act all innocent, offer *assistance* in order to continue to fulfill the terms of his agreement. All he had at the moment. He needed info, the lay of the operation. He was desperate.

Banks pushed the door open and held it for Jim to go through. Polite enough. Jim looked back toward the casino. Two men had moved in behind them. Shit. He knew he'd wasted what little luck he had on the slots.

The back end of the casino was like a bright tunnel, a white hall littered with white doors. Most unmarked. The *back room* was coming up.

"Are you sure? I talked to the Floyd woman quite a while. I might have some information the old man needs."

"I wouldn't call him that if I were you." Banks opened the last door on the right. A loading dock, empty except for three large wooden barrels with the lids lying next to them. Along with a hammer and nails. Not a pleasant thought, being killed and dumped into a barrel and then the lid nailed on. He internally shrugged. It would be a fitting coffin given the amount of barrel-aged Scotch he'd drunk in the past few years, but he wasn't ready for that just yet. Time to think on his toes. Follow a hunch about Banks he always suspected.

"You always seemed to like the girls, Banks. Hard to believe you'd be part of selling them off like dogs. And the abuse." Jim shook his head, tsked. "Hard to see you beating on your little girls like that."

His face twisted in anger as he moved in close. Jim didn't back up. "I ain't never inflicted an ounce of pain on any of my girls. I talk big, but they all know my job is to ensure they's safety." His attempts to cover his background in a higher vocabulary, like he had been in the casino, faltered with his indignation.

"I saw Lola and her friend. Beaten, raped—"

"Lola?" He grabbed Jim up by the shirt. Pressed the business end of a long sleek blade in the soft part of his neck just below his right ear. Deadly spot. Quick. Painless, at least.

"Figured she was one of yours. Pretty girl … once. Had that little beauty mark on her left cheek."

"Once?" Banks pushed the blade in harder. Punctured the skin. "What do you know about Lola? We thought she ran away from the Pony. I looked for her for two days."

"She didn't run, Banks." Jim tried to keep his balance, but it was hard with Banks holding him up high enough so his toes barely made contact with the ground and a shaft of steel pressed into his neck. "Zant is selling them. He's torturing your girls beyond even your imagination, then selling them."

"The hell you say." He shoved hard, sending Jim stumbling back and falling to the ground. He landed on his ass, banging his elbows on the concrete, facing Banks, who still had that blade in his hand and ready to throw. Instead he pounced on Jim, landing as if he were going to cut his throat, but not applying near enough pressure.

"We got her out. Lola." As Jim spoke, despite the blade compressing his voice box, Banks rolled them over, putting Bean on top, loosened his grip. Enough Jim could breathe, anyway. Jim would probably still have more than a shaving nick across his throat, but Banks was still playing the game. Listening. Yet not killing him. "We found her and a little blonde at a small ranch south of town. She'd been in a dog crate. Beaten. Drugged to stupidity." The rough man's face fell like a lost little puppy. "Zant... he sells them to the high rollers as sex slaves. I have tapes of the torture, the rapes. I can prove it to you."

Banks shook his head. Pretended to struggle and then rolled them back over. A big knee pressed into Jim's chest. Banks swung and gave Jim a halfhearted punch to the face. "Even that fucker is not *that* crazy."

"Yes. He is." Jim still had to shake off the weakened punch, happy Banks believed him enough to go light. But he hadn't stopped. "That's why Chris Floyd was dancing at the Pony. Working undercover to try and get girls out. She'd figured it all out. Four or five girls he takes out of the clubs several times a year. How many went missing on you over the last few weeks, Banks?"

He held tight, but his thoughts were clearly with his girls. "Three, out of my club."

Jim got his feet under the man's meaty thigh and shoved. He lumbered back. Even scrambling to stand as fast as he could, Banks had recovered just as quick. Quicker. A jaw-rattling punch landed across Jim's chin. He fell back to the cement floor. *Dang*. He had to kneel for a moment to clear the stars. The metal taste of blood filled his mouth. Jim spit, looked at Banks. He was about to run out of time. Erica and Chris were missing. He had to convince Banks that Zant was hurting his girls.

The small glance Banks made to the camera in the corner was almost imperceptible as he picked up his lost weapon. This was a performance for the benefit of the viewing end of that feed. It had to look like he was beating up Jim for the camera, while he was deciding whether he really wanted to beat Jim to a pulp or believe the story.

"You can beat on me all you like. But he's doing it. Zant's taking your girls. Selling them in Mexico."

"Motherfucker." He looked down. Shook his head. Walked toward Jim, knife pointed at the ground. "Gonna have to. Private feed in his office. If I don't kill you ..."

So Zant was watching. Evidently with no sound. Banks pulled Jim up off the cold concrete once again and gave him a blow to the ribs, still holding him close. "Tell me about Alexis." The punch connected, but it wasn't as hard as should have been. Jim overreacted, jerking. "Is that what Zant did with her?" His big eyes narrowed.

Jim balanced himself. So, Banks *did* know Jim's cousin. Most had. She'd lived with Zant for over a year. She thought the scumbag was going to marry her. Delusions of a young dancer in Vegas. A showgirl, taken in by the money, the jewelry, the nice trips. But she learned who Zant was in a hurry and she'd wanted out. Not many people got to walk away from the man with the knowledge Alexis had—thanks to Jim's doing some things he hated. All that and he'd ended up still owing Zant in the long run.

She'd asked and Jim had intervened, made her disappear. The same way he had from Ohio eight years before. New name. New city.

New everything. Even Jim had no clue where she'd ended up. Cost him every dime he'd manage to save and gamble for. Found a body, set it up to look like she was dead. After the funeral, Zant nailed him. Jim hadn't put a thing over on the fucker. But he gave Jim a deal anyway. Zant was to leave her alone, never search her out. And Jim would owe him … *favors*. And the big man had called on that marker more than once.

Each time Jim got the call, Zant toyed with him. Had him do things, small things. Make one piece of evidence disappear, supply another to take its place. None of it had hurt anyone so far. The biggest cost had been Jim's integrity. Amazing how much a guy missed something like that. Something unseen was virtually irreplaceable. It was a gaping hole that Jim tried to fill with Scotch as often as possible.

Here stood Banks. The big man looked concerned about Alexis. As Jim suspected, there was a soft spot for the ladies. "You knew her?"

"Was her protection for a while. She was a sweet girl."

Jim tried to go on the offensive. Landed one punch to the chest before Banks threw him off.

"Is she dead?"

Jim rolled away. He again found himself on his knees. "No. She's not. Last I knew, she was in a safe place. But Zant appears to be unhappy with me. And that's my weakness, isn't it? Puts her at risk again."

Banks lifted Jim to his feet. "I got no orders to kill her. Just you. Fuck. I always liked her. Was afraid she'd been dead this whole time and he'd lied to me about you and the arrangement." A good punch to the breadbox made Jim double over. He spit some blood from the cut lip for show.

"I can't take you being easy on me much longer, big guy. He'll use Alexis too if I can't stop the trafficking now and nail him. He'll have her killed as soon as he can find her. And we both know he'll find her."

Banks slowed. His big leathery face contorted with the strain of such a large decision. Let Jim go or kill him. "I have to hurt you."

"No. You don't."

He pulled Jim up. "Yes. I do." He placed the blade at his shoulder and shoved. "Sorry, man."

Jim growled, maybe screamed. He wasn't sure what it was. It fucking hurt. Banks's aftershave and his own blood made for a very unpleasant odor and it filled his senses, mixing with searing pain as the sting of the metal tore through his shoulder.

Oh shit. He was going to pass out. Couldn't do that. The floor beneath his feet was undulating like a breaking wave about to crash over him.

"Hold your shit, Bean." His body jerked as Banks maneuvered them so *his* back was to the camera. Zant couldn't see more than broad shoulders and bald head. "Take the knife, return the favor, and go. Keys are in the red van, over the visor."

"Really?" Seemed too easy. Jim didn't have time to think, much less the ability. He head butted the big bouncer. When Banks's head whipped back, Jim did an easy spin and kick move. None of which helped his own brain function, but even with the major miss, the little contact of his boot to Banks's upper arm and the whiplash took the bouncer off balance. Jim grabbed the blade and twisted, hard. Banks let it go. Jim stabbed with little aim.

The blade penetrated Banks's upper thigh as he fell backward. The big man yelled in pain and rolled to grab his wound. Jim hoped he hadn't just castrated the guy.

He glanced up at the camera. Time to go. Jim hoped it had all happened fast enough to be convincing on film. If Zant knew that Banks had let him off that loading dock, even with a stab wound and a busted lip, Banks would be a dead man. The bouncer was not the only killer on Zant's friend list.

And that was now Jim's number-one problem.

36

"THEY GOT THE GIRLS back too."

The words were like acid on Jim's tongue. His rage at Zant for taking Erica was about to eat him alive. Somehow knowing the asshole had the girls was like salt in an already burning wound. He needed to act but they were at a dead end. They still had no real lead on the Thin Man. Hitting Zant in his office would be a suicide mission, and they had no way to know he was even in the country, much less his penthouse.

Inactivity was churning in his gut.

They were in the emergency room getting his shoulder fixed up when Ely had called. The ambulance carrying Lola and Connie had been carjacked at a rest area. The driver hurt, the girls gone.

Miller shook his head, though painkillers slowed his actions. "How the fuck?" The detective was in a hospital room. His arm had been cleaned and stitched and his right leg had been set from a nasty compound break and was hanging in a strange contraption with pulleys and ropes. He was alive. It had been a close call, though. The rolling sedan had almost crushed him.

"I don't know. The whole thing was a crash and grab. Someone working with Sister Nora had to have leaked it." Oscar peered around the curtain of the tiny hospital room window. "We're out of allies and not likely to acquire many more since most everyone who has helped us has ended up dead."

His words were cold, slow. The calm worried Jim. And now Miller was a sitting duck, too injured to get out of the hospital.

"How did they know the route? It was last minute, untraceable. I feel like they're sleeping with us." Jim paced back to the door and looked out into the hallway. A woman shuffling along with an IV tower. A nurse. Nothing threatening.

Miller sipped water through a straw, then croaked out one word: "Broady." He tried to sit up but the IV lines in both his arms made it hard for him to adjust. O rushed over to help.

"Broady took Erica. Recognize the bike. Those black and yellow leathers. I was out on a scene one night and he stopped by. I teased him about those leathers for weeks. The asshole looked like a fucking bee." Miller moved his arm. Inspected the bandage. "And that was his gun. Polished nickel."

Jim paced, then propped his weight against the far wall of the room as the nurse came in. "So Detective fucking Broady put out the BOLOs and someone spotted your car on the move. Good luck for him, bad for us. He closed in and took you out. With more flair than he would have liked, is my guess." Jim seethed over the thought of the dirty cop having his hands on Erica. It was time to get proactive.

"I know you are cops and all"—the nurse scanned the room, then looked at Miller—"but you need some rest." She then gave the other two men in the room a glance.

"We're about to finish up."

She keyed something into the computer in the wall, updating his chart. "Good."

"Miss?" She looked up. Oscar flashed her that heart-melting smile. His face changed from cold and deadly to one of a mother concerned for a sick child. "You know how it is after an accident ... especially one with a cop involved. There'll probably be some other reporters, maybe even other cops who want to ask him a bunch of silly questions that can wait a few days. Just in case, I'd like to send a friend over to keep watch over our young detective here. Some pretty shady characters have threatened him. I promise, my guy will stand at the end of the hall and not get in the way of all the good work you ladies do."

His charm worked.

"I guess. If he's out of the way and don't scare the other patients."

"No, ma'am." He grinned again. "Scout's honor."

She snapped the lid closed. She looked skeptical. "He best not, or out he goes. And you two need to scoot. Soon."

"Yes, ma'am."

"Detective Miller needs some peace."

"Ma'am." Oscar winked as she left. Jim was sure he heard her giggle.

"How do you do that shit? Women fall all over you," Miller said with more clarity than he'd managed a moment ago.

Oscar shrugged. "I mean what I say. Honesty is something women feel."

"We'll go talk to the nun. See what we can get out of her, who she thinks is the weak link in her chain. There has to be something connecting all this. Chris's cartoon signature being in that bathroom stall was a crumb, a message." Jim patted the blanket-covered foot of

Miller's uninjured leg. "You feel better. Call if you need us." Jim gave him a clean cell.

Miller opened it, glanced through the preprogrammed numbers. Jim, Oscar, Ely. "Got it."

"I'll have someone here in ten minutes. You won't see him. But he'll be watching." Oscar slipped the detective a small .380 pony under the sheet by his good hand. "For vermin and such."

Miller nodded. "Thanks."

———

"Broady is the man in the yellow shoes, only the shoes weren't shoes at all. Motorcycle boots." He shook his head. Seven-year-old girl wouldn't have known that. "But Broady's beer gut eliminates him as the other player in the hotel, the Thin Man."

"Yep." They were pulling up to the church. It was getting late, dinnertime. He wondered if the sister would be there.

"If this is a dead end, we need to pay Zant a visit. Get proactive."

Oscar looked over at Jim's arm all tied up in a sling. "How'd that go for you last time?"

"Shut up."

O nodded and put the Escalade in park. "You may be right, but I think it best we know who's at the table before we throw all in, don't you think?"

"I think about Erica being in one of those crates and I *think* I'm ready to kill Andrew Zant and all his demented friends right up in his penthouse office in front of that giant snake tank." Jim took a deep breath. Nothing got a person into more trouble than uncontrolled emotion in this business.

Oscar got out, Jim followed. Oscar made it to the door first but turned back to Jim, blocking his entrance. "You change your mind about a gun? The stakes are high. Someone's gonna die."

He chuckled. O looked like he was waiting on Jim to have some Dr. Phil breakthrough. "Don't you worry. I saved your ass at the ranch, didn't I?"

Oscar seemed to search his face to make sure he was ready for the coming storm. He must have found something convincing enough. "Lucky break." He entered the church. Sister Nora was exiting the sanctuary. She hustled to them.

"You have news?"

Jim hadn't expected that. They were here to question her, not give her an update. "We were hoping you could help us, Sister." Jim tamped down his anger to prevent making the nun skittish. "We want to find the girls, but Erica has been taken as well. We believe a police officer aided in her abduction. What we need to know is who may have assisted from within your organization."

"Mine?" She backed up a step, put her hand to her heart in surprise or insult. Jim really didn't care which.

"Who knows the route and destinations when you start this enterprise? Who is privy to the underground railroad?"

"Only a few know most of the players, and they don't know each other." She took a deep breath and started walking toward her office. "Even I only know the first, sometimes maybe the second handoff. It protects the girls and the participants. And it changes frequently. I mean, it's a text and telephone network. I call my contact, I get a runner that helps, and then that contact arranges the next drop, and that contact person arranges the next."

She opened the door and held it for them. She shuffled behind a dark wood desk so large it made her look like a child. "We give them a letter that indicates the number of jumps. For this one I was obviously A. The next will be B. The idea is that there are five jumps so pimps, abusive boyfriends, husbands, or family lose track even if they try." She glared at the wall. "Most don't bother, but it does happen." She turned back to Jim. He was standing behind the chair facing her desk. "On E, we place them somewhere for short-term needs. Medical, psychological, rehab."

"So who all knew about today's jump?"

"Me, the medicals, the driver."

"You know the driver?" Oscar sat, stretched out his long legs.

Jim was too wound up to sit.

"Deacon of a Baptist church here in Las Vegas." She sat. "Not likely one to be convinced to divulge anything. He was injured but is at home now."

"And the others? The medicals?"

"Tricia is a trauma nurse who has been involved with this church for years. Highly unlikely." Sister Nora sifted through some notes and papers on her desk. Stopped to think. Jim noticed her Bible, tattered and loved, as she picked it up to retrieve a slip of paper underneath. He wondered what all she considered safe stored beneath its passages.

"Keith Worth." She handed O the slip of paper. "It was his second time working with us. He's missing."

"So he could have taken off with the girls?" He took the paper.

"Possible. Jonathan, the driver, had a head wound. Doesn't remember much that would be helpful."

Jim thought back on the morning, dropping off the girls. Tricia had carried Connie. "I don't remember much about Keith. Do you interview people prior to using them in the program?"

"Of course."

Jim came around the chair to be more intimate with her, to calm her. To not seem like a looming authority in the back of the room. He sat next to O, tried for relaxed. He was failing, but it was better.

She relaxed a little, even sat. Thought for minute. "I interviewed him a few weeks ago. He helped with a young runaway the other night."

Oscar looked at the paper. "Describe his face for me."

"Middle-aged, but not too wrinkled. Narrow nose. Brownish hair." She clasped her hands.

"His build?"

"Terribly thin."

Jim thought back and tried to picture him. The man hadn't been his concern at the time. He was usually pretty observant. Maybe the condition of those girls had shaken him enough to miss something that important. Still, lots of guys were thin. "I don't remember him being that thin."

She shrugged. "The EMT uniform goes a ways to hide it, those full shirts. Supplies in his pockets. He was in a suit the first time I met him. On his way to Bible study, he said. The slacks and the fitted jacket made him look as though he was close to starving."

He and Erica had been that close to him and had no clue. "The Thin Man."

Oscar sat up, and his size seemed to double as he leaned forward. "You checked his references?" He held up the paper.

"I did." She looked at the desk. "You think this man was not who he represented?"

"I'm sure of it." Jim stood. "What were his credentials?"

She riffled through more papers on her desk. "Westside Medical transport for four years. He was laid off last year." She handed him the sheet. It had an address and phone number. All most likely faked.

"I have one more question." Jim brought her attention back to him.

Sister Nora also stood, not to be intimidated by him. He liked that. "Yes?"

"Chris Floyd. You recognized Erica's name and her face, but you didn't say anything. Chris has been here before?"

She sighed. "Of course. She is also part of the team, so I would not bring her name into any conversation with anyone without her consent. Chris has made some nasty men in the area very angry by sneaking their wives, girlfriends, or working girls out of the city. Several cases a year come from her. Her day job is unique for finding those that need our special kind of help, and she said once she had some kind of inside contact. The troubled go looking for money before spirituality, Mr. Bean. She offers them a way out. She is a wonderful human being."

"Was she ever here when Keith was in the building? Was she working the other case last week when he was here?"

"Yes. They were both here for the runaway. Keith checked her. Cleared her to travel and left."

"He left before Chris?"

"Yes. She and I waited with the girl until her transport arrived. A man from over the California border. We've used him often for those heading west."

Oscar glanced at Jim, then back to the nun. "Was that a week ago Friday?"

She flipped to the back of that Bible, which Jim now realized was hollowed out and filled with blank pages and handwritten notes. "Thursday."

"She must have suspected something of Keith. Put the drawing in the stall so if someone managed to figure out she was part of this railroad, they'd know we were on track." Jim wished his shoulder wasn't throbbing, but he didn't want to risk any meds slowing him down.

"And he got her Friday or Saturday, according to the timeline."

"Anything about him you remember? Anything?" Jim asked.

She looked down at the paper with Keith's information on it as if it would talk to her. "He did odd jobs after he was let go from the ambulance service. Something about that place up north. The fancy golf course. Said he was the only one to live up there for a while."

All roads led back to Coyote Springs. The girls had to be there. Made sense. The crates behind the club and the deserted warehouses.

They stood to leave. Oscar took her hand. "This is a dangerous mess, Sister. Keith Worth is part of a large trafficking ring. I suggest you leave Vegas tonight. Visit a friend or relative for a few days."

She gave him a quick nod. "I may do that."

"Not may. Do it."

Jim looked back at the nun. She was pale, and her fragile hands shook. "Did I get Chris abducted? And Erica for that matter?"

"No. None of this is your fault, Sister." Oscar was quick to relieve her guilt.

Jim might not have been.

37

THEY'D STOLEN A CAR. Actually, Jim had. One that was not being searched out under the trumped-up BOLOs. A white Camry. Plain Jane. Nothing worth raising an eyebrow over. Nothing that went as fast as Jim would have liked once they hit the open, desolate highway. Probably best O was driving. Jim watched the terrain drop off into the darkness, just as he had when he and Erica first drove to Coyote Springs. Nothing changed. Not out there. Stone and sand, unfeelingly and unyielding. The car tires chattered on the broken road that led to the dream that had been Coyote Springs.

He rechecked the clip of the 9mm in his hand.

Ely's had been a bust. Watched from every conceivable corner. Oscar's place was just as buggy. No way in. "Wanna break into the shooter's club? Lots of guns there." O had offered.

Not really appealing. Too risky. He rattled off a verbal inventory to make sure he wasn't missing anything. "A rifle, two handguns, two knives, and a stun gun against Zant and his little army?"

O had given him that look that said *no worries, man*, and shrugged. "I've seen worse odds."

They zoomed past the anonymous hotel, the diner, and the strip club.

"Pull over here." Jim tilted his head to the east just below the service road and the warehouse on the west side of the highway. There was nowhere to hide the car in the open deserted town. Best they could do was pull it off the road a few yards and pop the hood so the Camry looked like it'd been left on the shoulder over engine trouble. Happened out here. It was a desert.

They gathered what gear they'd rescued from O's Escalade and the red van he'd taken from Banks. That added night vision goggles, a baseball bat, a coil of rope, two smoke bombs, and (thankfully) a handful of ibuprofen to the arsenal. Not the way he'd like to go in, but it'd have to do.

Jim swallowed the pain reliever before they jogged all the way north of the warehouse on the wrong side of the road, then cut back south and west to come around the far side of the building. They avoided the service road altogether.

"Last time I was here, there was one panel van outside this warehouse. No lights. Nobody home." Now they were looking at three cars, the panel van, and an RV. The place was lit up like a hotel on the Strip. "They're not even trying to hide."

"Why would you be out here?" Oscar assessed the building. This was his forte: getting people out of places they don't want to leave. The bounty hunter had it in his blood. His eyes darkened as he thought things through. His usually jovial face hardened. He took a deep breath. "Smells like a rat's nest to me."

Jim looked at the death in Oscar's eyes. Ten years this guy had been looking for redemption for his wife being taken, sold, and killed by these men. And here they had a chance to face down the entire operation. Slay all his demons in one shot.

Double O glanced back at Jim. "You want any left to prosecute?"

Jim felt killing wasn't usually necessary. Maiming worked just fine and gave the person something to think about in the future

"Keep at least one to testify against the top rat. As for the rest…" Jim shrugged. "I really do like the thought of Zant decaying away in orange cotton and using community piss pots."

They eased around the side of the structure, looking for weakness, a quiet way in. As they circled around the front, car lights swept across the open yard in front of the steel building. Dead bushes stood sentry on a path that led to a double glass door.

Jim ducked behind the RV. Oscar fell in beside him. They were each propped against a tire. No chance their legs could be seen under the chassis.

The car stopped at the far end of the building, past the vehicles. Lights stayed on, leading the way to a side door. Oscar took a quick look around the RV. "I recognize that one."

Jim looked as well. BMW limo. High-dollar ride. Real gold trim. Vulgar in its narcissism. "We have the head rat. Interesting. Why would he be out here for this?"

O's face was chiseled into stone-cold hate. "Don't care. Now they all can die."

"I'd still like to see Zant do the time."

"Zant would still be in business on the inside."

True enough. And Alexis and her son would still be at risk. The driver jumped out and rushed to open the back. Andrew Zant emerged, taking a moment to survey his surroundings. His smugness wafted through the Nevada heat like the stench of roadkill.

Jim glanced back the way they came. "We need to get inside. Get a head count. Make a plan."

O nodded and slipped into the dark, easily avoiding the floodlights as he made his way to the back of the structure. There was a second-floor window. An office. With any luck, it was empty.

Jim resituated the sling his arm had been enjoying. The rest of the night's activities were going to be painful. He'd turned down the narcotics the ER doc had offered. Needed a clear head. The shoulder hurt, didn't want to cooperate, but it worked. Banks had good aim. He'd done little more than cut through skin and nick some muscle. Jim was sure he hadn't been as expert in return.

He ran after Oscar. They positioned themselves under the window. "Want me to push you up? Can you get in with one arm?"

Jim nodded. "It's not like I can hoist your big ass up there."

"Upsy-daisy, then." He held his hands in a cup for Jim to step into.

Jim pushed up, O hoisted. Jim stepped onto his shoulders. The window was at chest level. The latch was not locked. Lucky. He pushed up the pane slowly. Bathroom. Not an office. He listened carefully for sounds. Let his nose check as well. Stale. Unused. O shifted.

Jim used his good arm to pull his weight to the sill and dragged his legs through. There was nothing below, so he turned and dropped. His shoulder complained. He ignored it. There would be time to heal later. Erica and Chris were here somewhere. He hoped.

He secured the rope to the post at the end of the row of stalls and tossed it out for O to climb up. The big guy made it up and in easily. Wordlessly, O removed the rope and tucked it in a pantry full of cleaning supplies.

Jim crouched down low, eased the door open. A couple of dark empty offices with large windows open to the warehouse floor below spread out to his right. The setup was intended for the managers in the glass rooms to oversee the production on the first floor. From the recessed bathroom door, he was too far back to see over the rail above the work area. He heard voices from below. Someone was heading this way. He signaled O to follow, then crouched and moved quick and quiet to the nearest office, closing the door behind them without a sound.

He turned and looked down from the window behind an empty steel desk. Lights were on in the main open area. Movement. A couple of girls he didn't recognize were milling about. Coolers and crates were stacked close to a table just inside three roll-up garage doors.

"Holy hot cars, Batman," Oscar whispered. "Look at that collection."

Voices in the office caught his attention. He wanted to go in there and just blow everything away. But not till they knew how many targets were moving around this warehouse. And where the head rat had taken root.

Jim looked long enough to see several sports cars lined up against the far wall, maybe fifteen yards away from the girls and the boxes. "That has to be a million bucks in scrap metal right there."

"More than that—the gold one's an Ascari A10..." He glanced at Jim. His lack of car enthusiasm must have shown. "It's basically a race car with turn signals. Has to go for eight hundred grand. And that Aston Martin is another three hundred."

"Bond car?"

"Yep."

"I like James Bond. Did you see the last one?"

"Yeah." O resituated his vest.

"Effects keep getting better."

"And the women hotter."

"I know the Rolls, but what are the other two? I don't recognize them at all." They looked like race cars too. Shiny. New. Expensive. Gluttonous.

"Not a clue."

The garage bay door opened. The RV pulled in.

"They're going to move the girls in that. Probably across the border into Mexico. Lots of little airports there with less than tight security. We can't let that thing leave here."

There were voices coming from the office next door. Some not so subtle.

One was Erica. Cursing

38

THEY HEARD FOOTFALLS. Jim guessed three, maybe four people. They eased back into the restroom. He hovered above a john. In the next stall O was doing the same thing. The hall fell quiet. Luckily no one needed to take a piss.

Voices wafted from the office. When he was reasonably sure no one else was in the hall, he eased the door open a crack, stuck his mirror out. Erica was in the receptionist's area. He could see her back clearly in the reflection.

"Affirmative," Jim heard a deep male voice say. Then a moment later the guard moved into his view. He was silent for a moment, followed by, "Wilco."

Then two men were in front of Erica in a heartbeat. Both had high and tight cuts, matching dark suits, and ear set radios. "Are you pilots?" She giggled.

Drugged. Not good. She'd be harder to handle, slower to move when Jim needed her to. Her arm was wrapped in bloody fabric.

It must have been injured in the crash. Her head was bleeding in the spot Banks had knocked her into the wall. Given that the car had rolled a couple of times, she was lucky to have a pulse.

"Hey!" Ex-Marine Thug Guy A ignored her exclamation as he pulled her to her feet, even though he'd been nice enough and not grabbed the injured arm. Hell. Maybe he wasn't nice. Maybe it had just been by chance.

Ex-Marine Thug Guy B caught her up when her legs refused to play their part and hold her weight or participate in the dynamics that were required to place one foot in front of the other. He also grabbed the top of her jeans and not her arm, so Jim knew they had some sense of her injuries and no real wish to make them worse. For now.

The ex-marine thug guys dragged her into the inner office as if they were helping her past a finish line.

To keep an eye on her, he had to move, possibly expose himself if he got closer. But Zant was likely in there. He needed to hear what they said. There was no choice. He'd like to have a plan for all the players in the building, but this was urgent. He had to go out. He glanced at Oscar. Got the nod.

O signaled that he was going to check the rest of the layout with a twist of his finger. Jim nodded.

He crawled into the outer office that Erica and the thugs had just exited and ducked behind a secretary's desk. He lay flat. The position gave him a view under the front panel of the desk that faced incoming guests. Part of the room was blocked, but he could see her. And Zant.

Zant stood behind a pretentious black lacquer oriental desk. It hadn't been that long since Jim last saw the man, and as usual he turned Jim's stomach. The guy's features were small, as was his stature.

Jim always fixated on his little mouth. It was tiny compared to his head. Should be on a boy. But very grown-up shit spewed from those lips. Jim had once pictured him as a small-mouthed bass, all face and a pie hole so small he probably had someone cut his meat into tiny bites in order to eat it.

Jim's focus drifted to the dead gaze of Zant's equally thin eyes. He needed to visit the same barber that the ex-marine thug guys used, because his hair was wavy and reached well past the collar of his four-thousand-dollar suit.

Erica was on the floor before the desk. She tried to hold herself upright in that kneeling position, but she faltered and swayed back and forth a couple of times. She caught herself since her hands were tie-wrapped in front of her. She closed her eyes tight, took a deep breath. Coughed.

Get your shit together or this bastard is going to kill you.

Zant appeared disgusted. "Give her some water. I didn't want her dead. Who is responsible for the bruising and bleeding?"

That was good news. Zant picked up a gold cigarette case with hands that were also in proportion to his mouth and his eyes. Manicured fingers took out a small black cigarette, tapped it on the shiny lid, and placed it between his skinny fish lips. All of his movements were smooth, exact.

The twisted trail of smoke that left his mouth was as compact as the man. No big show of the act of smoking. No wasted effort. He'd smoked often and for years. Maybe he was already being eaten alive with cancer. Brain cancer *might* explain how his mind was so twisted. Jim could only wish.

"Broady said the car flipped four or five times." Ex-Marine Thug Guy A handed Erica a full bottle of water. "Water should help move the drugs through your system quicker."

She drank it down fast, even as he tried to pull it back from her. "Easy, girl."

Jim saw her grab her stomach and look up at Zant and his immaculate appearance, that glaze gone for an instant. Maybe she wasn't as drugged as she was letting on. Then Erica let it go, vomiting, making sure the trajectory was in Zant's direction, as if she wanted to sully him.

"That's an antique Afshar carpet. Do you have any idea how much that cost me?" He tossed his lighter to the desk and glared down at her, but the man wasn't rattled, didn't come closer to her.

Ex-Marine Thug Guy B rushed to attempt to clean Erica's stomach contents off the rug.

She burped. "Excuse me."

With that, Zant did stalk around the desk. "There is some nasty stuff still in your system. Short-term unconsciousness is difficult to manage." He leaned back against the front of the desk, crossing his legs at the ankles, relaxed and making sure his presence allowed Ex-Marine Thug Guy B to continue to clean the evidently very expensive carpet. Jim thought her contribution was more an improvement to the busy red pattern than a distraction.

Without a word Zant watched, then took a long toke from the cigarette. Or was it a little cigar? And why did Jim care enough to consider the distinctions?

Zant motioned for Ex-Marine Thug Guy A to give her the bottle back. "Slower this time." She took it and nodded. "Leave us," he said to the big men. The thugs hesitated. "Her hands are tied and she's still fighting the effects of the injection. I'll be fine."

They dutifully filed out, moving as one. Jim ducked his head and pulled his legs in to be as small under the desk as possible. They weren't expecting trouble out here, so they weren't being overly careful. Neither did a visual scan as they left the office. Cheap muscle had no clue what they were up against.

Jim listened as they marched down the stairs, then he resumed the position that gave him the best view of the room and the quickest access to get Erica if needed.

He wanted her out of that small room, down in the open where he and O could take them all out. Zant gave Erica an appraising look, tilted his head. "I was going to kill you once you got to the city. Clean. Simple. Let your pretty little sister go with the others and kill you outright. Maybe even do the deed myself." He inspected his smoking hand, his right hand, like he was giving himself a moment to imagine what joy that might have brought him. "But kismet intervened in the little script of our association for a second time."

"Second?" She took another, slower drink from the bottle.

"Yes. The first was the wonderful revelation that Chris Floyd—the woman nosing about my business, costing me money—was none other than your baby sister. It was like a Christmas gift from the universe all wrapped up just for me." He shrugged. "Things fell into place. It wasn't hard to feed her a few extra bits of information, make sure she got close enough. Not often do things fall in line like that. And she was so pretty. Much like you." He bent forward, putting his face only a few inches from Erica's. "A shame it will take a while for that beauty to show through again. Very headstrong, that girl."

Jim heard O moving in. Held his hand up for him to stay put. They needed to know what Zant was planning, and the megalomaniac wouldn't be able to contain that kind of plot, keeping it for himself. No, he was going to lay it all out to frighten, to torment Erica. This guy was all about wielding power.

"She's alive?" Jim could feel Erica's relief from the other room as she sagged forward, dropping the water bottle.

"Of course." Zant sucked on the cigarette, taking a moment before letting out a long puff of stale smoke. "She's graduated. You, on the other hand, will not be trained. I can't risk the entire operation to put you into the pipeline now. Schedules are tight, preplanned for months. Lots of logistics to this business, you know."

"Trafficking sex slaves? I can only imagine."

"Commodities, Miss Floyd." He turned his back on her to look out at the warehouse below. The cars lined up, the girls dressed like pros—all toys to him. Smug. Showing he was unafraid to turn his back to her. No way she'd manage to inflict any pain on him since she could barely move.

"You of all people should understand that. *Everything* is a commodity in the modern world. You work with that reality constantly."

"People are not commodities."

"Really." He spun back to her. "You trade on labor forces all the time, don't you? Investing in companies who outsource to third-world countries, Miss Floyd. What kind of people do you suppose do that cheap work? And how are they treated?" He arched an eyebrow, as if she would give him an answer. "You simply choose to ignore what you do not have to *see* firsthand."

"That's not rape and torture." She tried to yell it, but it came out squeaking, like her lungs lacked the anger her heart did.

"You know this to be true? In those dirty little factories producing widgets for companies *you* funded, you *know* the little girls and boys toiling for long hours in horrible conditions are never molested or beaten to ensure productivity? Maybe in front of the rest of the workforce to make an example." He took another slow drag.

It snaked around his head as he let it out. "You're a hypocrite. You and your corporate kind."

Jim now saw anger in his dead eyes. He didn't want the man mad.

"So you want me dead for not funding the Lionbridge projects?" She shook her head. "It was a small deal for you. Do you kill off every businessperson who goes against you?"

"You have no appreciation for the depth of my business and the—how shall I say?—temperament of some of my associates." He smashed out the remaining bit of his smoke. Quite quickly, his face again became an emotionless mask. He was void. Empty.

"In that particular deal, we were looking for a vehicle to clean up a great deal of cash reserves. Your denial of the project left my business associate with a load of cash that he was unable to move, and with the research you did, he was linked to a past associate with whom he would rather not have been connected publicly. That managed to put him on a list. An FBI list."

His lips tightened enough to look like an asshole. "So, he lost his money and his ability to move about freely. He is most unhappy."

Even with her hands tied in front of her, Erica's fingers drifted to her forehead. "I don't under—"

"We needed the bank and the developments to help this South American associate get his cash *unsullied*."

"Jesus Christ." Her face tightened. Her spine straightened. She now apparently understood something Jim still did not. Big business financials were beyond his usual economics. Lately, anything beyond poker and beer money was beyond his economics. "We would have asked you for an up-front cash investment. He had it cooling somewhere. You were going to make the down payment in dirty cash and use the bank and the land sales to get clean money back."

"We *were*—" He stopped short. Jim saw that he was watching someone coming down the hall. He was as still as he could make himself as another man walked by. The newcomer stopped with his back to Jim.

"I brought your friend. He's admiring the cars." The man shrugged before he glared down at Erica. "She good to go? I'm ready to start the next batch." He turned, giving Jim a profile. An aging, balding pudge of a man in a tacky leisure suit. His neck, his wrist, and two fingers sported chunky jewelry. What was left of his hair was combed back and sprayed stiff to stay in place. Tasteless Vegas stereotype if he ever saw one.

"Gregory, you are a man with a singular track of attention. I admire that about you. But this one is to remain pristine."

Fat man made a tsking noise. "Doubt she's a virgin."

"Mr. Dubai doesn't want a virgin. He wants one to break himself." Zant looked at Erica. Jim saw a hint of glee in his eye. The crazy fuck was enjoying this game. Jim was about to rain on his parade. "I'm afraid his methods may not be as civilized as mine."

"Nice name." Gregory Lake snorted. "Those guys piss cash. I hope you charged a premium. Getting her across the border untrained will be a nightmare for the driver."

"Triple. For that and the fact he wants to inspect her *personally* before the shipment. That's why I had you bring him out here."

"Risky."

"Profitable."

Lake sneered down at her. "She looks like shit. I wouldn't pay seven hundred and fifty for that."

"This guy did. More, actually. He's a sick fuck." Zant took two steps closer to her. Bony fingers locked on her chin. He tilted her head to make sure she was looking at him. He wanted the audience. She closed her eyes. His grip tightened until Erica had no choice but look at him to stop the onslaught of more pain. "You embarrassed me. Cost me a few million in apology money. I have a reputation of being reliable. That's been strained. Unacceptable."

He dropped her chin, turned to the fat guy. "Have the boys take her to the others."

"Knock her out?"

"No." The answer was fast and firm. "He'll want to see the fire of her anger, the concern over her sister. Clean up the injuries. Dress her in something … fitting for the occasion. I'll go entertain Mr. Dubai while you get her ready."

Erica grunted as Lake yanked her to her feet. He led her out of the offices and to the stairs. Zant lingered and straightened his tucked-in shirt. He took a moment to let them get on down the stairs. He smiled at his reflection in the glass. He wouldn't be smiling much longer.

They needed a distraction.

Jim backed out. O was in the bathroom. Time for the assessment.

"Four 'men'—two have the potential for being trouble, two are minions loading the RV. Zant, Lake, and *the guest*." O shifted the holster at his waist and unlatched the leather that held it in place. He clicked the safety off the other. "And three girls."

Zant waltzed past. Jim heard his shoes tapping on the walkway. They waited a full minute before easing back into the empty office and looking over the floor.

Lake had dragged Erica down to the main area and into the RV. It was time to move.

Jim and Oscar made their way to the end of the catwalk over the open floor. Tucked back by a small stairway intended for emergency use only.

Double O stood up straight and pulled his shoulders back. Something cracked. "Outnumbered. Under gunned." He handed Jim one of the handguns.

"Shame if something happened to one of those expensive cars."

"Damned shame."

39

OSCAR DANGLED THE REACQUIRED rope over the rail at the farthest reaches of the building, next to a metal-encased elevator, away from the lights and the row of cars. All attention was on the RV, and that made the best opportunity for them to get down there.

"I'll go first. Then I can catch you."

O's voice was so low Jim had to play it back to figure out what was actually said. Once they hit the floor they would go silent. He checked his equipment over one more time to make sure he knew what was tucked where.

He heard some laughter. Zant's. A slow burn of anger crept up his spine.

Oscar shimmied down the rope and held it taut. Jim slipped his arm out of the sling and left the empty fabric hanging around his neck and back, grateful the drop wasn't more than a story and a half. Going it one-armed, he slid down faster than he intended. He made it without falling, but the thud and the tiny grunt of pain from his injured shoulder echoed as he hit the concrete floor. O scowled at the loud landing, but he was down. They crept along the wall until they were able to see the far southeast corner of the warehouse floor. All attention was still on Zant and the wealthy Middle Eastern–looking man with him walking down the billion-dollar row of cars. Mr. Dubai, Jim presumed. So named for his country of origin and not his actual surname. Being a pervert was an equal-opportunity gig.

The warehouse was a simple rectangle. They'd come down in the northeast corner behind some industrial equipment stacked near the apparently non-working elevator. The cars were directly across the building, backed against the south wall with a couple of tool chests and a workbench behind them. To the right of the cars, along the west wall, were two big roll-up doors. Luckily, the girls and the RV were situated along there, far enough away from the cars and Jim's planned distraction. The bay door on the right, closest to another couple smaller offices in that corner, had been left open. One of the offices had a light on, but Jim couldn't see inside. A few grocery bags and a radio sat on a wood picnic table close to the RV. There were several sleeping bags on the floor and four backpacks. Ready to travel.

The lights at the far east end of the floor had not been turned on, but it wasn't pitch-black either. Not the best cover. He still had to make sure no one was paying attention as he made his way along the east wall, under the big offices where Zant had been earlier.

Every step seemed to echo like a drum beat in the big empty chamber. Thirty-three seconds to the southeast corner. O worked his way closer in the other direction as Jim crouched and scurried behind the row of cars, stopping beside the workbench.

279

Zant and his guest had chatted and meandered their way past the cars and over to the RV. Casual. Unaware.

Jim eyed the cars. The biggest of the lot, the Rolls-Royce, was parked in the middle of the row. It was about twenty yards from the men, the girls, and Zant.

He pulled the sling over his head. Unbuckled the long strap.

The traveling sounds worked to his advantage here. Once he approached the Rolls, he was close enough to hear the ex-marine thug guys talking about the need to get the girls across the border in Mexicali around six a.m. The Thin Man was double-checking provisions. Lola and Connie were there along with another unknown girl.

Erica was sitting facing away from him at the end of the picnic table. Zant and his guest were heading her way. The pair were holding drinks and laughing as if they were strolling through a nightclub or restaurant, not about to auction girls off as slaves. Jim had to bite his lip to keep his cool. There were at least six grown men in this room and none of them were the slightest bit offended at the atrocity that was so calmly being committed.

Deep cleansing breath.

Zant and Mr. Dubai were still chatting about the rarity of the fucking race car at the end of the row as they made their way toward the RV. Ex-Marine Thug Guy A grabbed Erica up off the bench. She slumped back down but was now facing him. Closing his eyes, Jim fought visions of gutting the man who was here to *buy her*. Fuck.

The two men were moving closer.

"She should be awake."

"Should be." He nudged her with his knee. "Playing possum."

Between the cars Jim could see Zant bend to one knee. "I suggest you cooperate, Miss Floyd. You know what happens when my associates are unhappy. Someone pays."

Jim could see her look up at him, not moving her head but glaring through her loose bangs.

"My friend would like to meet you." He glanced at Ex-Marine Thug Guy A and gave him a nod.

The thug reacted by cutting her bindings. She flexed her fingers and wrists as blood rushed to her hands, squeezed her fists.

"Get her up."

She stumbled as she tried to stand on her own. Ex-Marine Thug Guy A held her until she had her balance and then left her to her own means to remain upright.

Erica looked over the man who intended on making her a slave. She held her head high. "What do you want with me?"

He didn't answer her. He took a long sip from his glass and looked back to Zant. "So she has not had any of your *training*?"

"As advertised. And she's a fighter. Her sister was as well. Took us a little longer than normal with her. But you intend on indulging in the … *pleasure* of her training yourself, so you can make that process last as long as you'd like." He also took a long drink. "I suggest you not stretch it out too long. They tend to die on you, or worse. We found four weeks is about as much as even the strong ones can take before they become useless."

They were talking about rape and torture and he shrugged casually, as if they were talking about training dogs or circus animals.

"But then, my friend, that depends on what you wish the final product to be."

Mr. Dubai left them and sauntered over to the table. Lola was sitting on top of the picnic table, her feet on the seat. She showed no fear. He brushed Lola's cheek. "I like the nature of the product you have tonight." Lola was cleaned up and dressed in what would be normal vacation attire. She grinned up at him and opened her legs a bit as if to invite. "Yes. This is acceptable."

Jim saw Erica bite her lip. He knew her temper. Knew she was struggling with her instincts to rant and fight. Knew she was smart. Fighting at this point would play into Zant's hand. He had said the client was looking for feisty and untrained. She needed to remain calm, docile. Unappealing to the monster. Jim doubted her ability to do so for long.

"I suggest you don't extend the training too long, then. I can have my man explain the process in further detail."

"Not necessary." Mr. Dubai turned back and slithered his way back to Erica, his tunic dancing around his pant legs. She looked down. Not challenging him, not threatening. "Her look is distinctly American. I like that. However, Mr. Zant, I requested a blonde."

"And"—Zant shrugged—"she's not."

"That should reduce her cost."

"It did."

Erica continued to stare at the ground. Her toe was tapping. How mad was she that she was being discounted for having brunette hair? Amazing. But instead of getting angry she started to cry. Jim didn't know if it was from wondering what Chris had gone through or because she wanted to appear weak. Either way, it worked.

Zant grabbed her chin and made her look up.

Jim dipped the woven fabric strap from the sling onto the gas can he'd slipped off the tool bench. When it was moist, he crept back to the Rolls-Royce. Center car. Far enough away to keep the RV from danger, close enough to cause some havoc. He opened the fuel tank lid and forced the fabric into the pipe. Erica would not be docile for long. It wasn't in her nature. She'd try, but was going to get herself hurt in a hurry. He needed to act. He shoved at the fabric with a screwdriver, pushing it down into the fuel tank.

"Where is the feisty girl who puked on my twelve-thousand-dollar rug intentionally?"

She shook her head and looked back down, her hands clasped at her waist.

"A shame to put that pretty makeup job Lola did for you to waste. Mr. Dubai here needs to see what his money is buying, Erica." Her name came off his lips as if he were a lover, sweet, sultry. Jim's stomach turned. "Be a love and show him for me."

She didn't respond.

"Fine." He turned to Ex-Marine Thug Guy B, who was standing near Lola. "Get the sister."

The thug jogged behind them to the smaller offices. Jim couldn't see his eventual destination, but in less than a minute Chris came waltzing out in front of the thug with a bit of stagger. She too was drugged, maybe more than Lola and the others. One side of her face was bruised, and a baggy lime-colored T-shirt hung loose on one shoulder, exposing another bruise.

As Jim watched he realized that Chris was freely going to Zant. No hate, no anger, even no fear. Erica's face tightened. Her eyes narrowed. *Hold on, baby.* Jim assessed Chris. The dead look in her eyes made him think back on something Oscar had said when they first met. *She may be better off dead.*

But Chris was very much alive as she was ushered up to Zant by Ex-Marine Thug Guy B. An empty smile greeted the man who had brainwashed her and tortured her. She glanced over at Erica. No recognition. No emotion. It was as if she'd never seen her own sister.

"The baby sister. Blonde." He pushed Chris's hair off her face. Ran his thumb over her lip. She glanced over at Mr. Dubai. "The bruising is all but gone, so she is almost ready. She was not picked for her appearance. She was interrupting our process. You could finish off her training."

"For the money I'm paying you, I want a feisty American girl. I want to beat her into submission myself. A gift to share with my boys."

"Your *sons*? Are you fucking *insane*?" The words were out of Erica's mouth before she had the sense to stop herself.

Jim cringed and worked the fabric fuse harder. He only hoped O was in place.

40

"**Ah.**" **Zant turned and** gestured back to Erica. "There she is. I told you. This one will fight you every step of the way, because she's smart. Has an advanced degree, experience in banking and finance. She has lived independently for years."

The man grinned. "Yes. Much to take out of her, then."

"Acceptable? Seven hundred and fifty, as we agreed?"

Erica started to hit the man. Jim saw one the big guys grab her in time.

"Shut the doors, Broady."

Jim lit the end of the fabric dangling from the fuel tank of the Rolls. Depending on the amount of gas in the tank, the fire he'd set would make a nice explosion in a matter of a couple of minutes. Timing was subject to the ratio of liquid fuel and vapors in the tank. An unknown. But ... boom. He needed to take cover.

He signaled O. The clock was ticking. O was around the northwest corner, on the far side of the RV and the conversation. He should have gotten even closer, unseen, hiding behind the industrial equipment almost as far as the two offices on the lower floor. Jim backed to the corner behind the sturdy workbench. His plan was to come directly at them. Straight across the open floor. A shock-and-awe campaign. The plan may have a few big-assed holes in it, but it was all they had.

He needed to get between the huge open door and the men. Which was not likely with only one gun.

"Someone smell smoke?" Broady entered the garage from the big open door.

This was a problem. A cop. With a gun. And no respect.

"Our driver is here. That means all our players are in the area?" The Thin Man came from behind the RV.

"Yes, sir."

Jim glanced at his watch. Hour and a half since they'd left Vegas. Little less than an hour since the call O made to Miller. He looked at the Rolls. Black smoke trailed up from the tank opening. Gasoline was burning. Fumes were building. He needed it to blow. *Now*.

Broady headed toward the black smoke. Zant held up a hand. "Don't bother. That will only expedite matters. Shut the doors."

What the hell was he talking about?

"Jim Bean," Zant shouted. "Mr. Olsen." He turned a circle. The smoke was getting thicker by the second. He laughed.

Jim's blood went cold. Shit. They knew he and O were there. Maybe even planned it. Too late to go get the igniter out of the tank.

Mr. Dubai relaxed and sat facing the line of cars on the picnic table. No fear.

Jim covered his ears.

Just as Broady shut and locked the large rolling doors, effectively shutting them all in the warehouse, the mix hit its happy place.

The tank exploded. Glass and bits of the car flew like bullets. The girls screamed, hit the ground. The ex-marine thugs barely flinched. Combat vets, he guessed. Mr. Dubai didn't move at all.

Fortunately, unlike in the movies, the explosion was not so spectacular as to take out the other cars around it. However, the flames that now engulfed the real wood and hand-tufted leather of the Rolls would grow and eventually take the entire building, given that there was little out here to stop it. The alarm of one of the other cars starting blaring its annoying horn. The echo was thunderous in the closed-off warehouse.

The burning hunk of extravagance did what burning cars do best. Mountains of thick black and gray smoke were rolling through the area. Zant didn't panic.

"You have about fifteen seconds to get front and center, boys," he called. He motioned Broady over. Jim saw the cop standing next to Zant, gun pulled. Boy, was he in deep.

"Ten seconds." The eerie sense of glee in his voice made the hair on Jim's neck stand up. Even with its large size, that part of the room was quickly filling with acrid smoke. He was going to lose his line of sight.

Jim looked at him over the hood of the Aston Martin convertible. "Let them go, Zant!" Even *he* knew he sounded like a beat cop in a cheap movie.

Zant's twisted laughter echoed in the cavernous warehouse. "Or?" He jerked Erica up by her injured arm. She tried not to scream or react, but he could see the pain on her face. Jim didn't move. Knew O was close and would wait to follow his lead.

"Not enough?" He put pressure right on the fabric wrapping the spot. Erica was dancing, trying to remove his hand from her arm. Tears were streaming down her face.

"Fine." Zant indicated the girls huddled behind the table. "Shoot the whiny one."

Jim heard the report, saw the golden flash through the smoke. There was screaming, but he couldn't see who was hit.

"You son of a bitch!" That was Erica. Jim let out a breath as she shouted it, probably struggling even harder. Jim wouldn't gamble another life. He stepped out and dropped the gun. No longer needed it. Screw the vision of Zant behind bars; he was going to kill him with his bare hands. Smoke billowed between him and Zant, leaving his vision blocked. Another piercing scream that he was sure was Erica's echoed through the vast metal room.

"I'm coming." He stepped closer to Zant, parting the smoke like a plane descending through clouds. When he could see, he found Mr. Dubai sitting causally on the table, Chris by his side. Chris was looking a little stressed even in her drug haze. The smug man didn't seem too concerned at all about the fire, the smoke, Jim, or Zant with a gun. Stupid fool. He was now target number two.

Broady was pulling Lola off Connie's dead body. He held a gun. That moved him up to target number two. Dubai could die later.

O materialized through the smoke just to Jim's right, equally unarmed as far as Jim could tell. Knowing him, there was plenty tucked into his vest. Given the hell in the big man's eyes and the deep-seated hate in his own heart, their odds still looked pretty good. Zant was a dead man. Jim just needed to get the civilians out of the line of fire.

"Told you they'd follow the trail and be here." Broady sauntered around the table.

"I am impressed, Officer. You delivered. All my nuisances in one room." He glanced at the burning car. "And *you* even started the fire yourself, Bean."

"Set up," O grumbled.

Broady shrugged. "I still have to take care of Miller. But I think with the trail of bodies you two left along the way, that'll be easy enough."

Zant nodded. "Fair enough. May I see your gun?" The cop handed over his gun. Jim thought that might be the moment they needed to move, but Zant pointed it at Broady's head. "You win the prize." He pulled the trigger before Broady could open his big mouth to protest. Erica gasped as brain matter blowback spattered her shirt.

Zant calmly tossed Broady's gun away. "I've wanted to do that since he first came to my office. Slimeball. Gave me the creeps."

Jim figured Zant was right, but to creep him out, one had to be pretty low on the evolutionary scale.

Ex-Marine Thug Guy A coughed. "Getting dark in here. Time to move, Mr. Zant."

Zant looked at his gaudy gold watch. "Ah. Yes. It is. Mr. Dubai, are you ready?"

He gestured affirmative and got to his feet, brushing the dust from his tunic. The thugs stepped up to stand on either side of Zant.

"Kill them both. Make it look like they killed each other or something. Leave them to burn with the cars." Then he turned away.

Keith Worth, the Thin Man, pulled Lola and Chris toward the offices. Jim saw there was a red emergency exit sign on the wall just to the right. They were all heading out that door.

They would not make it very far.

Jim assessed. Everyone was in eyeshot except for Lake. He was old, fat. Probably ran when the car exploded. Jim would worry about him later.

Another car hit its happy gas mixture. It blew. The blast and fire flash made everyone jump. Jim reacted. O followed his lead.

Both ex-marine thug guys had guns drawn but neither got to shoot. Jim guessed they got nervous seeing the boss shoot his cop flunky. The pair wouldn't make it past this job either. Probably were realizing that they'd get it in Mexicali, when they delivered the girls. Nerves made them slow to react after the second blast.

O fired a snubby he'd been palming. Hit Ex-Marine Thug Guy A center mass. Two shots. The big man's eyes widened. His gun fired two wild rounds before it clattered to the concrete. Sadly, his buddy followed his instinct to help. Bad decision.

With his good arm, Jim grabbed the guy's shoulder, pulled him around. A quick tight jab to the solar plexus with the slapjack. While struggling to breathe, Thug B tried to fire at close range. Jim heard the round go by his head. He jabbed again, this time to the man's throat. He went down, gagging and choking.

Jim headed to the door. O wasn't beside him. He looked back and saw Thug B take one to the head. O had motives Jim did not. Years of pain. Years of effort to stop these guys from doing to other women what'd they'd done to his Chloe. Didn't matter if this guy had been on it all along or if today was his first day on the job, he was going to atone for the sins of the masses.

"Oscar." The big man looked up from the two dead guys. He was a blank. "More bad guys."

He nodded. He retrieved the weapon Ex-Marine Thug Guy A no longer needed and handed it to Jim as he passed. "Use this, Bean."

"Do my best."

41

DUST AND GRAVEL PELTED his head as Jim exited the warehouse. It was dark. The limo was just starting, but the RV was already on the way out of the parking lot. Oscar fired at the moving limo. Jim didn't dare fire blankly at any vehicles. No telling what he'd hit or which vehicle Erica was in. Oscar fired wildly at the limo. Rounds pelted the doors, windows, and ricocheted into the night.

Bulletproof.

It slowed but didn't stop. "Use grenades. Stop the limo!" O shouted as he ran toward the car.

"Grenades?" Jim looked at his vest. Two smoke bombs hung off the right side. Grenades. Not smoke bombs. Shit. Grenades, hanging off his chest as he'd started a car fire. They'd been dangling there as the cars exploded. He yanked one off, pulled the pin with the action. O was getting an ass whooping when this was over for not informing him they were live grenades.

He was running as he threw it. Tossed high and long like a football pass. He hoped his throwing aim was better than his shooting aim. His intention was to land it just in front of the moving car, not on it.

Bull's-eye. It blew. The limo met the percussive explosion and jerked up and to the right, hard enough to lift the front tires off the ground.

O was there when it landed. The front tires were lost to the grenade's explosive pressure, leaving the limo stranded. The sunroof opened. Lake stood and leveled an MP5 at O. He held it too loosely, and the powerful kick sent the rounds far afield. He was no better than Jim with a gun. Comical, really. Bad guys who can't shoot. But then again, the guy was a dry cleaner by day.

Then there was O. He fired once from the snubby, on the run, and created a new orifice on Lake's face. He fell over the windshield, feet still in the sunroof.

Jim caught up, ran up on the trunk, pulled what was left of Lake out of the opening in the roof. O was there. It was quiet. Jim stood over the sunroof, looked in. Empty. He quickly stuck his head in enough to see that the windshield was blown out. The driver slumped to the side on the seat. Jim's aim was better than he thought.

"They're all in the RV," Jim concluded. Which was well down the service road. Too far to chase on foot. A third explosion rocked the warehouse behind.

O smirked. "I think we can catch them."

Jim was already on his way back into the building. "Get the door, would ya?"

"Of course." O headed to the big rolling doors. Jim headed to the Aston Martin. He may never be an FBI agent, but he was about to play Bond, only the guy with the Double O moniker was going to be the passenger.

Holding his breath, he busted the steering column. Jim Bean did have some talents, and that hot little ride was purring in about twenty seconds. O got in. The bounty hunter looked like a caricature in the convertible car. A G.I. Joe action figure in a Lego car. He took possession of the gun tucked at his waist.

Vegas PD had to be getting close. "Miller will have convinced someone to come. Let's just hope they bought his story and they arrest the right people."

"If there's anyone left to arrest." Jim looked at O at that. His face was still veiled in hate. "You know he'll still have power locked up. Even in the tightest security. That's *if* he ever serves jail time. Fuck face owns this town, Bean. We need to end this tonight. Now."

Alexis. That was why he needed Zant alive. Jim had been so wrapped up in the urgency of extraction, he hadn't considered if Zant had set them up to be in that warehouse tonight, he'd known Jim was involved with Erica all along. Alexis was already in danger. Being hunted. There was no time to explain it to O.

Jim refocused on driving. "I need some info from Zant, O. I need him alive. Give me two minutes anyway."

They caught the RV about two miles south of the Showgirl. O shot out the back tires. The lumbering RV swerved and skirted off the side of the road. Jim and O sped past as the *tat-tat-tat-tata-tat* of rapid fire left a hole or two in the Aston.

Jim slid the car around. They were now face-to-face with the RV. The Thin Man shot through his windshield from behind a huge steering wheel. The round shattered the front glass of the Aston Martin as well. O fired back.

They spun around again, like some kind of modern joust with automatic weapons and hollow-point bullets instead of wooden poles.

Jim saw a hint of blue lights in the distance. The cavalry. Once the cops got there, Jim would not be able to question Zant. "Shit. Take 'em all out. I don't care. Give me one minute to question Zant."

"I'll try."

Jim had stopped behind the RV, off to one side. There were no windows on it to give the asshats a good angle to fire from. "Three of them. Four girls. They're gonna use the girls as shields."

The side door opened toward Jim and O. "You can have your girls, Olsen." It was Zant. The door blocked him, but Jim knew it was him. "Let us take the car. You keep the girls. I'll forget this all ever happened. We'll be all square."

"I find that my trust level for you is low, Zant," Oscar answered.

"Jim knows I keep my word. Don't you?"

He didn't answer. Considered their options. Girls in the RV. Guns in the RV. He needed the guns out.

Zant shouted, "She's going to be a dead woman, Bean. I'll find Alexis. You cross me and she's dead."

He mouthed the words *trust me* to O. His friend hesitated, then stepped to the side.

Jim emerged. "Look, fine. I got no beef past these two. Give me the girls. You take the car."

"Drop your guns where I can see them."

They did. Oscar looked none too happy. "You know he's going to blow our heads off when he gets in the car," O whispered.

"Won't get that far."

Zant and Mr. Dubai eased from the RV.

"Wait, boss. What do I do?" Keith, his skinny self, stuck his head out the door.

"I'll get you out." Zant and Dubai hustled toward the car, guns trained on Jim and O.

"You won't make it long enough for that," Oscar said, his voice silky and scary. He stepped toward the RV.

"You shut up." Keith then fell, flailing for balance, out the door. Pushed from inside. Probably Erica. O acted. Retrieved a gun from the ground. Fired at the car. Hit Dubai in the chest. Keith regained his composure and tried to fire, but Jim threw his knife, penetrating the meaty part of his hand between his thumb and finger. Erica jumped down and kicked the gun away as he rolled.

Zant was trying to push a very wounded Mr. Dubai off the driver's door of the Aston. Selfish bastard right to the end. Jim stalked up and took the little freak by the neck. "Is she being hunted?"

Zant shrugged. "Fuck you. I can still make this all you. I own the department. I own her."

Jim was tired of this guy. Oscar had the right idea. Kill them and let the chips fall where they may. "Tell you what, *Andrew*." Jim pulled the last grenade from his vest. Zant's eyes got big, further exaggerating the fishy look of his little mouth. "I'm going to put an end to all this. Right now. I don't give a shit about my pathetic life, and you know it. You used that fact to manipulate."

"Now, Bean, I'm—we can negotiate this." He was trying to back up, crawl away, but Jim had him by a good forty pounds. Used his good arm to press him harder into the car door.

"No. No more negotiating for you." He pulled the pin with his teeth and pushed the grenade down Andrew Zant's five-hundred-dollar slacks. He counted, "Three."

Zant's eye got huge. "She's fine," he stammered. "In the Keys, last I was told. Haven't touched her. Too valuable. I swear. The boy's my kid."

"Two." He lifted the man and pushed him back into the car and ran as fast as he could the opposite direction. He kept counting in his head.

"One!" He hit the ground and covered his head to protect himself from flying Aston Martin debris.

42

ANNIE SAT QUIETLY IN his lap, her purr the sweetest sound on the planet, her tail softly brushing his arm. Most of his body hurt. The surgery on his shoulder had been a success for the most part. His doc was worried over range of motion. He wasn't. His door was hanging crooked in its frame from the SWAT team entrance. The busted thing was also letting in a great deal of heat. Oscar was reading over the instructions for the new one on the floor.

"Why do they make this so complicated?"

"Why are you reading directions? Just hang it."

"You want it square?"

"I want it closed."

Ely pushed open the broken door and waltzed past Oscar with a small salute. He plopped on the couch across from Jim's chair. "How's the wing?"

The question made Jim move his arm a little. "Hurts like hell."

"Good. Glad to hear it."

Jim and O exchanged glances.

He shrugged. "Pain is healing, cleansing."

"I'll take those *healing* killers any day, then." He nodded at the prescription bottles on the coffee table.

"Your choice, man. In Nam, I let the pain be a pathway to enlightenment."

Jim guessed the Viet Cong did not offer Vicodin to their prisoners. Jim was happy to have the pills.

"Anyway, dude. Mrs. Lake called."

"That can't be good."

"She wanted us to know that she's donating most of 'the bastard's' money to women's shelters and asked if there was any other organizations that keeps girls off the street and away from that shit. I gave her Sister Nora's number. Told her the church was friendly to street people."

Jim had managed to keep the sister's name out of the police statements. It left some holes, but the prosecutor who had taken all their statements had said it was the worst clusterfuck of a case he'd seen in years. What were a few holes? Whatever. He'd believed them for the most part and was working all the angles to make the charges stick.

"What's the word on Zant?" Ely leaned back and crossed a gangly leg over his knee.

Oscar piped up. "Unfortunately, he'll live."

Zant had managed to get the explosive out of his pants, but his throwing arm and decision-making process sucked. The grenade detonated about eight feet from him. He hadn't put the car between himself and thing either. His injuries were severe, but he *was* alive.

"I hope it blew his dick off." Erica had come in the back door. Without knocking. Again. As she had every day since the surgery.

"No such luck. Head and chest wounds." Oscar lifted the new door and leaned it against the wall. While Jim had lain in the hospital, he and Erica had cleaned up Jim's apartment from where the cops had tossed it. "How's Chris?"

Her face fell. "She's … um … never going to be the same again. We all know that. But the doctors say she's trying, and that means something. They won't predict anything after only five days."

This had aged Erica. Hardened her. He could see it in her eyes and in the away she carried herself. She needed some help too. Maybe staying in town to be here for Chris would help her deal with the trauma. Shit, what did he know? Maybe it would make it worse.

She would eventually go back to Boston. He'd stay in Vegas and mostly he would be part of her memories—her nightmares, when the things she'd seen here, the things Zant had done, came to her in the night. That was when she'd remember Jim Bean.

Korey Anders, he was dead. And Erica now understood why.

"At least Zant can't do *that* to anyone ever again." Annie got up out of his lap and went to Ely as he spoke.

"My guess is prison will not be as kind to Andrew Zant as you think, O. The man walked on people, let guys take the fall for him. He won't be very popular. Especially if the feds keep his money frozen."

Jim would stay in Vegas at least that long, to see Zant facing his peers and wearing orange. After that, who knew?

About the Author

J.D. Allen (Raleigh, NC) attended The Ohio State University and earned a degree in forensic anthropology and a creative writing minor.

She's a member of the Bouchercon World Mystery Convention National board and president of the Triangle Chapter of Sisters in Crime. She does workshops on the basics of crime scene investigation, voice, and public speaking.

———

Readers, I'd love to hear from you. Visit me at www.JDAllenBooks .com to read about upcoming events, reviews, and more books. You can also sign up for my newsletter to get a free award-winning short story. Connect with me on Facebook at J.D.AllenAuthor.

Reader reviews and recommendations are vital to authors; if you've enjoyed my books, please tell your friends.

www.MidnightInkBooks.com

From the gritty streets of New York City to sacred tombs in the Middle East, it's always midnight somewhere. Join us online at any hour for fresh new voices in mystery fiction.

At midnightinkbooks.com you'll also find our author blog, new and upcoming books, events, book club questions, excerpts, mystery resources, and more.

Midnight Ink Ordering Information

Order Online:
• Visit our website www.midnightinkbooks.com, select your books, and order them on our secure server.

Order by Phone:
• Call toll-free within the U.S. at
  1-888-NITE-INK (1-888-648-3465)
• We accept VISA, MasterCard, American Express, and Discover
• Canadian customers must use credit cards

Order by Mail:
Send the full price of your order (MN residents add 6.875% sales tax) in U.S. funds, plus postage & handling to:

> Midnight Ink
> 2143 Wooddale Drive
> Woodbury, MN 55125-2989

Postage & Handling:
Standard (US). If your order is:
> $30.00 and under, add $6.00
> $30.01 and over, FREE STANDARD SHIPPING

AK, HI, PR: $16.00 for one book plus $2.00 for each additional book.

International Orders: Including Canada
> $16.00 for one book plus $3.00 for each additional book

Orders are processed within 12 business days. Please allow for normal shipping time.
Postage and handling rates subject to change.